CASPIAN'S FORTUNE: INFINITY'S END BOOK 1

ERIC WARREN

Part of the Sovereign Coalition Universe

CASPIAN'S FORTUNE – INFINITY'S END BOOK 1

Cover Design by Dan Van Oss www.covermint.com

Content Editor Tiffany Shand www.eclipseediting.com

ISBN 978-1-0929-4602-5

To Meagan, Always and Forever

The Sovereign Coalition Series

Short Stories

CASPIAN'S GAMBIT: An Infinity's End Story

SOON'S FOLLEY: An Infinity's End Story

Novels

INFINITY'S END SAGA

CASPIAN'S FORTUNE (BOOK 1)

TEMPEST RISING (BOOK 2)

DARKEST REACH (BOOK 3)

A BRIDGE TOO FAR (BOOK 4)

The Quantum Gate Series

Short Stories

PROGENY (BOOK 0)

Novels

SINGULAR (BOOK 1)

DUALITY (BOOK 2)

TRIALITY (BOOK 3)

DISPARITY (BOOK 4)

CAUSALITY (BOOK 5)

Sign up on my website and receive the first short story in the INFINITY'S END SAGA absolutely free!

Go to www.ericwarrenauthor.com to download

CASPIAN'S GAMBIT!

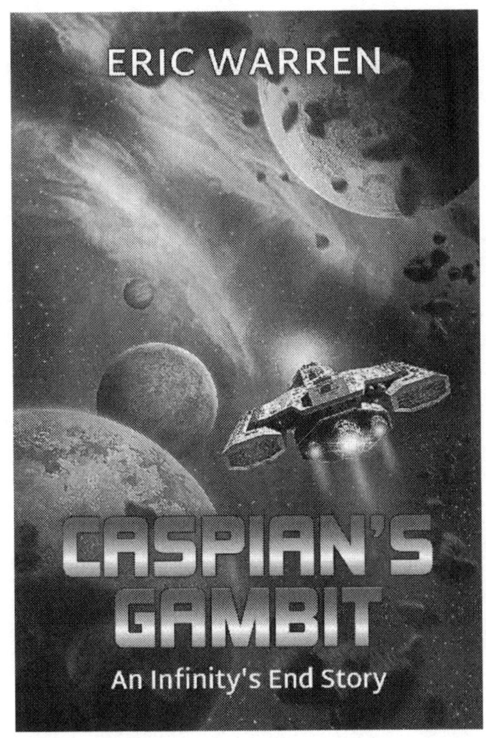

1

"Why must you disappoint me, Cas? Next time come visit *my* side of the ship," the elegant woman said, descending the long metal ramp.

Caspian Robeaux raised his fist to his chest in salute, ignoring the insinuation. The princess knew full well if Caspian so much as looked at her the wrong way he'd see the end of a shooting gallery by the end of the day. But that didn't mean he couldn't at least be cordial.

"I can only…apologize if everything wasn't to your satisfaction," he replied.

She reached the bottom of the ramp, gliding over the surface as if she were on a portable hover, her long sapphire dress concealing any hint of actual legs underneath there. For all Cas knew, maybe she didn't even have legs. Perhaps there was a rolling device that replaced her entire lower body. It was better he kept that image in his mind rather than where his imagination wanted to direct him.

A sweet, flowery scent filled the air as she moved into his personal space. Cas tightened his fist, pressing it into his chest as hard as he could as her copper eyes studied his own. The princess was almost exactly his height, and she stopped inches short of their faces touching. Caspian tried not to breathe her in but it was impossible and intoxicating at the same time. "You know, Cas," she said, her voice low. "We could always extend the trip. Your...*skills* could be put to use in places other than the engine of your ship."

Cas suppressed the urge to wet his lips. "Begging your pardon, your highness, but I'm afraid we wouldn't have the time. You're due for your ceremony in only a few hours."

She reached up with her slender fingers and drew them down the stubble on his cheek. He felt the ache of desire bloom within him, but he held steadfast. He really wished for that mechanical torso right about now. "I can be quick if you can," she whispered.

His body wanted to shudder at the suggestion but he planted his resolve. One finger out of place and he was dead. Her father, his Royal Highness of Cloistria would make him suffer ten different ways before granting a merciful death. Still...the temptation was strong. If he suspected she was doing anything other than toying with him he might actually consider it.

"Alas," she said, dropping her gaze. "You're correct. And I mustn't keep my family waiting. You performed your duty admirably."

Cas drew a breath. The first he'd taken in the last two minutes. The princess moved past him, still gliding as if on a cloud of air. He dropped his fist and turned to watch her leave.

"Your accommodations were satisfactory," she added. "But next time I'll expect the *deluxe* package."

Cas had to keep from rolling his eyes because even though the princess had her back to him, her two guards who had disembarked before her stood facing Cas, their stares boring into him. Making a move on the princess would have been the last voluntary action Cas ever took as a human being.

He pulled a small rectangular device from his pocket, checking his balance on the comm unit. Something was wrong. "Er…Princess," Cas called, jogging to catch up with her. The two guards immediately advanced on him, moving on either side of the princess and each grabbing him by the bicep. "For Kor's sake, I just want to ask a question," Cas spat at them. The princess turned to face him again, gliding forward. He wrenched his arms free when the princess raised her hand to indicate he could speak.

"Change your mind?" Her eyes twinkled.

"Your payment didn't process through," Cas said, holding up his readout.

"Oh." Her shoulders dropped as she seemed genuinely disappointed. But it quickly hardened back into her normal confidence. "I transferred your payment to your partner's account. He gave me all the proper credentials. I assumed you two split everything fifty-fifty."

Cas did his best to keep from lashing out at her. "My…partner." He meant it as a question but also didn't want the princess to see his confusion.

"Yes, Mr. Maddox explained it all quite expertly."

Cas bit the inside of his lip, forcing a smile. "Yes. Of course. Sorry for the confusion. I hope you enjoyed the trip."

She smiled back. "Not as much as I could have, I suspect." She reached up for his face again, but stopped mid-way and retracted her hand. Then she turned on her cloud of air and was off toward the entrance to the Elongorium. And with a sharp snap of her fingers her guards turned and followed her.

As soon as she was through the sliding doors Cas raced back up the ramp into the ship. "Box! Box, get me coordinated on Maddox *NOW*!"

Box poked his rectangular metal head from around one of the corridors. "Maddox?" he asked in his Mancunian accent. "Wot's he got to do with anyfin'?"

"And drop that damn accent!" Cas yelled, reaching the cockpit of his ship. His hands flew over the controls, retrieving the ramp and moving through the pre-flight checklist faster than he should. He didn't care. There was no time to waste.

"Sorry, boss," Box said in his normal voice as he entered the cockpit, his bulky mechanical frame slumping down on the pilot's seat. "Last known location was Devil's Gate, as if he would be anywhere else."

"Great," Cas fumed. "Just fantastic. That's six hours away. It'll all be gone by then."

"Stole your money again, huh?" Box asked in the superior way he always did. "I never did like that man."

"Then help me get us the hell out of here so we can steal it back," Cas yelled, finishing the pre-flight sequence.

"Boss, I don't think you're supposed to—"

"He's not getting away with it, not this time," Cas said, hitting the thrusters. The *Reasonable Excuse* jumped to life, lifting off from the landing pad and spinning one-hundred-eighty degrees as it blasted away from the Elongorium.

Box turned his attention to the controls, making the adjustments Cas had forgotten in his haste. "How'd he do it this time?" Box asked.

"Conned the princess. Told her we were *partners*," Cas yelled.

"Boss."

"What?"

"You're yelling. There's a finite amount of oxygen."

Cas gritted his teeth. "Give me a break. We have reserves for weeks."

"Fine," Box said, folding his spindly, metal arms behind his head. "Don't complain to me when the air runs out. I don't need it. In fact, keep screaming. It means I inherit this ship sooner."

"Robots can't own ships," Cas said, seething. He wasn't even focusing on Box. All his thoughts were on Maddox and how much of his payment the man had already gambled away. In six hours, he'd be lucky if there was even one kassope left.

"Robots can't lie either," Box said with a smugness that could never show on his featureless face. Box was a typical class 117 Autonomous Mining Robot which meant he was built for labor. He sported a transparent visor across his "eyes" and a metal mask across the rest of his "face" but there was nothing underneath there except a speaker for a mouth and two yellow optical sensors for eyes. It was designed to protect his components from the harsh weather conditions of whatever assignment he'd received. Fortunately for Box, he'd never seen a day of labor in his life thanks to Cas.

Cas rubbed his temples. He needed to get to Devil's Gate quicker. "How close is one of the undercurrents to the gate?"

"Approximately fifty billion kilometers," Box replied. At least he was good for that much, Cas never had to consult the nav system.

"And how close are we to the undercurrent?"

"Vetar has an entrance at the edge of the system. Thirty minutes at this speed." They'd already reached the uppermost layers of the atmosphere of Vetar IV, home of Her Royal Highness and surrounding court. It wasn't a place Cas had visited before and he didn't see what all the fuss was about. It was just another blue and green planet with a purple atmosphere. The only reason it was even important was because it was in Sargan space. Had it been part of the Coalition…

"We're taking the undercurrent," Cas said.

"Boss, that will cut less than an hour off the trip *and* put extra strain on the ship. Maybe you want to get her serviced before another undercurrent jump."

He swiveled to Box. "Tell me this, smart guy. How am I supposed to pay for any repairs without any money?"

Box shrugged. “Steal? I noticed the princess had some fine jewels on her person.”

He wasn’t going to dignify that with a response. No, he was going to go get what was owed to him and nothing more. Except this time he needed to make things clear to Maddox. The fat lip and black eye he’d left the man with last time hadn’t been enough.

“You could always ask for another loan from Veena,” Box suggested.

“Any more loans and *she’ll* own this ship. Is that what you want?” Cas asked, going over the controls for an undercurrent jump.

“She’s probably nicer than you. I bet she’d give me a bed,” he replied.

“You don’t sleep!”

“That doesn’t mean I don’t like to lay down every once in a while,” Box retorted. “Rest my creaky joints. My old servos. Put up my ambulatory units.”

Cas’ eyes narrowed. Even after five years in space with Box he still had trouble knowing when he was being serious or not. Typically robots had zero use for any recreation, but ever since Cas made the modifications, Box had been more interested in non-robot things.

“Maybe if you’d stop lounging around watching net dramas all day your joints wouldn’t hurt as much. Movement is a good thing.”

“I need them to relax.”

Cas pushed away from the console, standing. “Just input the coordinates, and let me know when we’re ready to jump. And for once in your short life, don’t complain about it.”

“No promises.” Box kept his focus on the controls in front of him.

Cas shook his head and made his way back down the main corridor, the doors to the cockpit sliding closed behind him.

He couldn't believe he let Maddox get the better of him again. And after everything he'd done for the man! Cas had to learn his lesson the hard way. Life outside the Coalition was hard and it was unfair. And that was probably the most difficult part to get used to. You get screwed over by someone, there was no justice system in place to right the wrong. You either took care of business so it didn't happen again or you allowed yourself to become a victim; another casualty of the Sargan Commonwealth. And he refused to be a victim.

As Cas passed the quarters where the princess had stayed while he'd ferried her from Tau Hydrae that sweet scent reached his nose again. He stopped a moment and inhaled, holding the smell inside for a moment.

By Kor, he needed a drink.

2

The blaring of the alarm startled Cas awake. He fell off his shelf of a bed, smacking his face on the hard metal floor. "Box, shut that thing off!" he yelled into his communicator.

"Sorry, boss, just thought you'd like to know we're five minutes out from Devil's Gate."

"No, you're not," Cas replied, pushing himself back up.

"You're right. I'm not," his voice said through the overhead.

"I'll be up there in a minute," Cas grumbled, shutting his comm down and moving to the sparse sink in his room. One would think as captain he'd get the nicest room on the ship, but no. Those were reserved for the guests. It was the only thing he had to offer over other couriers and it didn't help his competition kept upping the ante on him. Now he was expected to have vidscreens and fancy soap in *every* hab suite? That combined with his interest payments to Veena and pretty soon he wouldn't be able to pull a profit at all.

Cas splashed some water on his face then cupped some and drank it greedily, his week-old stubble scratching his hands. He'd managed to finish off one bottle of Scorb from his stash before passing out but it always made his throat dry. Not to mention the always-present headache. Headaches were par for the course whether he was hungover or not. He checked himself in the mirror and ran his hands through his dark hair a few times to adjust its stubbornness. Once marginally satisfied by what he saw he made his way to the bridge.

"Busy today," Box said as he entered the cockpit. They had exited undercurrent space to find at least forty ships in various positions around Devil's Gate. The station itself was quite large; a giant, upside-down domed disk a couple of kilometers across. Below the disk were dozens of levels for things like entertainment, shipping, storage or habitation. Devil's Gate was one of the larger stations in this part of Sargan space.

"Anywhere to park?" Cas asked, surveying the top of the disk.

"I think I can squeeze in," Box said, jerking the controls. The ship lurched forward at considerable speed and Cas grabbed his seat so he didn't fly off.

"RE-12, slow your approach vector!" a voice snapped over their comm systems.

"Acknowledged!" Box said before cutting the comm. He sped up.

"There, right there," Cas said, bravely taking one hand off the chair to point at a space where another similar-sized ship was leaving. A third ship was waiting to take the spot above it. "Can you make it in?"

"Watch me." Box's metallic fingers running over the control pad while the other hand remained on the throttle. The parked ship pulled away as Box came screaming into the airspace. The ship waiting above them made a move to take the spot. "Not today," Box said, jerking the ship around so the rear thrusters decelerated them instantly as he dropped the ship into place, landing it perfectly.

"I knew there was a reason I gave you the piloting job," Cas replied. There was no way a human—even an amazing pilot—could have pulled that move off.

"It's what I do," Box replied, his glowing yellow eyes flickering with appreciation. Cas was glad Box didn't have a human face. He'd never wipe a smug look off it. Box turned the comm back on only for it to light up with three different feeds coming in at once. "The station flight controller is angry with you," Box said. "As is the ship we cut off. Erustiaan I think." He paused a minute. "And the ship we almost clipped on the way in would like a word as well."

Cas rolled his eyes. "It was your doing, you deal with it," he replied. "I'm going to find Maddox." Cas initiated the rest of the docking procedures, making sure they had a hard lock to the station.

"If you think I'm missing that you've gone crazy, boss," Box said in one of his accents.

"I told you, stop doing that," Cas replied.

"Sorry, boss," Box replied in his normal voice. "Docking procedures complete. I'm sure these guys can wait a while." He cut the comms again, shutting the ship down.

"C'mon," Cas said. "Let's get out there before he finds out we're here. I don't want to spook him."

***

The hypervator doors opened on level thirty-five. It was primarily an entertainment level, with a few spaces reserved for goods and storage. But it was also Maddox's favorite level—where all the gambling tables were. If he was anywhere on this station, it would be here.

They got off the lift with a dozen other people, most human but a few non. Cas had noticed one of the Erustiaans in the lift eyeing him suspiciously and he couldn't help but wonder if they had been on the ship Box had cut off. The only problem with pissing off an Erustiaan was they were, on average, over two meters tall and all muscle. Not to mention the hard pieces of bone or hoof growing out of their fingers so when they made a fist and hit you, it felt like being hit by a sharp brick. It was not an experience Cas looked forward to repeating and he made sure to avoid eye contact.

Once they were out of the lift the Erustiaans had gone their own way while he and Box made their way down the main promenade, checking the different establishments for Maddox.

"He won't be hard to find." Cas tapped his sidearm underneath his jacket just to confirm it was still there and he hadn't accidentally left it on his ship. It was a weapon of his own design, a class-L Boomcannon; the only one in existence. Of course it was probably illegal to have a weapon that not only fired a plasma pulse but a projectile at the same time, but it wasn't as if the Sargans were strict on weapon control. It was in their best interests for people to arm themselves out here because it meant squabbles might turn into firefights. Firefights meant less competition on quality goods. And the Commonwealth had no problem with that.

"I dare say," Box emulated in a bad British accent. "I do believe I've found him." He pointed through a window of the next establishment. Beyond the crowd was a man of medium build, blonde hair pulled into a ponytail, spinning one of the Lett'ra wheels. He proclaimed something in a drunken slur causing the women on each of his arms to burst into manufactured laughter.

"Maddox," Cas said under his breath as he narrowed his eyes. He pushed his way into the crowded and noisy room, Box right behind him. The speakers blared some electronic noise from Esook or some other Coalition planet while the smell of the room was a combination of body odor, perfume, and alcohol, all jumbled together. Cas suppressed the urge to stop by the bar first and instead pushed through the crowd, moving people out of the way. Most were too drunk to care. His gaze didn't leave Maddox who only continued to spin the wheel before downing a gulp from his considerable glass.

As Cas reached the second-closest Lett'ra table Maddox finally locked eyes with him and his expression went cold. He dropped his glass, turned and took off running in the opposite direction, leaving the women surprised at his sudden departure.

Cas was ready for it. In three steps he vaulted the Lett'ra table and broke into a sprint after Maddox, who pushed his way through one of the back doors to the establishment. Adrenaline surged through Cas's system and pushed the last remnants of the headache away.

"Box, go around!" Cas yelled, pushing through the same door. But he didn't check to see if Box had heard him or not. He wasn't about to let this man get away again. Cas found himself in a long hallway, filled with chemical, industrial and mechanical equipment. The door had soundproofed the noise from getting into the casino but in here it was loud enough to obscure someone's footsteps. Maddox could have gone in either direction and there was no sign of him.

Cas glanced down. A puddle of green discharge covered a small part of the floor. And leading away from it was one footprint every meter or so. Maddox had caught one foot in the puddle. "He's gone to the east," Cas said into his comm.

"Understood," Box replied. He wasn't sure where Box had gone but he hoped he had a better understanding of the layout of this place than Maddox did.

Cas followed the footprints until they began to dry out, causing him to slow. He didn't want to miss anything. The noise wasn't as bad this far down, there had been a gravity generator right behind the casino, and those tended to put out a lot of ambient noise. Probably a backup in case the station lost power the casino could keep everyone's chips where they were. Total gravity loss inside a money haven like that could turn into a bloodbath.

The sound of metal hitting metal echoed through the hallway and Cas took off toward the sound. It wasn't far away. As he rounded the corner at a T-junction, he saw someone stumbling down the hallway. It didn't take him long to catch up. Maddox glanced behind him and with a panicked look on his face tried to pick up speed only to trip over his own feet and fall face-first into the wall. Box appeared at the other end of the hallway.

"Looks like you didn't need me after all," Box called.

Cas didn't respond, only approached Maddox who moaned as he tried to push himself back up to a standing position again. Cas grabbed his jacket from behind, jerking him into a standing position, then swiveled the man around and threw him against the wall. Maddox winced and slid back down. His eyes were half-closed.

"Oh no you don't." Cas grabbed him and kept him upright. "Did you really think you could get away with it, Theo? You don't steal another courier's money." Box came up behind Cas.

"I…I needed it," Maddox said in a pitiful voice.

"You needed it," Cas replied. "For what? Gambling? You needed to throw away *my* money."

"No, no, it's not like that," Maddox said, his words slurred. "I was doing really good on the tables."

"I don't care if you're a millionaire," Cas replied. "You don't steal from me."

Maddox smirked and put his hand on Cas's shoulder but Cas brushed it away. "Yeah, but you're okay Cas. You won't kill me like those other guys. You're the only one I *can* steal from."

"Oh yeah?" Cas said, pulling his boomcannon from under his jacket and pressing it to Maddox's temple. "You want to test that out?" Cas caught Box begin to reach for him, but the robot apparently thought better of it and pulled back.

Maddox began sobbing uncontrollably. "C'mon, Cas," he pleaded. "You don't want to kill me, we've been in this a long time together. It'll never happen again. I promise. Please."

Cas pressed the tip of the gun harder into Maddox's skull but his finger remained off the trigger.

"I'll give you everything I've won. You can have it all," Maddox pleaded. Cas waited a beat, watching the pathetic man. His eyes were slammed shut as if he expected the hand of death at any second.

Cas pulled the gun away and re-holstered it. "All of it. If you steal from me again—"

"I know, I know," Maddox rushed his words, putting his hands out. "Never again. Thank you. I knew you were one of the good ones."

Ten minutes later the three of them had returned to the casino, Cas more than once propping Maddox up so he could keep walking along the way.

"Cash it all in!" Maddox yelled to the tender on the other side of the ornate gate. He pressed his thumb to the small pad in front of him.

"All of it sir?" the robotic tender said.

"Yes. All of it," Maddox pronounced, sticking his chest out. Cas shot a glance to Box, shaking his head.

"Here you are, sir." The tender handed Maddox a receipt showing his full balance. Cas snatched it away from his hand as soon as they were clear of the tender.

"What the hell is this?" Cas asked, shoving Maddox back. Remarkably he stayed on his feet. "I thought you said you were doing well on the tables!"

"I did!" Maddox protested. "This is the best I've ever done!"

"There is less than a quarter of my money here!" Cas replied, his body tensing. "That's all you have left?"

Maddox shrugged, then stumbled down into a chair beside him. "It's what I owe you," he slurred. Then he lurched forward and his head hit the table in front of him. A soft snore came from his mouth.

Cas rubbed his temples. His headache had returned. "I should have shot him."

"Probably," Box said.

Cas looked at the slip. It had Maddox's transfer number on it. Which meant all he needed was a scan of the man's thumb to get the money back into his account. "I'm not leaving here empty-handed," Cas replied. "Grab him. Let's go find a terminal."

"As you command, sire." Box bent and hoisted the unconscious man over his shoulders.

3

"I don't believe this," Cas said, staring at the terminal outside the casino. Maddox lay in a heap beside the machine, still snoring.

"Don't tell me. He was lying and he's actually ridiculously wealthy," Box prompted.

"He's got less money in his account than I do," Cas replied. "His *winnings* are pretty much it." He tapped a few controls confirming the account status. Maddox was dead broke.

"What about his ship?" Box asked.

"Highly leveraged from what I can tell. I could take it and get at least a portion back of what I'm due." Cas gripped the sides of the terminal so hard his knuckles turned white. "Which leaves him stranded here."

Box scoffed. It was a strange sound coming from a robot. "You already know what you're going to do. Can you just do it already so we can leave?"

"You go back to the ship," Cas said. "I'll take care of this."

Box hesitated, then left him alone with Maddox. The rest of the promenade was fairly busy and he disappeared into the crowd. Cas turned back to the terminal and transferred Maddox's winnings into his own account, using Maddox's thumb to confirm the transfer. He *should* take the ship. It would serve Maddox right for betraying him. But Cas couldn't do it. He couldn't leave the man stranded, regardless of what he'd done. He shut down the terminal then hunched over and patted at the drunk man's jacket. All he had on him was a small data recorder in his inside pocket. Cas smacked him across the cheek.

Maddox startled. "Wha…?"

"I'm taking this," Cas said, holding the recorder in front of Maddox's eyes. He'd get a pittance for it but he didn't care. It was something. "Don't steal from me again."

"You got it," Maddox slurred before falling asleep again. Cas stood and made his way down the wide corridor. Security would come get him and let him sleep it off in the drunk tank. Cas wished he was ruthless enough to have taken Maddox's ship; it would have gone a long way to settling his debt. He could have broken it down for parts, sold them off one-by-one and doubled his profit. But he wasn't built that way. Despite his current situation, it wasn't how he was going to live what was left of his life. He needed to be better than that.

Cas found another terminal a few shops down. He didn't want to make a secure transfer with a drunk and unconscious man leaning against the terminal. Especially when it was as important as this. After a quick log on he confirmed the money was in his account and he transferred almost all of it to Veena. He didn't want to think about what would have happened if Maddox had burned through more than her cut.

Yeah, Veena, you know that last job? With the princess? I don't have your portion. If you'll spare the beheading for a few more weeks I can probably scrounge up another payment.

He made sure at the end of the transfer to submit his best wishes as well.

"And a merry fuck-you too," he said under his breath. A man passing by had turned his head as Cas spoke and Cas leaned over the terminal closer until he was gone. "You better appreciate this," he added, unsure if he was talking to Veena or Maddox.

On the way back through the station Cas stopped off at the exchange shop to turn in the data recorder. As expected he received a pittance for it, but at least it was enough for a couple of drinks at the bar. As he passed back by the casino he was glad to see security had already come and picked up Maddox; the man was nowhere to be seen. Drunken and disorderly people collapsed outside of establishments were generally bad for business.

Cas made his way down a few more doors until he came to an establishment called *The Pit*. It was a place he knew well and frequented often. Though not as often as Maddox hit the casinos.

"I'll take a firebrand and a tooth melter." Cas plopped down on one of the stools and pressing his thumb to the pad.

A robot bartender similar in appearance to Box glided over and poured the drinks.

"So. Hear any good jokes lately?" Cas asked the bartender.

The robot's yellow eyes flashed while he continued to pour and mix the drinks. "Two blind men walk into a bar. The third one ducks."

Cas eyed the robot, wishing he'd kept his mouth shut. Maybe he shouldn't have told Box to go back to the ship. He was good for some entertainment when he wasn't in one of his moods.

The bartender slid the drinks toward him. "Tipping is not a planet in the Caledon system," he said.

"I'll try the drinks first. Then we'll see," Cas replied, sipping the firebrand. True to its name it burned all the way down. But accompanied with that was the sense of relief knowing he wouldn't have to dwell on thoughts of how to pay for the repairs to his ship without any more money. In a few minutes he wouldn't even care and based on how much he got for that data recorder he should be able to suck at least a few hours out of this place.

Cas wasted no time in taking the tooth melter—a sickeningly sweet drink that helped chase the firebrand. The ol' bartender hadn't done a bad job. Maybe not tip-worthy but certainly not bad by any means.

Cas waved to the robot. "One more round." After that he'd have to switch to something he could nurse.

"Not often you see rugged ship captains order fruit drinks," a female voice said beside him. Cas wheeled around, dizzy by all the alcohol infusing his blood and it took him a moment to comprehend what he was seeing. She was a mercenary, tall and wearing a long cloak that reached the backs of her knees. Her dark brown hair was done into a braid that fell down her left shoulder and her emerald eyes glittered like the jewels they stole the name from. But the most noticeable thing about her was the broad sword strapped to her back.

"Excuse me?" Cas said.

"Your choice of drink. It's unusual," she said.

Perhaps his luck hadn't run out after all. How often did beautiful woman approach him in a place as seedy as this? Though the sword was concerning. Cas leaned back away from the bar to get a better look at the weapon strapped to her back. He didn't recognize the hilt. "What's with the sword?"

"I use it to cut off the heads of my enemies," the woman said, deadpan.

Hiding his expression, Cas leaned forward again and took the second firebrand the bartender had poured. "Join me?" He knocked the drink back.

"I don't drink."

"Of course you don't." So much for luck. Cas took the second tooth melter and knocked it back as well.

"What is that supposed to mean?" the woman frowned.

"Nothing," Cas said, waving to the bartender again, who'd barely gone two meters. "Give me a rank, whatever you have on tap."

The bartender nodded and glided away.

"You really should clean yourself up," the woman snapped.

Cas screwed up his face. "I'm sorry, is there something I can do for you? Since you're obviously not looking for any company would you please leave me alone?"

The woman's eyes narrowed. "Your demeanor is unbecoming," she said. "Especially for a captain."

Cas sighed. "Let me guess. Veena sent you. If she wants another courier job she's going to have to wait. I need repairs and I—"

"Veena didn't send me," the woman interrupted, crossing her arms. "I want to hire you, freelance."

Cas couldn't help but laugh. "You want me to work for a mercenary? You really don't know who I am, do you?"

"You're Captain Caspian Robeaux. That's all I need to know."

"And who might you be?" Cas asked.

She stiffened. "Evelyn."

"Does Evelyn have a last name?" The bartender brought the rank, it was tinged green with a good amount of foam on the top. Just how Cas liked it. He took a long draw from the mug.

"That's not important," she replied.

"Well, *Evie*. I hate to disappoint you, but my ship is in no condition to be doing freelance work. Not to mention if my boss found out I was making money without cutting her in she'd cut *me* off if you get my drift." He took another draw. "Sorry. You'll have to find yourself another captain." It didn't escape his notice she bristled when he called her Evie.

Evelyn took one look at his glass and then at him again. "It appears you're quite comfortable where you are then," she said, her eyes boring into him.

A wave of shame bloomed up from within and it took every last ounce of the rank to drown it before it became unbearable. But the entire time he drank he didn't take his eyes off Evie. And she didn't take hers off him, though they were filled with disgust.

Cas took a breath and slammed the mug back down on the metal counter. Evie sneered and turned away, disappearing through the doors.

That had been the right call, hadn't it? He couldn't take a mercenary's job even if he wanted to, not with his ship in its current state. It needed at least a dozen new parts before he was confident he could pull anything off. Perhaps the universe was reaching out with one hand, trying to give him a chance. Then again perhaps Veena already knew about his troubles and was testing his allegiance to her. But Evie hadn't seemed much like Veena's type. In fact, she hadn't even seemed that much like a mercenary, except for that head-chopping comment. Regardless, the woman carried a sword. Not the kind of person he wanted to trifle with. No, he needed to keep his head down and figure out what he was going to do about his cash-flow problem.

But even that could wait. Cas motioned to the bartender one more time and if he wasn't sure it was impossible he could have sworn he saw the bartender glance at him with exasperation. But robots didn't have emotive faces. Except, maybe spending all this time with Box had taught him how to read them better.

"Yes, sir?" the bartender asked, approaching him. Definitely some malice in there. Had to be.

"One more round," Cas said.

4

The alarm tore through the air and Cas shot straight out of bed, puking on what remained of his sheets. "Dammit." Cas wiped his mouth. The smell of vomit permeated the room. "Turn that fucking thing off!" Cas yelled in the comm.

The alarm went silent. "Everything alright, boss?" Box said through the speaker.

"It would be a lot better if you stopped waking me up with an ear-splitting siren." He clutched his pounding head, recalling the brief image of a woman with a sword. Had he dreamed her?

"Sorry, boss. But I do love hearing you retch in the mornings," Box said.

Cas coughed and spit what remained of the vomit into the spreading pile on his bed. He'd clean it up later. "What time is it?"

"Nine hours have passed since I brought you back to the ship," Box replied. "You need to hydrate."

Cas pushed the sheets to the side and staggered to his sink, splashing water on his face and down his throat. It didn't help. "You brought me back?"

"Carried. You were too drunk to walk. Again."

"Tell me I didn't do anything stupid," Cas said, hanging his head over the sink as the water droplets dripped down his face into the basin.

"No more than usual."

That was a relief. Cas hadn't meant to let it get out of control. He hadn't even thought he'd had enough money to buy that many drinks. He'd underestimated how much he'd gotten for the data recorder. "I'll be up there in a minute," Cas said.

It was hard to concentrate under the shower. Each stream of water felt like an exhaust blast on his skull. He shouldn't have gone overboard but what else was he supposed to do? He was almost as bad off as Maddox. At least Maddox had a functioning ship to make runs. Cas would be lucky to launch from Devil's Gate at all. And he still had no clue what to do about his money problem.

No. He knew what he needed to do. He just didn't want to do it.

Cas finished the shower and threw on his cleanest clothes. If he had to do this he wanted to at least make a good impression.

"Morning," he grumbled, ambling into the cockpit.

Box's attention was focused on a net drama playing on one of the screens. "Coffee is brewing in the kitchen. Sleep well?"

With each step a miniature shockwave blasted its way through his brain. "Don't start. What's the ship's status?"

Box paused the feed and turned to him. "Thruster four on the port side is dead. You have two magnetic coils that need to be replaced and the undercurrent targeting system is off by twelve percent. It will need to be switched out with a newer model…unless you want to get lost in the deep reaches of space."

"That would almost be preferable." Cas slumped down in the captain's chair. Really it wasn't the captain's chair, this ship was too small to have anything so grand. Box always took the pilot's seat, so if he was really honest with himself it was the co-pilot's chair. He was the only one who thought of it differently. "Maybe I can take a look at the targeting system, realign it in some way."

"Hab suite two has a pressurization problem, but it's localized," Box added. "Also two of the landing gear struts are rusted from that landing on Calfour Straxus. Which, if you'll remember, I warned you about."

"Okay, okay, stop," Cas said putting one hand up and rubbing his temple with the other. "How much do we need for repairs? Minimum. To get the ship in working condition?"

"If we ignore hab suite two and a few other non-essentials, approximately four hundred and twenty-five thousand kassope."

Cas slapped his hands to his face and screamed into them, despite the pain it caused his head. When he removed them Box was staring at him. "Would you like me to leave?"

"No," Cas said, standing. "I hoped I wouldn't have to go to Veena. But I don't see any other way out of this, do you?"

The robot shrugged. "It's not too late to take Maddox's ship. We could leave him yours."

"I'm not giving up the *Reasonable Excuse*. This ship has been the one constant in my life for the past five years."

"What about me?" Box complained.

"You weren't you in the beginning. You were just like all the rest." Cas made his way into the kitchen and poured the slimy coffee from the maker into a chipped cup. It might as well be tar. Still, he downed it as quickly as he could without burning his throat.

Box appeared at the entrance. "I'm serious. There are people worse than you out there. People who deserve to have their ships stolen. It isn't like you'd have to make it a regular thing."

Cas shook his head. "I'm starting to think you're right. Making an 'honest' living out here is impossible. I've already had to concede to carry Veena's *goods* along with the passengers. But it looks like that might not even be enough anymore." He placed the cup in the autocleanser. "But I'm not taking another courier's ship."

"You seemed pretty serious with Maddox last night," Box said.

"That was to scare him. Sometimes I think he's worse at this than I am."

"Except he's willing to break a few rules."

Cas turned to the one window in the kitchen. Beyond was the surface of the station, hundreds of ships docked beside one another. And after that the blackness of space stretched to infinity, only occasionally interrupted by a speck of white. "It could be worse," he said. "She could have me working down on Vetar. At least here I'm in space, even if it is the same few routes over and over again." The thought of the woman with the sword crossed his mind again and he turned around. "Box."

The robot looked up.

"What would you think about taking a mercenary job?"

"Veena would cut off your balls," he replied.

He arched an eyebrow. "Only if she found out."

"If you're willing to risk it. I'm not sure I'd be so careless with my genitals, if I had them."

"Let's take a moment and be thankful you don't." Cas immediately wiped *that* image from his mind. "I think something happened last night."

"It must not have been up to your usual standards, I didn't catch it on the vid feeds before I came to pick you up." Box moved into the kitchen, his yellow eyes blinking in what Cas recognized as amusement.

"No, not that. A woman approached me. A mercenary. Said she had a job for me."

"What did you do?"

"I think I laughed in her face." Cas shook his head. "I don't know, maybe I imagined her. I was already drunk when she came up."

"A random mercenary comes up and offers you a job out of the blue. You." Box said. "I agree, it was probably an alcohol-induced hallucination brought on by your fear of facing Veena and perhaps even guilt over what you did to poor Maddox."

"You just said I should steal his ship!"

"Doesn't mean I can't feel sorry for him, especially after you pointed a gun in his face. Tsk, tsk, captain."

Cas' eyes narrowed. "I really hate you sometimes."

"No, you don't. If I weren't here you'd end up talking to the coffee maker. And *nobody* wants that." Box turned and left the kitchen.

"Thanks for the help!" Cas called after him, knowing it was futile. "I guess I'll go off and sign the rest of my life away!"

Box didn't reply. He'd probably already plugged back into his net drama. Cas smoothed the front of his wrinkled shirt, then grabbed his worn jacket from the floor and dusted it off before slipping it on. He hated himself for what he was about to do. Even if he wanted the mercenary job he didn't have the ability to do anything worthwhile. Not unless this possibly fictitious woman paid for all his repairs.

As he strolled out of the ship and down through the airlock into the connecting corridor he winced as he imagined the look on Veena's face when he asked her for a loan. She'd toy with him, that much was guaranteed. And she'd hem and haw over it and try to make him think he wasn't worth the extra risk. But the truth was she'd love it. Because it would mean Cas would be indebted to her so deep he'd never be able to get out. He'd be a part of the Sargan Commonwealth for the rest of his life, and there was little he could do about it. It wasn't as if he could go back to the Coalition, what with the warrants for his arrest and all. Not that he ever would anyway.

Cas made his way through the main promenade, looking exactly as it had last night. The only difference being it wasn't as crowded as it had been the night before. It seemed everyone only came out later in the station's cycle, which was synched up with the closest planet: Vetar. Vetar had a twenty-two-hour day. It was better than some of the more exotic planets, but also made adjusting difficult. He kept the *Reasonable Excuse* on a twenty-hour cycle, despite operating in this sector of space for over five years. It was something he didn't want to let go of. Not yet.

As Cas passed *The Pit* with zero memory of Box retrieving him from the place, he happened to glance over only to catch sight of the same woman from last night. He almost stumbled, but managed to keep his composure and his stride. She was leaning up against the side of the doorway, her arms crossed with the long sword still strapped to her back. As he passed her gaze bore directly into him, following him down the corridor. Cas thought about calling out to tell her to mind her own business but thought better of it. Instead, he turned away and focused on his destination: Veena's chambers. He hadn't made an appointment but it wouldn't matter. She'd see him if for no other reason than to give him a hard time. It seemed to be her favorite pastime.

Before Cas rounded the corner, he risked one look back toward *The Pit* only to find the doorway empty. *Finally. Go find someone else to bother.*

Maybe he should mention to Veena he was being headhunted by a couple mercenaries. See if she wouldn't up his pay. But why would she? By Kor, he'd be lucky if she didn't decide to impound his ship. But that definitely wasn't happening. He tapped the boomcannon under his jacket. *No one* was getting that ship.

A pair of strong hands grabbed his lapels, yanking him inside a room adjacent to the corridor. He hadn't even seen them coming. By the time he got his bearings and the fog of his hangover allowed his eyes to adjust he found a very long and sharp blade pressed to his neck. And the person holding it was none other than Evie.

5

Cas breathed heavily as Evie pressed the blade to his skin. "Is this because I said no?"

"By Garth your breath stinks," Evie replied, screwing up her face. "Ever hear of a mint?"

Cas surveyed the room. It was a normal hab suite with a bed and adjacent room with a head and shower, but it appeared unused. A window on the opposite side of the room showed the starfield beyond. "I'm not really into the kinky stuff. If you're going to make me do this you might be disapp—"

"Shut up," Evie said. "How any woman would want to have sex with you is beyond me."

"Then, if you'll just excuse me," Cas said, "I have a meeting and I don't want to put it off any longer otherwise I'll lose my nerve and have to pay another visit to the bar."

Evie lessened the pressure on the sword, still keeping it close to his throat. "I don't care about your schedule," she replied. "You're coming with me whether you like it or not."

"You sure you're not into kinky stuff?" Cas asked. "Because the sword seems to be turning one of us on and it's not me."

She withdrew the weapon, sheathing it with a simple, practiced movement. Cas worked to hide his awe.

"My name is Lieutenant Commander Evelyn Diazal of the Sovereign Coalition of Aligned Systems. I was ordered to retrieve you from Sargan space and that's what I'm going to do," she said as if it was obvious.

Upon hearing the words *Sovereign Coalition of Aligned Systems* Cas recoiled, pressing himself further into the wall despite the lack of a weapon making him do so. "I don't think so, lady."

"You don't have a choice," she replied, matter-of-factly.

"No, you don't have a choice," he said, heat rising in his cheeks. "*I'm* not part of the Coalition anymore. I can do whatever I want."

"Mr. Robeaux," she said, her voice dripping with disdain. "I don't think you understand the pred—"

"I understand perfectly, *Evie*," he said, pushing past her. "The Coalition decides maybe I'm better off back in jail so they send an errand girl to do their job for them. I don't think so. You'll actually have to use that sword on me if you want me to come back with you."

"Jail? What are you talking about? I was ordered to bring you back to Coalition space, to Starbase Eight." She narrowed her eyes. "Why were you in jail?"

"You don't know?" he scoffed. "That's surprising. And here I thought I was infamous. I'm sure someone will tell you if you ask. But it's not going to be me because I'm not going back."

"Until recently I was stationed out near Epsilon Lyre. We don't get a lot of gossip out there." She seemed to reset herself. "Regardless, it doesn't matter. The admiral made this mission a priority one, which means come with me willingly or unconscious. Your choice."

"Neither." He grabbed the handle of his pistol but kept it in the holster. "I told you, you'll have to take me in a body bag if you want to have a chance of getting me back into Coalition space."

Evie's eyes went to the pistol and she stiffened. He hadn't even meant to do it, it was a reflex. But if the Coalition had sent her, how many other officers were out there on the station waiting for him? She might be right, he might not have a choice. If she was alone he had a good chance of getting past her. But if there was a small army on the other side of that door waiting to ambush him…he'd never have a chance. And the longer he stood here arguing with her the more paranoid he became about it.

Cas released the handle of the gun, leaving it in its holster. Evie relaxed her shoulders. "Look," he said. "I don't have a quarrel with you. But if you try to take me back I'll be forced to shoot you in the leg. And neither of us want that. Don't make me do it."

She seemed intrigued by the prospect. "I have my orders."

"How many more are there? To take me back?" he asked when she cocked her head as if she didn't understand what he was talking about.

"Just me."

Cas nodded for a moment. "I have no doubt you know how to use that sword, but I also know you won't use it on me. Not if you're *really* from the Coalition." He turned toward the door. "If you want my advice," he said. "Get out while you still can. Before they make you do something you can't take back." He took another breath then pushed the pad beside the door and it slid open. It was a gamble, turning his back on her, but he needed to get out of there. To get out from under her accusatory stare.

To his astonishment, the door slid closed behind him sealing her back inside. Cas's hands shook. Coming so close to the Coalition after five years of nothing had rattled him more than he'd expected. He hadn't set foot across Coalition space ever since *the incident*. As far as he was concerned, the crime-ridden, slimy underbelly of the Sargan Commonwealth was much safer. Everything in the Coalition was too…structured. Too easy. At least that's how they made it seem. That was the whole recruitment slogan. *Come join the Sovereign Coalition of Aligned Systems! Share in our resources! Eliminate your planet's problems!*

Yeah, and the only cost was any sense of self-determination.

The supporters would disagree with him, saying not only did people have the right to choose whatever they wanted, they could do so without consequence. Want to be a painter? Great! The Coalition would provide for all your expenses. Prefer to lay on some exotic beach for the rest of your life? No problem, the Coalition had you covered. Want to explore the stars in an advanced starship? Absolutely! Have the time of your life! Except sometimes you might have to do a few things you might find questionable. We are a military organization after all. And there has to be a tradeoff for all those painters and people lying on the beach all day. It all has to even out in the end.

Ugh. Cas tried shaking his hands out as he made his way back to the main corridor. He couldn't see Veena like this; she'd play him like a Valderan squrn. No, he needed to get his head straight.

He passed *The Pit* again but the last thing he needed at the moment was more alcohol. He'd made the mistake of meeting with Veena drunk once and it had not gone well. Apparently it was difficult to make contract negotiations for what you're agreeing to haul for someone when you're intoxicated. He was still paying for that one.

No, he needed to go back to his ship. Get his head straight. Otherwise he might as well curl up beside the wall like Maddox and wait for station security.

6

"That was quick," Box said as Cas re-entered the ship. He'd moved to the kitchen and had switched off his regular net drama to some other program.

"I didn't get to Veena's, tha—" Cas paused. "What are you *watching*?"

"Hm?" Box said, looking up. "Oh, this? It's an old program called *World on Fire*. It's about this woman, Janet, whose husband has been cheating on her, but she doesn't know it, and then her teenage daughter finds out he was actually cheating with *her* best friend, but she doesn't want to tell her mom because she thinks her mom will think it's her fault because she's the one who invites Rebecca over all the time and it will tear their family apart and there's all this drama and it's just great! It was on for forty-seven years. I'm on season three."

Cas stared at him, dumbfounded. "You know what, I'm sorry I asked." He rubbed his temples again. "I need to go lie down. I assume nothing else has broken in the thirty minutes I've been gone."

"I don't know, I've been engrossed." Box turned his attention back to the display.

As Cas made his way out of the kitchen Box called to him again, "What stopped you from reaching Veena? The smell of the bar?"

"No, smartass," Cas said, returning to the entryway, his mouth firmly set. "That woman showed up again. I didn't dream her up after all. She's from the Coalition."

Box reached up, turned off the screen then swiveled around to face Cas. "Spill it."

Cas fumbled a moment. "There's nothing to spill. The Coalition wants me back. I said no. End of story."

Box took a step forward. "You said no? You think they're just going to let you go about your merry business? What the Coalition wants—"

Cas waved him off. "I know. And as soon as I splash some water on my face I'm going back to meet Veena. I'll get the money to fix the ship and then we're gone. The Coalition can't operate in Sargan space forever without being detected. And if she tries to stop me again I'll just blow her cover. She'll have to go back empty-handed."

"What's her name?" Box asked, reaching over for the portable terminal in the kitchen. It booted up easily.

"Lieutenant Commander Evie Diazal. Evelyn Diazal," Cas corrected.

"Evie huh?"

"Don't start." Box's fingers raced over the interface, breaking through the Coalition's primary firewall in seconds. "I knew there was a reason I kept you around."

"I know, it's my winning personality," Box replied. "Here. Lt. Commander Evelyn Diazal. Born 2568 on Sissk. That's pretty far outside the inner ring."

"And a hell of a long way from here," Cas added.

"Entered the Navy Academy at the age of eighteen, quickly rose through the ranks. Her parents were/are in the

Coalition as well, but it looks like their files have been redacted. I can't seem to find anything on them."

"Anything else pertinent?" Cas asked. The more he knew the better. Despite his warnings to her, he knew he hadn't seen the last of the Lieutenant Commander.

"A few commendations for service. Her postings have been all over the place, but mostly around the outer rim. She's stayed away from Horus and the central planets."

"Probably explains why she doesn't know about me. And why they chose her to bring me in. Lack of prejudice."

"Anyone else would have smashed your nose in first," Box said, his eyes flickering with laughter. "Oh. She's also got one hell of a piloting record. She might even be able to keep up with me."

"Great." Cas sighed. "So even if we do get off this station in one piece she'll probably be waiting for us." He tapped his foot, pondering. "See if you can locate any ships with a faint Coalition signature. She'll have no doubt masked it, but maybe if we know what we're looking for we can—"

"Found it," Box replied. "About half a kilometer away, pad 076 Delta. It's tiny, a two-man shuttle with undercurrent capability."

"The Coalition has been busy," Cas said. "Those were still in the development phase when I…left." He stared at the screen. Pad 076 Delta. It wasn't that far away. He could get over there quickly enough. There was even a good chance he could get on board without triggering the alarm systems. "Are you thinking what I'm thinking?"

"Probably not," Box replied, spinning back to face him. "What if this is a good thing? What if they genuinely want you back? Not *everything* about the Coalition is bad, you know."

"I'm not even going to dignify that with a response." Cas turned his back on Box, passing back through the entry into the corridor.

"Think about it," Box said, raising his voice to follow Cas down the hall. "It's the perfect opportunity to get away from Veena. You'd have the Coalition's protection."

Cas' face flushed. "Yeah, all four walls with ample amounts of bread and water. No thank you. I'd rather take the risk."

"What if it isn't to send you back to prison?" Box asked.

"Let's be honest. We know what this is about. And if they aren't going to send me to prison then the alternative is much worse. Either way it's a bad deal. At least with Veena I know what her motives are. I know she's trying to manipulate me. She's upfront about it. But the Coalition likes to pretend it is this giant benevolent whale, just gliding along making sure everyone is safe when really it's just another alpha predator. It will do anything and everything it needs to survive. The only difference is the Coalition lies to you about it. They'll pretend like nothing is wrong, that you will always be safe and secure and happy. And the truth is there is no safe, secure and happy. It doesn't exist. That's what most people in the Coalition don't realize. I'm not going back to that fantasy. I like it better in the real world."

"Tell me how you really feel about it," Box replied.

"I don't know why I even bother with you," Cas said, extricating himself from the situation. Box loved to get him fired up; he just couldn't seem to help himself.

"You sure there isn't something you want to get off your chest?" he called, his tone slightly mocking. Cas ignored him, trailing the hallway down to his quarters. He opened the door to his room only for the stench of vomit to smack him in the face. He had to suppress the urge to relapse and instead went to the small en-suite and closed the door. The stench in here wasn't as bad but still present. He might just have to incinerate those sheets.

He ran the tap and splashed a generous amount of water on his face, noticing his hands had stopped quivering. The anger over the Coalition had won out over any fear they might actually be able to take him back. Water ran down the sides of his neck, seeping into the shirt underneath. He took an extra few minutes to clean his teeth before giving himself a last once-over. He could do this. So what if it meant he knew how the rest of his life would turn out? There were worse fates. Maybe in another ten, fifteen years working for Veena he might even be able to move up in the organization. Though…he shuddered at the thought of what she required of her lieutenants. Perhaps it was best to stay in transport. To stay out in space.

Wide, open space.

***

This time Cas took the opposite direction outside the hard lock with his ship. Since Devil's Gate was a giant disc it only made sense he'd get to Veena's by taking the long way around, except he had a stop to make first.

The upper corridors weren't as spacious as the promenades of the lower levels, most of them having been designed with function in mind rather than comfort. More than once he had to duck under pipes and squeeze through small spaces to get to adjacent landing pads. The first thing through his mind was Claxians would have a hell of a time fitting through here which was an odd thought to have considering he hadn't even seen a Claxian since his court-martial. But it seemed the appearance of Evie was drawing out all sorts of unwanted and repressed memories.

"Zero seven six delta," Cas said to himself as he approached one of the locks. "Let's see if anyone is home or you're still out there waiting for me." He pulled a scanner from his pocket and did a quick search for heat signatures, finding nothing out of the ordinary. The shuttle was remarkably small. Had she slept in it? Coalition space was at least five days away with the nearest undercurrent. He crept into the lock itself, walking up the ramp to the shuttle door. "All we have to do is make you think there's a coolant leak inside." Cas tapped a few commands on the access panel and the door slid open.

It was sparse. As all things Coalition tended to be. A small bench to his right doubled as a bed, a locker sat to his left which had been left unlocked. He peeked inside to find three identical uniforms and a smattering of other personal items. A small door beside the locker led to the onboard utilities, also very clean and *not* smelling of vomit. The front of the ship had two chairs and a viewscreen. According to Box all the Coalition had done was apply a layer of electronic paint and altered the engine signatures. It was enough to pass if anyone wasn't looking, but for someone with experience with Coalition ships, and shuttles in particular, he'd had no trouble identifying it.

He'd almost forgotten what it was like.

Shaking the thoughts away Cas quickly went to work, removing one of the side panels to the shuttle to access the primary undercurrent generator. Two minutes later and the system had been permanently disabled. She'd need either a brand-new generator—which she'd have a hard time finding here without revealing she was Coalition—or wait for rescue. Either way, she wouldn't be following Cas once Veena approved the loan and all the parts were installed. Neither of which should take more than half a day at most.

Cas dusted off his hands, replaced the panel and made his way back down into the lock, careful to leave everything as he'd found it.

One problem down, one to go.

7

Taking the long way around to Veena's Cas didn't pass *The Pit* again, but he kept an eye out for Evie anyway. He wasn't about to be ambushed a second time and she seemed to have some kind of superpower allowing her to get right in his way.

At the same time, he practiced what he would say to Veena. He needed to be firm and yet grateful. He'd do what he had to do and get the hell off this station. At least out there *he* was in control. And while he didn't relish the idea of ferrying any more princesses across the Sargan Commonwealth things could be a lot worse.

Cas approached the giant cylindrical dampeners near the center of the station. They were at least thirty meters in height and ran up through multiple levels. But if not for them, anytime a cosmic trench would pass through the system every person on the station would go flying. He thought of them as gigantic metal guards, since they were situated on the opposite sides of the entrance to Veena's section of the station; one of the most lavish and unnecessarily large spaces he'd ever seen. He approached the doors nestled between the dampeners and pressed his thumb to the pad.

The twenty-meter-tall doors swung back, revealing the inner entrance, complete with human guard this time. He was tall yet muscular, wearing a derby hat with what appeared to be the tip of a spear sticking out of the top.

"Kort," Cas said, passing the guard standing beside the scanning portal.

"Robeaux," Kort replied, tapping a few buttons. Cas felt a tingle as the scanners electronically probed every part of his body.

"Gun," Kort said, holding his hand out. Cas unholstered the boomcannon and slapped into Kort's hand, butt first.

"Do everyone a favor and keep the safety on," Cas said.

"Someone's feisty today," Kort replied, placing the gun in a drawer which slid shut. "You're gonna need it."

"Why? What's wrong this time?"

Kort smiled, revealing two missing teeth and two more platinum replacements. Cas hadn't seen it but another one of Veena's lieutenants told him Kort pulled them himself. Apparently, he was working toward a set of specially engraved teeth. "You'll find out. I just hope you haven't come to ask for anything."

Cas sighed, pondering how far he could get the *Reasonable Excuse* before it completely fell apart. "Thanks for the advice," Cas replied. Kort hit another button and the second set of doors opened, revealing what Cas referred to as the *long walk.*

Past the second set of doors was a massive, open room, thirty meters high, just like the dampeners. In front of him a long walkway a hundred meters long, decorated with a red velvet carpet straight down the middle. On either side of the carpet the floor extended another ten meters before dropping off into nothing. Below housed the guts of the station itself and at least a two-hundred-fifty-meter drop. Veena told him it was where she disposed of all the people who disappointed her over the years. She often joked it was becoming too full, which was impossible as anything that fell was incinerated halfway down from the heat the station generated.

Regardless, it provided a creepy atmosphere with the orange glow emanating on both sides as her "subjects" as she liked to call them approached her. At the very end of the walk sat—what else—but a giant throne, complete with steps leading up to it. Behind the throne more dampeners gave the room the appearance of a church with a very large organ. Cas grumbled to himself as he walked, not allowing himself to be intimidated by the space or her for that matter. He'd never seen her *actual* quarters, this was just where she tended to do business. And considering she owned the station itself, it was only fitting she chose the center as her lair. Off to the left and right of the throne were areas where the floor was not missing and presumably led to her private sanctuary.

Today it looked as if he'd come at a good time. Typically she was on the throne, mirror or console in hand, either preening herself or watching something entertaining. Though one time he'd walked in as she'd ordered an execution, watching as the man had been tossed over the edge. She had been in a particularly good mood that day.

Cas marched along, taking less time than he normally did to get up to the throne. "Rasp, you're looking well," he said to the light-skinned man standing off to the side with his hands clasped in front of him.

"Come back later, Robeaux," Rasp replied in a deep voice. "You don't wanna be here today."

"I'll make it quick," Cas replied. "Let me see her."

Rasp shrugged. "It's your life." He turned and disappeared behind one of the walls to the left.

Cas waited off to the side of the stairs. He didn't like being directly in front of the throne. It felt wrong somehow; too ominous. The only sounds were the occasional swoosh noises from the dampeners and the general hum of the station.

Otherwise it was silent, which was impressive for such a cavernous room. He imagined it could be quite peaceful in here. Maybe that's why she liked it. After all it—

"And what does *he* want?"

The screech came from behind the wall where Rasp had disappeared. The relative calm of the room was destroyed as Veena's voice echoed throughout the entire room, bouncing off every surface over and over again.

The distinct sound of heels striking the floor made Cas glance up to see Veena appear from behind the wall. But this wasn't the typical together, everything-is-in-its-place Veena. This was a frantic Veena, a side of her he'd never seen before. "I don't fucking believe this," she huffed. She ignored him, making her way up the stairs to her throne, her long green dress dragging on the ground behind her as it always did. Her dark hair, typically in some kind of ornate braid he could never figure out, fell over her bare shoulders while her green crown remained perched on the top of her head. She had vibrant blue eyes which complimented her dress except today they were hidden behind a sheer veil attached to her crown. She adjusted herself then sat in the throne, crossing her ankles and grasping the armrests on either side before turning to look at him. "Approach," she said.

Cas swallowed his pride and made his way up the steps, stopping at the very last one to take a knee. "High Priestess Veena," he said, bowing his head.

"Caspian Robeaux. What a *surprise*." Her tone caught him off guard, but he wasn't about to let it derail his plans. Veena liked pomp and circumstance and it wasn't out of the ordinary to spend at least five minutes singing her praises. But everything about this meeting seemed out of the ordinary. He wasn't sure what to expect.

"I'd like to thank you for taking the time—"

"Save it, Robeaux," she snapped. "We both know why you're here so get on with it and leave me be. I have more important matters to attend to."

Cas raised his head and stood, drawing a deep breath. "I need a loan."

She let out one short, but loud, laugh and sat back in her chair, glaring at him. "A loan." Her eyes dashed to the left. "And what, pray tell, would you need with a loan?"

"My ship is in need of repairs and if you wish for me to continue making *supply runs* for you, you'll help me out."

A wicked smile spread across Veena's face. *This* was more like it. This was what he'd expected. She relaxed her shoulders, not releasing him from her gaze. "And just how much do you need? *If* I were to grant such a request." Her long nails tapped against the armrests in a strange rhythm.

"Four hundred and twenty-five thousand," Cas replied. It was a lot. They both knew it was a lot. But he wasn't going to back down now.

"Oh, Caspian," she said, her voice suddenly saccharine. "That's an *awful* lot of money." She tapped the armrests again. "And what might I receive in return for this...*investment*?"

"Extend my contract. Until it's paid in full with interest."

Veena seemed to consider it, then turned her head to the side, revealing a series of earrings sparkling in the light just underneath her hair. "I heard you had a little encounter with our mutual friend Maddox yesterday."

"You could call it that." What was she getting at?

"As I understand it, he wasn't very fair to you." She turned back to him, her grin widening. "And you had to take matters into your own hands. Things got...heated."

"Your point?" Cas asked.

"It just seems to me that my little boy scout is growing up," she said, her voice still dripping with honey. "Maybe you're ready for something more...serious."

He struggled to maintain his composure. "I'm fine out where I am; ferrying diplomats and your other illustrious guests. You need someone you can trust out there." Suddenly coming here seemed like a bad idea. He hadn't considered she might take the opportunity to renegotiate his contract. There were plenty of couriers, she could always use someone else. And why would she give him a loan when she could easily reassign him? He mentally slapped himself in the face. How could he have been so stupid not to see this before?

Her long fingers traced imaginary lines on the armrests. "I don't know, Caspian. I hate the thought of you out there all alone, just you, your ship, and that pathetic robot your only source of company." She leaned forward. "I think we can find you something much more suited to your particular…skills."

"That's enough," a female voice announced from somewhere off to his left. Veena recoiled as if she'd been bitten; the smirk on her face transforming into a visage of loathing.

Stepping out from behind the same wall Veena had appeared from earlier was none other than Evie, arms crossed and a smug look on her face.

8

"What are you doing here?" Cas said, stiffening.

"And here I was hoping it was all a bad dream," Veena said, examining her long nails.

"What is going on?" Cas asked, unsure of anything at this point. Why would Evie be conferring with Veena? Her story about being in the Coalition hadn't been a ploy, Box confirmed that much. Which meant she had either gone rogue or was more determined than Cas gave her credit for.

"This...*mercenary*," Veena said, distain dripping from the word, "has purchased your contract." She put her hand down.

"What?" Cas took a step back, broaching the edge of the stairs. He righted himself just in time before tumbling backward. "You allowed that?" He glanced from Veena to Evie and back again.

"It wasn't an easy decision, I assure you," Veena said, her chin higher than before. "But it was too good of a deal. Though upon reexamination...I think I might have been cheated." She narrowed her eyes at Evie.

"We have a deal," Evie replied.

Veena scoffed, flitting her fingers. "So we do."

Cas's comm unit beeped. He checked quickly to see it was Box on the other end. "Problems?" he asked.

"A team of Veena's people are here," Box replied. "They want access to the ship." Cas caught Veena's gaze.

"I *have* to get my goods from your hold if you're no longer going to be in my employ," she said. "I can't allow you to walk away with two million in untraceable equipment, now can I?"

"Two million?" Cas yelled. "That's how much I was carrying?"

Veena's smile stretched wide as she sunk back into her throne. "Don't blame me if you don't know what you're carrying. Weren't you the one who—how did you put it? *Didn't give two shits about what's in your cargo hold as long as you didn't have to deal with it*? Maybe I'm paraphrasing."

"Box, let them on. They're going to lighten our load." Cas said, tapping the comm unit to cut the line. He couldn't believe she'd put that much on his ship. It was possible she just did it to goad him. Had he actually looked at any point during the journey he would have realized he'd had more than enough to trade for all the parts he needed to fix his ship and then some. With a couple million he could have stayed in deep space for a few years, just cruising. And all he'd needed to do was take it and run.

"How long will it take to unload?" Evie asked, her arms still crossed.

"An hour or so," Veena replied, no longer interested.

Cas watched Evie. The answer seemed to satisfy her as she still wore that smug look on her face. She knew she'd won. Veena no longer had any vested interest in him. How much had Evie paid? By purchasing his contract, she'd eliminated any protection he could have expected from the Sargans when the Coalition came calling. Evie would be able to drag him back into the Coalition one way or the other now.

Unless he blew her cover. If Veena found out she'd been paid off by the Coalition she'd lose her mind; it was the one organization she refused to do business with, no matter how good the money was. He respected that about her. It was what drew him to her in the first place and had been the one thing they shared in common. He'd never gotten the whole story but from what he'd put together through the years her hatred of the Coalition had something to do with how her parents were treated while citizens.

Cas took stock of the room. Rasp was right behind Evie. Kort was down the hall and Veena had two other guards whose names he didn't know standing off to the left and the right of the throne. If he did blow Evie's cover Veena would have no qualms about dropping her into the pit. Even with the sword she didn't stand a chance against four of Veena's guards. Veena would probably even order Cas to help them which was unacceptable.

"Wait, you can't just let some stranger purchase all my debt from you," Cas protested, trying to think of a way out of this. "I don't even know this person."

Veena stood and took two steps toward him, placing her hand gently on his shoulder. Even through his jacket he could sense her skin was bitterly cold. "I don't care," she said, her voice soft. "All I know is I've lost a good asset today, but the price to keep you was just too high. Contrary to what this mercenary thinks, you're not worth that much." She gave him a brief smile before dropping her hand.

He couldn't exactly protest. He'd wanted a way out, though preferably one that didn't lead straight back to the Coalition. Although, there might still be a way he could turn this to his advantage. "What about the repairs to my ship?" Cas asked, indignant. He thought he caught Evie's smile falter. "I can't exactly do any jobs for *anyone* without an operational ship."

Veena turned to Evie. "I can of course repair his…ship." Even when he was helping her she couldn't keep the revulsion out of her voice. Though standing in this room it was obvious Veena only liked the best. "For a price."

"I don't think that will be necessary," Evie said.

"What?" Veena said with mock concern. "Who spends so much money on a courier who can't transport anything? Or perhaps your interest is in something other than his skills delivering goods back and forth." She drew her long fingers down through Cas's hair to the base of his neck, making him shudder. He didn't dare face her.

"Thank you, but we'll find repairs at the next port over," Evie said.

Cas brushed Veena's hand away as she chuckled. "It won't make it that far," he replied. Evie snapped a look at him with fire in her eyes. "I doubt I can even open an undercurrent in the state its in."

"You won't find anyone else on this station with the appropriate parts either," Veena sneered at Evie. "But don't worry. I'd be happy to give you…a five percent discount."

"How generous," Evie said through clenched teeth.

"It's my pleasure," Veena replied. "After all, you did give me a once-in-a-lifetime deal." She'd lost any trace of her earlier anger. And that made Cas nervous. "Rasp," Veena called out. "See to it repairs begin immediately. We don't want to keep our new friend waiting too long. Though," she turned back to Evie, "I'm sure you can find *something* to do with him for a few hours."

"Yes, Mum," Rasp replied, turning and disappearing behind the wall.

Evie clenched her fists, dropping her arms. "I'll transfer the second payment to your account as soon as we leave."

Veena grinned, nodding but not responding. All of a sudden she'd reverted back into the collected, regal woman Cas had always known. She resumed her place on the throne and tented her long fingers together as Evie approached Cas.

"Let's go," she ordered, marching past him and onto the red carpet for the long walk.

Cas took one last look at Veena who seemed content now and turned to follow.

***

"What the hell was that?" Evie whispered as soon as they were beyond the outer doors and back in the main corridors of the station. Cas had made sure to check his ammunition when he retrieved his boomcannon from Kort. He couldn't afford sabotage now.

"What?" Cas said, feigning ignorance. He needed a drink. Badly.

"That crap about repairing your ship. You could have put my life in danger," she said.

"You did that the moment you stepped on this station," he replied. "It's not my fault you went to one of the most dangerous people in the sector to accomplish your mission."

"Well, it doesn't matter. She can keep your ship for all I care. You and I are going back to Coalition space and we're leaving right now. And in case you haven't noticed, you're all out of excuses." She picked up her pace and Cas took longer steps to keep up with her.

"Well, actually, we're not," he said.

She stopped cold. "Look. Unless you want a battalion of Coalition marines on this station tomorrow dragging your ass out of here I suggest you cooperate. And don't think I can't do it. I told you this was a priority one order which means you don't get to say no."

"What I mean is, we're not going anywhere because I disabled your shuttle." Cas smirked. "And it looks like my ship is getting the repairs it needs so in a couple of hours I'll be saying *adios* and you can just wait for rescue."

Her jaw hung open slightly but her eyes burned into his. “You…how could…only a Coalition—”

“I told you, I’m an engineer. I know how stuff works.” He turned and made his way down the hallway, leaving her standing there. “But thanks again for getting me out of my contract *and* for the repairs.” He tickled the air with his fingers at her as he sauntered off in search of the nearest bar.

9

"Why is it seventy-five percent of the times I've seen you it's been in or near a bar?" Evie strolled up to the counter inside *The Pit*.

Cas moaned and took another gulp of his rank, relishing the fizz going down his throat. "Give it up already, you've lost. In a couple of hours I'm leaving this station once and for all and you'll never see me again," he said.

She sat on the stool next to him, unhooking her sword and laying it on the bar beside her. The robot bartender glided over. "Yes?"

"What he's having," she said. The bartender turned to the taps. "You're absolutely right," she said to Cas. He arched an eyebrow at her. "You've got me. There is not a thing I can do to make you come back to the Coalition."

He took another sip as the bartender set her glass in front of her. "Why do I feel like there's a but coming on?" he asked.

"No buts. No more tricks. Here's to you, as clever as they said you were. You've bested me." She held up her glass. He furrowed his brow but lifted his own and clinked it with hers before taking another draw.

"I thought you didn't drink," he said.

"Now is the perfect time to start, don't you think? Every good failure needs a pick-me-up."

"What does this mean for you?" He couldn't help but wonder what the failure of a priority one mission would mean for her. "Going back empty-handed?"

She shrugged. "Who knows. They'll probably reassign me. Or maybe even demote me. Doesn't matter though."

"If you're trying to guilt me into coming it isn't going to work." Cas finished the rank. "I'll take another," he said to the bartender.

"Guilt you? Ha! I'm not sure that's an emotion you're capable of," she said. "I envy you. You have this uncanny ability to put yourself at the top of this little pyramid and everyone else around you just slides down to the bottom." She made a sliding motion with her hand. "But hey, you get to stay there at the top so no harm done, am I right? I'd just like to know how you do it." She tipped the glass back and drank half the liquid in one move.

The bartender set the second glass in front of him. "That's not how it is," he said, taking a large gulp himself. She was steering him into treacherous territory.

"Whatever you have to tell yourself." She finished off the rank and set the glass down. "Another," she said to the bartender. Cas glanced at his own glass. "Maybe I'll be like you," she said. "I'll just stay here on Devil's Gate. Pick up some work here and there. Earn myself a ship. I'm not going anywhere for a while so I might as well make use of my time." She yanked the second glass out of the bartender's hands before he had a chance to set it down. "Cheers." Evie raised it slightly before downing half of it again in one gulp.

"By Kor, slow down. If you really haven't had anything to drink before you're gonna topple off that stool."

"What's that?" Evie asked, sitting up straight. "Was that concern I heard?" She glanced around like she hadn't known who it had come from, making a small spectacle of herself.

"Did someone just express concern about my well-being? Nah, not here. Not in *Sargan* space."

Cas shushed her. "Keep your voice down unless you want people to start asking questions."

"You know what I can't figure out," Evie said, slamming the glass down on the counter and staring him directly in the eye. Her eyes wavered slightly. If she wasn't careful she'd end up on her ass before she managed to finish her second drink. "I can't understand why you didn't just out me to Veena. Why not tell her my true identity? It would have been a lot easier than sabotaging my ship. Which you did a magnificent job on by the way. I can't even figure out how to make the shower work anymore."

"It was necessary," Cas said. "I didn't have a choice."

"Answer the question."

He hesitated, staring into his drink. "You said you don't know who I am or what I did."

"No, and I don't care. If I'd needed to know they would have told me. It can't be that important. Either that or it's too important. But to me it doesn't matter. I just have my orders." She took another drink.

"And you don't know why they want me back so badly?"

She shook her head, rolling her eyes. "Above my pay grade."

"You don't get paid," he said.

"That's where you're wrong," she said, sticking her finger in his chest. "I do get paid. I don't need money to be happy. I get paid in fulfillment from helping my fellow life form, whether it be human or other. I get paid in the life experience I earn through my actions. I get paid in the access to the virtually unlimited resources of the Coalition. Why anyone would choose *this life* over one there is beyond me."

"It's because you haven't seen the seedy underbelly of the Coalition yet," Cas said, draining his drink and motioning for another. "But don't worry. One day it will all be clear. Then you'll think back to this moment and say to yourself 'Cas was right after all'."

Evie scoffed. "Doubtful." She'd finished her drink as well. The bartender brought them both a refill at the same time. She didn't bother toasting him this time, instead she greedily began drinking.

"Evie, seriously, slow down. That's a good way to knock yourself out."

"Just doing what you do," she said between sips. "Numb the world so it can't hurt anymore. It's all part of my new mission to understand alien life such as yourself."

"We're the same species."

"We definitely *are not*," she said, sadness reaching her eyes as she took another drink.

Cas cursed himself. No, he didn't need this. He was home free. In a few short hours he and Box would be off in the ship to some distant star, no longer concerned with the Sargans or the Coalition or any of this. Maybe he'd even discover a new civilization. Something no human had ever seen before. All he had to do was get past Evie.

All he had to do was leave her here.

He watched as she drained the rest of the third glass. He'd barely even touched his. "I didn't tell Veena because I didn't want to see you killed. You might be a pain in my ass but you don't deserve to die just because you were ordered to retrieve me."

She eyed him, rocking back and forth on the stool. "How generous," she spat.

"If I go," he said, testing the waters. "I want it in writing I will not be jailed." She stared at him, probably looking for any signs of deception. "And I will only stay in Coalition space for two days. After that I'm gone."

Evie stared at the empty glass in front of her. "I need certain concessions."

"Such as?"

"Such as your guarantee you won't run when we reach the border. That you'll cooperate with whatever it is they need you for." She turned to him. "I need to know you won't break your word." Cas stared at her in amazement. All traces of inebriation were gone; it was as if she were stone sober. Was her tolerance really that high? Even he felt the effects of the rank by now.

"If you can give me yours…I can give you mine," Cas said, not believing what he was saying. Why was he willing to go out on a limb for this woman? Probably because he would always wonder what would have happened to her if he left her here, alone. Not to mention he'd be looking over his shoulder for the rest of his life. The Coalition would keep sending people after him. At least if he went in now he could finally close this book. Because there was only one reason they could want him so badly.

"You won't run," she said.

"You'll keep me out of prison," he replied.

She stuck out her hand. He glanced at it, weighing the alternatives one last time. He grabbed his glass and drained it in one go then grabbed her hand and gave it a quick shake before he changed his mind.

"Thank you," she said.

10

Cas stumbled down the main thoroughfare toward the hangar bay. Box had needed to move the ship from the parking area to one of the repair garages on the outer edge of the ring itself. The walk seemed to take forever but it was probably hampered by the fact he's had another two ranks at the bar after agreeing to return to the Coalition.

Evie walked beside him, completely sober.

"Either you were lying about never having a drink before, or you're a sorcerer," Cas said, putting his hand up against the wall. The hallway stopped rotating around him as he did.

"Some people just tolerate it better," she said. They'd agreed since her ship had been disabled and his was in the process of being repaired they would take the *Reasonable Excuse* back to Coalition space. Evie argued it allowed her to keep a better eye on him and Cas had tried to argue back but when the urge to retaste the rank entered his throat he shut up. He didn't like the idea of her on his ship but he didn't see a better alternative. If he wanted this over quickly it was better to take her back now. And frankly he was in a hurry to get away from Veena. He still couldn't quite believe it was real, that he no longer owed her a cent. Which brought up something he'd been pondering.

"You do know that you just paid off a crime lord, don't you? All that money will go to people who build themselves up on the backs of others. Who make others suffer…" he paused, ensuring he wouldn't throw up. "…needlessly."

"I was told whatever it takes," Evie reiterated. "And yes, that included paying off a few criminals."

"That's what I was afraid of," Cas replied.

They reached the hangar bay as Cas's headache kicked in. Veena's workers swarmed the ship, replacing panels and wiring parts together. Off to the left of the ship was a pile of worn and damaged components. Box sat in front of the ship in a fold-out chair, his metal legs resting on a transportation crate while the holovid in front of him showed that stupid show he'd been watching.

"Box," Cas said as they approached.

"Huh?"

"Box look at me."

Box reached over and turned the holo off, turning to face them. "Oh Kor!" he yelled. "You look terrible! Why'd you want me to look at that? I was enjoying my show."

Evie stifled a chuckle while Cas approached him. "Are they almost done?" he asked, indicating the ship.

"Hm? Oh." Box turned to watch the workers. "They're ninety-two percent done. Boss," he said suddenly serious. "They pulled a lot of stuff out of the holds. I watched them carry it away."

"I know."

"We could have been rich off that stuff."

"I know, Box."

"Could have traveled the stars for years! Made it out to Omicron Terminus and back again." He was staring up at the ceiling twenty meters above them.

"Yes. Had either of us thought to look we could have done that." Cas held his stomach a moment. "As it is we're going back to the Coalition."

"But you said—"

Cas put his hands up. "I don't care what I said. We're going. For two days. Then we're out. Got it?"

"Got it, boss." His yellow eyes dimmed, indicating disappointment. Cas doubted Evie even noticed. It was something you only picked up if you were around 'bots a while.

Cas turned to Evie. "This is Lieutenant Commander Diazal," he said. "Evie, this is my…traveling companion Box."

To her credit, Evie held out her hand. Box examined it a minute then took it, giving it one shake. "That's rare," he said.

"What's that?" Evie asked.

"Not many people are willing to shake a robot's hand. Most think I'll crush it with my mammoth strength! Others are just assholes," he said.

"I've worked with artificial life forms in the past," Evie said. "You're no different to me than Mr. Robeaux here."

"I hope I'm a little different!" Box exclaimed. "He smells like Moogar excrement!"

Cas rolled his eyes. "Fine. I'll go shower. I assume the water pressure is working."

Box activated the holo again except this time a manifest showed up. "The pressure is…yes, you're clear to clean your balls, boss."

Cas turned to Evie. "Ignore him. He has an unhealthy obsession with genitals." Cas began walking toward the ship.

"No more unhealthy than humans!" Box called after him.

Evie caught up beside him. "Maybe you could show me where I'm staying. That way I can stay out of your way until we're ready to leave."

Cas reached the ramp to the ship, placing his hand on one of the struts. He took a deep breath. "I can't believe I'm doing this." He turned to Evie. "Follow me." Leading her up the ramp he took a right when they were past the second lock to the ship, down the primary corridor. "It'll take at least five days to get to Coalition space from here," Cas said, passing the hab suites. When he reached the last one he pressed his thumb to the pad beside the door which slid open. "So make yourself comfortable."

"I know how far it is. I flew here," she said, stepping into the room. It wasn't the nicest suite on the ship because he wasn't about to give a Coalition officer his best accommodation. She was lucky he didn't put her in an escape pod and tow her behind them.

The room was sparse, but functional. Not unlike Cas's room. Except the window was on the other side. "This will be fine, thank you," Evie said, removing her sword and laying it on the bed.

"We have limited food supplies, but it will be enough to get us there. Use the kitchen if you need it. I'll stay out of your way if you agree to stay out of mine," he added.

"Agreed. I'll be fine in here."

"Great," Cas said sarcastically. "Just great. I'm so glad we're doing this." He left her at the entryway, heading back to his own suite. All he wanted to do was lie down. He didn't want to shower. He didn't want to clean up. He didn't even want to think. He just wanted to try not to think about the mistake he was in the process of making. Not thinking about it was the best thing he could do for himself at the moment.

As the door opened the pungent smell of day-old vomit hit him and he doubled over, retching in the hallway.

"Is everything alright?" Evie asked from her doorway down the hall.

“Fine, fine.” He waved a hand behind him as he was still bent over. “Just stay over there. I’ve got it.”

“You sure?”

“Yes, under control.” When he didn’t hear anything else he assumed she’d returned to her suite. Cas tapped his comm. “Box get up here and help me clean up this mess.”

“What mess, boss?”

“The one in my room. And now the hallway,” he said, his throat burning.

“Drank too much again, huh?” Box asked.

Cas didn’t respond. Instead, he cut the comm and ventured into his room, pulling the soiled sheets off the bed and balling them up. He took them down the corridor to the lock, down the ramp and out into the garage, tossing them on top of the rest of the discarded equipment. Box came up behind him.

“I need you to print me a new set of sheets,” Cas said. “Before we leave. Use the station’s power.”

Box leaned down, putting his hand on Cas’s shoulder. “Are you sure we should do this?” he asked. “Why not just leave?”

Cas turned back to the ship as if he could see right through it. Right through to where Evie was probably sitting on the bed, wondering how she’d gotten *herself* into this situation. “Because I can’t run forever,” Cas replied.

11

Cas approached the door to Evie's room, pressing the button beside the door causing a chime to ring inside the room.

"Just a minute," she called.

He waited, wondering why he'd made the effort to come all the way down here when he could have sent a message through the comm. The door slid open to reveal her in her full Coalition uniform. He hadn't seen her bring it aboard but it made sense. She'd probably returned to the shuttle again before they'd left Devil's Gate while Cas was sleeping off his hangover on his sheet-less bed smelling of vomit.

"We're half an hour out," he said. "Just wanted to make sure you knew."

"I knew," she said.

Cas looked past her to see she'd hung the sword on one of the small hooks on the wall. "You going to take that thing back into Coalition space?"

She paused a moment, her eyes flickering back and forth over his face. "Not that it's any of your business but yes. It will go back into my personal storage."

"Not exactly Coalition-issue," he said. "I expect most citizens don't appreciate an officer walking around with a tool that slices off heads."

She chuckled. "No. It's just for infiltration. Plus, it doesn't hurt to have a family heirloom at my side. Helps keep me grounded." She stared at him as if waiting for him to say something else. Why *had* he come down here?

"Anything I should know before we arrive? I don't want to be shot down once we get in the Starbase perimeter."

She arched an eyebrow. "You know about that? Don't worry, I've already transmitted our description. They know we're coming."

"Did you get that agreement in writing yet?" he asked.

Evie tapped the back of her hand twice and Cas's comm unit beeped. He grabbed it, glancing at the document it'd just downloaded. "Official Coalition letterhead and all." He closed the document and replaced the comm back in his pocket. "I'm not stupid. I know once I'm on that base you can keep me there. But I'm trusting you'll keep your word. Don't make me regret that decision."

She watched him, her eyes scanning his face. "You're not the only one going out on a limb here. How do I know you don't have some plan devised once you get on the station to sabotage it? You clearly know what you're doing in that department. For all I know you could completely disable our closest defense to Sargan space."

Cas almost laughed. He hadn't considered sabotaging the station until she'd brought it up. But stations like that were different than a simple shuttle. Not that he couldn't do it, but it would be a much more complex and lengthy procedure. "I have a feeling that's going to be pretty hard with guards watching my back every minute."

"You know an awful lot about Coalition procedure," she said, staring at him under lowered lids. Somehow with her uniform on she looked taller. Cleaner. Cas supposed that's what the Coalition did to people. Polished them up and spat them out.

Cas shrugged it off. "I know a lot about a lot of things," he said, turning to head down the hallway. "Oh." He turned back. "When we get there, make sure they don't mess with my ship or my robot. I'm fond of both."

She nodded. "You have my word."

Cas continued down the hall. "It had better be worth something," he muttered under his breath. He returned to the cockpit where Box was monitoring the undercurrent. "How's she looking?"

"I think we'll get through with a clean run. No trenches detected so far. And we've only got another four minutes in undercurrent space." For once Box was paying attention to what he was doing instead of watching some program.

"How far from the station will we be when we exit the current?"

Half a second later, Box answered, "Eight-hundred thousand kilometers. Another fifteen, twenty minutes to the station itself."

Out in the distance Cas could see the Station, hanging in the blackness of space like a child's mobile, held up by an invisible string. It was like a giant white hourglass. At least from this angle. A wide, flat cone at the very top, thinning in the middle then expanding again down at the bottom. In the middle of the spire various pods and instruments were attached, each was specifically there for a purpose and could be removed or changed out as necessary.

A deep loathing welled up in the depths of his core. This was crazy. He should have just left Evie back with the Sargans and fled to an uncharted sector of space. Get out of the local area. Maybe he would have died in the blackness of the void. But at least he wouldn't have to live with this fear permeating his system.

"You must have impressed Veena," Box said, pulling Cas from his thoughts.

"What?"

"This new equipment, she set you up with some of the best stuff I've ever seen. Brand new thrust controllers, top-of-the-line undercurrent emitter, platinum coated actuators. The ship has probably never run so well. Not since you've owned it anyway."

Cas furrowed his brow. "Did you happen to talk to any of the installation crew while they were working?"

Box fell silent a moment. "No. I felt it was much better to just let them work and stay out of their way."

"You mean you'd rather watch vid programs than do your job." Cas took a deep breath. "Why would she go to the trouble? She wasn't happy about my leaving. At least, not until the end."

Box's shoulders jumped up. "Maybe your new *owner* paid her good money for you."

Cas exhaled through his nose, willing himself not to take the bait. "Whatever the reason, stay on guard. I don't want to be caught by surprise out here."

"Always, boss," Box replied.

***

Cas found he couldn't return to the sanctuary of his room. Every day they'd been in underspace the room had felt smaller, more closed-in. What had once been a place he could take refuge now felt like a flying cage. He'd spent more time in the kitchen and cockpit than normal, taking time to enjoy it while he could. There was no telling what would happen once they reached the station, but with any luck he and Box leave in a few days. Unless this had all been a giant setup.

He paced the hallways while Box initiated docking procedures. They'd come into the station's perimeter without issue and had been granted clearance. It should have made him feel better Evie had been truthful about that part but somehow it didn't. Piloting the ship into the docking bay had felt like just another set of bars closing down on him.

He'd managed to find some clean clothes for once. It was nothing more than a cotton shirt and his pocket trousers. He'd even rummaged in the back of his closet and retrieved his jacket, the one he'd gotten from his brief time with Liss. If he thought about it hard enough, he could even still catch her scent on the fabric.

Evie stepped out of her room carrying a small bag and the sword in one hand. "Have we landed?" she asked.

"Box is finishing the procedures now. Tell your friends if they plan on searching my ship to not break anything. I have some valuable artifacts in here and I don't need Coalition fingerprints all over them."

She flashed him a side-eye. "I'll see what I can do."

The ship shuddered and Cas recognized the sound of the exhaust systems purging their excess thrust. They had landed. "Box?" he called.

"Yeah, boss?"

"You're coming with us, let's go."

There was a loud *thump* and Box came trotting down the hall. "A field trip!" His eyes flashed in excitement. Cas pressed the button to lower the main ramp from the primary lock. Evie took a step for the door but he took her arm, stopping her.

"Don't make me regret this," he said, doing his best to keep his voice from shaking.

"You can trust me," she replied.

He nodded and let go, following her down the ramp and out the second lock into the vast space, Box close behind him.

When they exited, he couldn't help but be impressed by it all. After five years of seeing nothing but barely-maintained Sargan ports of call, the pristine station of the Coalition was a breath of fresh air. Unlike the landing pad at Devils' Gate, ships weren't crammed in the bay like sardines. The closest shuttle was a good thirty meters away and everything was clearly marked and easy to follow. They had landed on pad Charlie Sigma seventeen. A crew of four started their external check of the ship, as was standard procedure when a non-Coalition vessel docked. They checked for anything hazardous or any potential problems with the ship itself, which they would then present to the pilot upon their departure.

Smug bastards.

Evie handed her bag and sword off to an enlisted crew member in a gray jumpsuit and gray hat. He saluted her before taking her goods then trotted off in a different direction. "Let's go," she said. "We'll head through the civilian sector. It's the quickest way to the admiral's office."

"Perfect!" Box exclaimed, following along. "I was planning on going there anyway. Do you know how many drama programs I can download while we're here?" he asked. "And they're all free! My processors are gonna be full!"

"Yes," Cas said, "Free." He glanced up to the ceiling of the shuttlebay; a good twenty meters above them. He couldn't detect a bit of, dirt, dust, or exhaust anywhere. Just like it was supposed to be. Sterile. He turned to Evie. "I'm surprised we didn't have an escort waiting for us at the bottom of the ramp." Though it was standard procedure with potentially hostile vessels.

"I told them I could handle it. Think of it as a peace offering," she said, maintaining her focus forward as they walked to the closest hypervator.

"That's very generous," Cas said.

She didn't reply, only stopped at the door to the hypervator, pressing a button beside the door. Cas took a last glance back at his ship, hoping it wasn't the last time he'd see her. He couldn't help but stare past her at the starfield beyond the protective force field. Cas sighed, turning back to the hyper that had just arrived.

"Main concourse," Evie announced as soon as the three of them were inside. She glanced at Cas. "Here we go."

12

As the doors opened again Cas steeled himself for what lay ahead. The reality of the situation sank in. He was on a *Coalition* station. By choice. Being escorted by a Coalition officer. This was insane. He'd lost his mind.

Before him was a long, wide corridor with shops on both sides. The corridor curved out of sight, following the natural curve of the station. In some ways it was like Devil's Gate, and in other ways it was the complete opposite. For one, the concourse was much wider, about fifty meters, giving people plenty of space. No one was in any danger of running into anyone else here. Fountains of different liquids lined the center of the concourse, each demonstrating a different show. Above them a glass atrium curved over the entire concourse and beyond was nothing but stars. The concourse only had one level but above the shops on both sides were massive planters filled with flora from at least thirty different worlds.

It felt like a dungeon to Cas.

"There it is!" Box squealed. It came out as a garbled yowl. He took off toward one of the shops and Evie and Cas had to run to keep up with him.

"What is he doing?" Evie yelled.

"He found the entertainment store," Cas replied.

Box was already inside at the counter. He'd dropped an uplink cord on the counter with a thud. "Fill it up," he said.

The attendant peered around him at Cas and Evie entering the store. "Ma'am?" he asked.

Evie nodded. "It's fine."

"What, you have to get permission to download entertainment now?" Cas asked.

"No, it's just that a robot walking in and demanding something isn't…usual." She forced a grin.

"What would you like?" the attendant asked Box.

"As much as you can fit inside me," he replied, proudly.

Cas groaned, dropping his head.

"Y—yes, sir." The attendant took the uplink cable and plugged it into a device beside him.

"Oh yes. That's it, give me more," Box said.

"For Kor's sake, Box!" Cas yelled, walking over. He yanked the cable from the machine and swiveled Box around, pushing him out of the store. "He's had enough, thank you." He waved to the attendant who seemed speechless. Evie followed them out. "Do you have to make a spectacle everywhere you go?" Cas asked once they were back in the concourse.

"Yes," he replied. "Life is short. Make it interesting."

"We need to keep moving. The admiral expects you," Evie said, walking past them. Cas caught the hint of a smile on her face.

They continued moving down the concourse with Box following behind, completely enveloped in the information he'd downloaded. Every now and again Cas would catch the eye of someone, and they would sneer or turn away. He'd been fooling himself if he'd thought people had forgotten already. It had only been seven years ago. Cas was more astonished no one had told Evie yet.

Just as they approached a second hypervator in the center of the concourse a woman strode up to Cas, fire in her eyes. Before he knew what was happening her palm had struck him across the face. It hadn't hurt much, though it had been a shock. All around them people stopped moving.

"Do you know who I am?" she demanded.

Cas forced himself to look at her. He nodded.

"How dare you show your face here again," she said, raising her hand to slap him again.

"Ma'am, step away." Evie forced herself between them. "This is the Coalition; we don't assault people. Give me your hand, I need to scan you for security."

"Me?" the woman yelled. "He's the criminal." She pointed to Cas. "You're letting him walk around free and you want to arrest me?"

"For striking another life form, yes," Evie said, raising her hand to her comm unit.

"Evie, it's okay." Cas placed his hand on hers and guided it back down by her side. "It's fine," he reiterated.

"Are you sure? She just committed a class one infraction."

He nodded, not looking at the woman. "Let's just keep moving." They walked around the woman who continued fuming there in the middle of the concourse.

"Next time it'll be a class two!" she yelled after him. They filed into the hypervator and waited until the doors closed.

"What was that about?" Evie asked. "Are you okay?" She stared at his stubble-ridden cheek.

"Ask around, I'm sure someone will tell you," he said.

She turned her attention to Box who was still involved with his holo program streaming from his arm. "What about you? Do you know?"

Box nodded. "We're like soul sisters. We tell each other everything."

She turned back to Cas, a smirk on her face.

"He's exaggerating," Cas replied. The hypervator stopped, the doors opening on a very clean hallway. The sides were a neutral gray and the floor carpeted with something firm but pleasant. On the far side of the wall were a series of doors every few feet, each labeled with a different person's name. Some were transparent and others weren't but in the ones Cas could see through people worked at desks inside. They'd reached the main offices. "Where to?" he asked.

"Follow me." Evie turned right down the hallway. It sported a more pronounced curve, with all the doors on the outside with other, non-transparent doors lining the inside. She tapped her hand as they walked. "Lieutenant Commander Diazal with Caspian Robeaux proceeding to Admiral Rutledge's office."

Cas stopped cold. "What did you say?" he asked.

Evie turned to him as someone passed them in the hall. "What?"

"Which admiral?"

"Admiral Daniel Rutledge," she said, her words falling off a cliff. She really didn't know anything about him. Any of his history at all.

"I'm not going, deal's off," he said. He wasn't about to face that man again. Not after everything that had happened.

"Wait, you can't back out now," Evie said. "You gave me your word."

Cas had already turned back down the hallway to get to the hypervator. He might not make it far, but he'd be damned if he didn't to try. "You never said I'd have to deal with him."

"Captain, don't do this," Evie warned. "Don't force my hand."

He turned back. Box was leaning against the wall watching the program, oblivious to what was happening around him. "I should have known," he said. "I should have suspected he was behind this, but I didn't want to believe it.

That's my own fault. I should have been more honest with myself. Because there is only one reason the Coalition would want me back and it's sitting on the other side of a desk down there somewhere." He pointed down the hall.

"What is this all about?" Evie asked. "Why not just meet with him? He's the one who ordered me to find you."

"I can't say I'm surprised," Cas replied. "But I can't do it. I'd rather go back to Veena than face him."

Her features softened. "You told me I could trust you."

Cas cursed himself. He glanced down the hallway. More than likely there were guards down there, ready to grab him the moment he tried to run. His ship had probably been disabled so he couldn't escape without authorization. He glanced back at Evie, pleading with him.

He'd known it would come to this, someday. He'd just hoped he'd been wrong. He took a deep breath and turned back toward her. "Fine. Lead on."

She relaxed her posture but held his gaze a moment. Then she turned, leading them down the hall until they reached a door larger than the others. And based on how far the next closest doors were on either side Cas could only assume this was their destination. As confirmation the plaque on the door said: *RADM Daniel S. Rutledge, SCAS.*

Cas shoved his hands in his pockets so they couldn't see they were shaking.

"You might as well do it, boss, you're already here," Box said, his focus still on the program.

"Oh, so you *can* do more than one thing at a time," Cas said.

"Only on special occasions," Box replied.

"Ready?" Evie asked, concern in her eyes.

Cas nodded. She tapped the button beside the door.

"Enter," the voice Cas hadn't heard in over five years said. The doors slid open.

13

The office was clean and sparse; a perfect picture of how a Coalition Admiral's office should look. In the center of the room sat a large, wide desk made of some super polymer—Cas didn't want to guess which one—with a built-in command system that would appear at the touch of a button. He'd seen desks like these before, they were often called "war desks" due to their advanced tactical displays. Behind the desk was a giant map of Coalition space with the borders outlined in a dark blue. To the upper right was the Sargan Commonwealth outlined in green and down below, outlined in red, was Sil territory.

The man Cas hoped he'd never have to see again stood up from the desk, a grin across his face. His broad, stocky shoulders filled out his admiral's uniform well and his brown beard had gone a great deal grayer since the last time Cas had seen him. It seemed ten years had passed for Rutledge, not five. Though those years had hardened him, not worn him down. His eyes were lit with activity, scanning Cas, then Evie and then Box behind them. Cas had to work not shrink from the man. He'd never thought this day would come, and if it had, he imagined it going much differently. With Cas pulling the boomcannon Evie'd made him leave on the ship and blasting a hole right through the man.

"Commander," he said in his gravelly voice. "Well done." He stuck out his hand for Evie who took it, shook once then placed her hands back behind her. Her braid fell off her shoulder behind her back.

Rutledge turned to Cas. "I bet you never thought you'd see me again. Captain, is it?"

"That's right," Cas replied, trying his best to hide his anger.

Rutledge didn't offer his hand. "And this is…?" He motioned to Box.

"My associate," Cas replied.

"Ah." Rutledge studied Box a moment. "Glad you could both make it." He put his own hands behind his back and walked to the side of the desk. "Commander, would you mind taking the robot outside for a few minutes? The captain and I have a lot to discuss."

Evie's gaze flitted between them for moment before she realized she was hesitating. "Yes sir," she said, taking Box by the arm. Cas heard the doors behind him slide open and closed again but he didn't take his eyes off Rutledge. He swore he'd never turn his back on the man again.

Rutledge chuckled. "Gave yourself a promotion, I see."

"It's my ship. It needs a captain."

Rutledge scoffed, walking to the wall on the far side. A vidscreen was built into the wall and he tapped it, bringing it to life. "Right. Because if you can't get it through hard work and determination why not just give it to yourself for free."

"Save it, Daniel," Cas said. "Let's just get this over with. What am I doing here?"

"I think you know," Rutledge said, tapping the screen a few more times. An overhead map of local space came up, zooming in on their location. "I wish I could say it was good to see you again, but we both know that's not true." He paused. "You're here because of the *Achlys*."

"I find that statement shocking," Cas said, deadpan.

"Cut the shit, Robeaux," Rutledge snapped. Whenever he'd gotten riled up in the past he'd start sweating on his forehead and Cas could already see the sheen reflecting off him. "She's missing."

"Good riddance," Cas replied.

Rutledge ignored him. "Ten days ago we lost contact with her," he said, "out near the Rekaa Quasar." The screen zoomed in to the space around the quasar. A red blip indicated where the *Achlys* had last been seen.

"What was it doing out there?" Cas asked.

Rutledge turned and smiled at him. "I think you know."

Cas struggled to contain his anger. "You got it working, didn't you? You finally built the fucking thing and they were testing it."

"First test was ten days ago," Rutledge said.

Cas failed at controlling his anger. "Then maybe they blew themselves up. Too bad you weren't on board."

Rutledge scoffed again. "This is bigger than just me anymore. We have people counting on the *Achlys* now. It isn't just some experiment."

"You still haven't answered my question. Why am *I* here?" Cas followed him as Rutledge walked back over to the desk, staring him down from the other side.

"You're going to help find it."

He took a step back. "Why me? Why bring in the one guy who doesn't want anything to do with the ship's experiments?"

"Because despite the need, most people don't know the…intricacies…of the project. They don't know what they're looking at, all they're doing is measuring results. I need someone who has seen this stuff up close. Who can identify it and tell me what went wrong."

"You forget, I was in jail by the time you finally brought one on board. I've never seen it," Cas argued.

"Technically you'd already run from Kathora by the time we brought it back. But it turns out they are remarkably close to the initial prototypes you developed. I need your knowledge here Caspian. If I had another choice I would have taken it, believe me."

Cas turned his gaze upward. "*That* I can believe." He took a deep breath. "I assume you knew what happened to me on Kathora?"

The admiral gave him a hard stare.

"I thought so. Guess I was harder to get rid of than you thought."

The admiral's penetrating gaze bore into him. "You're not here to rehash history. We can either leave that in the past, or we can waste time arguing about something neither of us can change. Which do you prefer?"

He was right. It wasn't as if Cas could go to a review board and plead his case. He had no proof. Not to mention he didn't know how many people were involved. This might be his only chance to get clear of this mess once and for all. He glanced at the map on the wall. "How do you even know the ship is still out there?"

Rutledge relaxed his shoulders. "We don't. But if it is, I want someone who knows what they're looking at when it's found. Things have escalated. I need to know what happened on that ship, why and if the experiment can be salvaged."

Cas nodded, taking it all in. He worked his jaw, crossing his arms. "And if I refuse?"

"We have a comfortable brig. You can have your old spot back."

Cas shook his head, staring at the ground. "I expected nothing less. I knew this was a mistake—coming here. And yet I came anyway." He thought about it a moment. "Fine. Toss me in. Impound my ship. Let's see what happens."

Cas swore he could see a vein throbbing on Rutledge's forehead. The older man watched him a long time and Cas watched right back. Daring him to do it. Because the fact was Rutledge was on a time crunch and Cas wasn't. He didn't care if the ship was ever found. If Rutledge had gone to all this trouble to find him and bring him in he wasn't about to toss him in the brig.

Rutledge turned away first. "It's too bad you can't order me to do it." Cas smirked. "That would solve all your problems, wouldn't it? Of course the last time you ordered me to do something it didn't go so well. For either of us."

"What do you want?" Rutledge asked, his back to Cas as he studied the map in front of him.

"I'll go find it, in my ship. Alone. When I find it I report the information to you. And then I'm gone. Forever. I want all records of me in the Coalition destroyed. Like I didn't exist."

"Out of the question," Rutledge said, turning back to him. "You'll run the first chance you get. It's what you do."

"I'm not—" Cas began but Rutledge put his hand up.

"I have a ship ready to depart, waiting for you. For the duration of the mission you will be a special advisor to the crew. If you find the ship, confirm what happened, report back to me. Once that's done," Rutledge said, raising his voice above Cas's objection, "then you can depart from there. We'll load your ship on the *Tempest*."

Cas shook his head, nails biting into the palms of his hands. "If you think I'm joining another Coalition crew you can—"

"It's temporary and I'll agree to your other terms. *Once* it's found." He sat back down in his chair, eyeing Cas as he leaned back. "Otherwise it *is* the brig and neither of us gets what we want."

"Fine." Cas clenched his teeth.

Rutledge showed the smallest hint of a smirk then tapped the back of his hand. "Commander, come back inside, please."

Evie entered while Box remained in the hallway. Cas turned just enough to see him displaying his vid on the far wall.

"Escort *Mr.* Robeaux to the maintenance yards. And arrange for his ship to be transferred over to the *Tempest*."

"Sir?" she asked, glancing at Cas.

Rutledge glanced over to Cas, his eyes piercing him. "He's going with you to look for the *Achlys*."

14

The doors closed behind them, sealing the admiral's office from the outside hallway. Cas took a deep breath, praying to Kor he hadn't gotten himself into something he couldn't find a way out of.

When he glanced up Evie was staring at him. "What?" he asked.

"You two know each other," she said.

He chuckled. "Yeah. We know each other. Who do you think threw me in prison for two years?"

"You were an officer?" she asked, her eyes widening.

Cas glanced to Box further down the hall, his attention rapt by the vidscreen projected on the wall. "Believe it or not."

"Why didn't I know that?" she asked, indignant.

"I guess Rutty in there didn't think it was important." He walked toward Box.

"I looked for a file on you before I left, but there was barely anything there. It mentioned you were a citizen. You had an altercation and you were no longer part of the Coalition. Nothing about serving in the Sovereign Navy, nothing about being an officer or being in jail," she said.

"Box," Cas said, ignoring her. "Put that away. We have work to do."

Box turned his head. "But it's on the best part, see this guy Antonio just found his half—"

"*Box!*"

He reached up and tapped his arm. The video disappeared. "Where to?"

"We need to get back to the ship. We have a mission."

His yellow eyes blinked on and off in confusion. "A mission? I thought this was the mission."

"You've been assigned to my ship," Evie said. "The *Tempest*. We're going out to look for one that is missing."

"And you agreed?" Box asked, his voice full of surprise.

"It's the *Achlys*," Cas said. He pushed past Box down the hall toward the hypervator.

"Oh," Box said. His and Evie's footsteps fell in step behind him.

"Did everyone know about your service record besides me?" Evie asked, catching up with him.

"It appears that way," he replied.

She sped up and stood in front of him, forcing him to come to a stop. "Rank."

"What?" he asked.

"What was your rank? When you were discharged?"

"Lieutenant Commander. Same as you," he replied.

She visibly relaxed. "That's how you knew how to disable my shuttle. How you knew so much about Coalition procedures."

"Once an engineer always an engineer." This was why he hadn't told her. He didn't want to reminisce about the past. About his time on his last posting. Before that things had been…better. Maybe not perfect, but better.

"Wait, were you the engineer on the *Achlys*?" she asked.

"No, I started out as the engineer on the *Hartford* but was offered to be first officer after a few years," he replied.

"That's my station on the *Tempest.* I was transferred before I went on temporary assignment to find you."

He raised his eyebrows, forcing a smile. "Great. Looks like we're evenly matched."

Cas stepped around her, trying to run the variables in his head. Could he really get away once they found the *Achlys*? Or what was left of it? He might need to make some modifications to his emitters on the *Reasonable Excuse.* If Rutledge double-crossed him, the *Tempest* might be able to hold on to his ship if he tried a forced escape. It would be tricky, but he couldn't drop his guard, not now.

He reached the hypervator, pressing the pad to call the car. Evie came up beside him again, eyeing him. Box appeared on his other side. "When we get back to the ship I want to do a full systems check," Cas said.

"But I just did one before we left—"

"I don't care," Cas replied. "Check everything again. We're going into deep space and I don't want to be caught off-guard." He winked at Box, making sure he was turned away from Evie.

"You heard the admiral. Someone will move your ship for you. We're going straight to *Tempest.*"

Cas shook his head. "No one moves my ship but me."

"Sorry, *Commander,*" she said, emphasizing the sarcasm. "Admiral's orders." Box tapped his metal arm as they waited.

The doors opened and they stepped in. "Shipyards," Evie said as the doors closed.

The hypervator shot past the civilian section of the station, speeding up. Below his feet Cas could feel the car vibrating as it reached high velocity. The shipyards were on the upper end of the station. As he was thinking about the last time he'd been on this station the back of the car turned transparent and he was treated to a view of the inner-workings of the spire as they rose through it. Floor after floor of either habitation, offices, or storage. And in the center, running through the entire station a large power core, providing clean energy to the station itself. Starbase Eight had been here since before Cas had been born and was one of the largest Coalition bases on this side of space. But you didn't feel the sheer size of it until you were traveling from one end to the other. Even at this speed it was taking a long time and Cas estimated they had to be traveling at least three hundred kilos per hour.

"Who is moving my ship again?" he asked Evie.

"A competent officer," she replied. "I can't take the risk you'll leave, transferring the ship means moving it from the civilian shuttle area to the shipyards. Which means going outside the station's defensive perimeter. I'm sure you understand."

"Then why didn't we just park in the shipyards to begin with?" Cas asked.

"Because you told *me* you were here for two days and then you were gone. I saw no need to expose you to sensitive Coalition technology. But obviously I'm the only person who doesn't know about your past. So I'll take responsibility for that one. My bad."

"I'm not letting anyone—"

"It's too late, Captain," she interrupted. "I've already signaled to have it moved. I did it in the hallway back there."

Cas grumbled but turned away from her just in time to see the shipyards come into view.

At least a dozen Coalition ships sat docked around a central core and hanging in midair as if by magic. But there was no gravity in the shipyards unlike the opposite end of the station. At least not in the area where the ships were constructed. Cas caught sight of a few he recognized: Ajax class, Hermes class, Waterfall class; all staples of the Coalition Fleet. But there was one he didn't recognize.

"Is that it?" He pointed to the smaller ship. It was compact, with what seemed to be wings flowing out from the main body, then reattaching again. Its undercurrent emitter was mounted on top of the ship unlike others where it was mounted on the bottom. He couldn't even see the bridge.

"Yep, brand new from Coalition Development," Evie said, sticking her chest out. "USCS *Tempest*, FCX-8001. Dragon class."

"Dragon class?" Cas arched an eyebrow.

"It's a new line of stealth vessels. The *Tempest* is the second produced, the first one in full service. She has modifications to the undercurrent adapters, it allows her to travel the currents almost twice as fast as any other Coalition vessel."

"How is that possible?" Box asked before Cas could ask the same thing. Coalition ships had a fixed speed in the undercurrents. It took as long as it took, there were no shortcuts.

"The Claxians came up with it, who else?" Evie asked. "They found a more efficient way to traverse the currents. Don't ask me to explain it, I'm not an engineer."

No. But Cas was. Now he wanted nothing more than to get inside that ship and inspect its engine. Figure out what made it so fast. Figure out what the Claxians had realized that they hadn't.

"You have a Claxian on board?" he asked.

She nodded. "He's our chief engineer."

Cas took one more look at the ship before it moved out of sight, replaced by a standard bulkhead. The hypervator turned back to opaque. "I can't wait to meet him."

***

The hypervator came to a stop and the doors opened on a large bay, much like the shuttlebay on the other side of the station where the *Reasonable Excuse* had been parked. Could they have moved it already? Cas was itching to get back as soon as possible.

Evie led the way through the expansive room, which Cas assumed was a construction bay located close or near to the center core where they could access the ship. Before they could get very far Cas noticed an officer approaching them. His uniform matched Evie's but his purple stripes near his collar indicated a captain's rank. Cas drew a deep breath, steeling himself for the inevitable confrontation.

He was on the older side, with a head of thinning hair and a stern look that seemed to be carved on his face. His piercing blue eyes didn't leave Cas as they approached each other, stopping only meters away.

"Commander," he said, his voice strong.

"Captain," she replied, placing her fist to her chest briefly. "Do you know—?"

"I know him," the captain replied.

Evie pinched her lips together. "Caspian Robeaux, this is Captain Cordell Greene," she said.

Greene didn't move, or stick out his hand, which didn't surprise Cas. He'd heard the name before, but never met the man. He had a reputation for being difficult to work with initially, but fair. And he was one hell of a captain from his reputation. At least if he had to go into deep space with a Coalition ship, he'd have one of the best captains the Coalition had to offer.

"I will be out of your hair as soon as humanly possible," Cas said.

"I should hope so." Greene nodded. "Who…" he trailed off.

"This is Box, my…assistant," Cas said.

Greene turned to Evie. "Is he coming too?"

"Yes, sir," she replied.

Greene seemed to mentally right himself. He returned his gaze to Cas. "I understand we are searching for your previous posting," he said, his words coming out stoic and solid. "I have requested more information about this mission but have been denied access. Information I assume you have." Cas didn't respond, though Greene stepped closer. "I'm in the unfortunate position of being required to trust you will not get me, or my crew killed. But rest assured, if I see something I don't like the mission is over, I don't care what the admiral says. I'm not risking my ship for an escaped convict."

"I didn't escape," Cas said, drawing himself up. "I was released on parole."

"And ran," Greene said.

"I won't do anything that will put your crew in danger," Cas said, only realizing what he was saying as the words came out of his mouth.

Greene didn't laugh, as most others probably would have; he only watched Cas. Cas was the first to break the stare.

Greene turned to Evie again. "Commander, when he's on the ship I want him under guard at all times."

"Aye, sir," she said.

"And this…robot too. Make sure they are both contained to non-essential parts of the ship."

"You mean I don't get to see the bridge?" Box complained. "But that's my favorite part!"

Greene only stared at him before turning back to Evie. "Carry out my orders, Commander," he repeated. "I'll see you aboard." He turned on his heel and left them standing there, walking with purpose back the way he'd come.

"He's…intense," Cas said.

"Is that true? Did you run from your parole?" Evie asked, watching the captain walk away. Cas couldn't read her. Was she accusing him? Or was she trying to understand?

"I didn't have much of a choice. And until a few days ago, had worked out pretty well," Cas replied.

"I guess everything comes back around…in the end," Evie said. She walked off too, leaving Cas and Box standing alone among the workers around them.

15

As they made their way through the connecting tunnel to the *Tempest* Cas caught a glimpse of his ship pulling into the shipyards and making its way toward them. He stopped on the walkway, nudging Box. "Who's driving?"

Box turned, focusing on the ship. "I have their image, as soon as we get in the ship I'll access the manifest."

Satisfied, Cas resumed the trip down the tunnel. Evie was ahead of them, waiting at the main port to the ship. It wasn't ideal, but Cas felt better about being on the *Tempest* than being on the station. At least he wouldn't have to stay in the same structure as Rutledge.

"Ensign Yamashita will escort you to your quarters," Evie said as they reached her. A young woman with jet-black hair stepped out from behind her, dressed in a scientist's uniform.

She glanced up to Box. "I've never seen an AMR in person before."

"Ensign," Evie said.

Yamashita seemed to remember herself. "Yes, sorry, sir." She faced Cas. "If you'll follow me." She indicated they should fall into step behind her.

Cas remained put with Box behind him. Yamashita turned when she realized they weren't behind her, glancing at Evie as if at a loss.

"Is there a problem, *Captain*?" Evie demanded.

"I don't need quarters. I'll stay on my ship. And he doesn't sleep." He threw a thumb back to Box.

"I watch *him* sleep," Box said, as if it was his duty.

Both Yamashita and Evie seemed at a loss for words. But Evie spoke first. "You can't stay on your ship, it's a security issue."

"Then talk to Rutledge, I'm sure he'd love that you'd have to bother him with something so petty," Cas said, ramping up his own hostility. If she could act like this then he could too.

"Ensign," Evie said, drawing her words out. "Inform Lieutenant Page our *guests* will be staying on their ship. Make sure he mag locks it so the ship can't leave." She turned and left the three of them standing there.

Yamashita shrugged. "I guess we're going to the docking bay. Do you know if your ship is in Bay One or Bay Two?"

"Which one's bigger?" Cas asked.

***

"Enter," Captain Greene said.

The doors slid open and Evie stepped through, her posture near perfect if she did say so herself.

"Relax, Commander," Greene said. He was behind his desk reviewing something on the screen in front of him. "Have our guests been settled?"

"He insisted on staying on his own ship," she replied. "I didn't want to bother you or the admiral with it."

Greene glanced up for a second then returned his attention to the screen in front of him. "Make sure Page knows—"

"Already taken care of, sir," she said.

"Good." He shut down the program and leaned back in his chair. "Please." He indicated the seat on the other side of the desk. Evie hesitated a second then decided it would be best not to be rude so she took a seat. "We haven't had much of a chance to get to know each other yet," Greene said. "But I want you to understand that I must have complete trust in my XO. You are not to protect me from any information you find pertinent." She began to nod. "If you have a dissenting opinion, I want to hear it. The only way this ship works is if all of us are honest and work together."

"I agree, sir." She took a breath. "And I'm not just saying that." A smile formed on her lips. This had been the assignment she'd been pursuing for almost four years. So it was a stealth vessel instead of an exploratory ship. So what? She wasn't about to screw it up now.

Greene showed a hint of a smirk. "You brought Mr. Robeaux in. I need to know everything you know. Tell me what he's likely to do."

"Unfortunately, sir, I seem to be in the dark about Ca—Mr. Robeaux. As I'm sure you know I've been stationed on the outer rim of Coalition space for a long time. Not a lot of news gets out there."

Greene nodded, leaning forward and tapping on the table, pondering. "You wouldn't have heard this. The Coalition redacted all his records. They didn't want the information getting out. But it happened right here, so most of the residents know who he is."

"Did you know him, sir? Before?"

Greene considered it. "Not personally. But I knew of him. Rising star in the Coalition. On track to be a captain of his own ship by the time he was thirty. Gifted engineer. No one could believe it when it happened."

"Sir…" Evie began, glancing down for a moment. "I know I don't have clearance. But what did he do? I don't want to give you an erroneous impression since I don't know all the facts."

"He was first officer aboard the *Achlys*," Greene said. "And the ship was thrown off course, it ended up in Sil space."

"That's pretty far off course," Evie said, building a mental map in her mind. They would have had to traversed a lot of neutral space, the large area separating Coalition space from Sil. "How did they get out there?"

"The report mentions a gravimetric storm, something we haven't seen before, but you'd have to ask the admiral. He was captain at the time."

Evie sat back. "Rutledge was his commanding officer?"

Greene nodded. "Apparently on their way back they ran into a Sil ship." Evie's hand went to her mouth. "The Sil didn't see them at first, but when Rutledge ordered Cas to ready the weapons, he disabled them instead. Then he sent a coded message to the Sil, telling them where the *Achlys* was."

"What?" Evie said, her mind trying to wrap around the idea. He'd betrayed his crew?

"They managed to get out of there before the Sil could do too much damage. According to the logs Rutledge saved them. But twenty-four people still died in the attacks. When they returned here, to Eight, Robeaux was court-martialed and Rutledge got a promotion."

"I don't understand," Evie said. "If he was such a model officer then why—?"

"Why betray the Coalition and put his ship in danger?" Greene shook his head. "The psychiatrists called it a psychotic break; the pressure of performing got to him. He temporarily lost control of what he was doing."

"Then shouldn't he have been rehabilitated?" Evie asked.

"That was the plan, and the reason he was only in prison for two years," Greene said. "But then he ran off to the Sargans and Rutledge had him banned from returning. There didn't seem to be a desire to go find him. A lot of people were angry at him, regardless."

Evie furrowed her brow. It was a lot to take in. And it explained a lot about Cas's behavior. But to betray the Coalition like that—to cost those lives. It was unthinkable.

"I'll be honest with you," Greene said, standing and going to his window that showed the rest of the shipyards beyond. "Rutledge ordered me to place him back under arrest as soon as the mission is complete."

Evie glanced up. "Sir?"

"He wants to make an example out of Robeaux. He's probably going to spend the next twenty years in prison."

She screwed up her face. "But Cas told me Admiral Rutledge made him a deal," Evie said. "That he could go free when the mission was over."

Greene turned back to her. "I don't like it either. But honestly, I'd feel better with him inside a cell. I don't like the idea of him roaming the ship freely. The man has no business being on any Coalition ship ever again." He paused. "That being said, I don't like being kept in the dark and the admiral has been very quiet regarding this mission's objectives. I need to know what I'm getting my crew into."

Evie pondered the situation a moment. "He hasn't said anything to me, other than he was the XO on the ship we're hunting. Which makes sense now. Are you asking if I trust him?" Greene nodded. "Before you told me what he did I would have said there was an eighty percent chance he'd carry out the mission without being a problem."

"And now?" Greene prompted, ridges in his forehead appearing.

"Twenty-five," she said. So far he'd held his word but it hadn't been easy. He'd seemed to her like a spooked rabbit, ready to flee at the slightest noise. Though, to his credit he hadn't needed to come at all. He could have gone off on his own and left her empty-handed. And if she'd come back without him there was a very good chance she would not still be assigned to this ship for its mission. "But—" Greene arched an eyebrow. "I don't know if its guilt or what, but I feel like he'll see this thing through. He's had more than one chance to run and hasn't taken it."

"That doesn't mean he won't, Commander."

"I'm just being honest, Captain."

Greene seemed to take it in. "Very well. See if you can find out anything else before we arrive. The last known location of the *Achlys* is a couple of days outside Coalition space."

Again? That ship sure did go outside Coalition space a lot. "Yes, sir," she said. She tapped her chest and rose from the seat.

"Dismissed."

16

"Crewman Robert Abernathy," Box said, using the terminal on the wall opposite of where the *Reasonable Excuse* had been "parked".

"That's him?" Cas asked, eyeing his ship. "Is he still in there?"

Box shrugged. The ramp had been extended when Yamashita had finally gotten them down to Bay One. The ship was a flurry of activity, everyone running around preparing for the mission. Most paid Cas no mind but the few that did glance up passed by with angry looks on their faces. Yamashita didn't say anything else on the way down, Cas couldn't tell if she knew or not. When they arrived a guard was already waiting for them at the door to the Bay. Yamashita had handed them off and Cas had stormed past the guard, intent on seeing his ship. So far, no one had stopped him and the guard hadn't said anything about Box accessing the terminal.

"I'm going in," Cas said, making his way up the ramp.

"Every punch is another four seasons on your record," Box reminded him. Cas stopped, took a breath. Box was right. It wasn't Abernathy's fault he'd had to move Cas's ship. No, it was Evie's fault. They could have easily gotten back in the *Reasonable Excuse* and flown down here rather than take that ridiculous propaganda ride. It wouldn't surprise Cas if visiting dignitaries got the same treatment during their application to join the Coalition. It was such a pony show.

A hiss of air above him notified him the lock was opened. Abernathy came strolling down the ramp but stopped short upon seeing Cas.

"Did you scratch her?" he asked, pushing past the boy—he couldn't have been older than twenty-one—and making his way into the ship.

"Scratch her, sir?" He turned to Cas, confusion on his face.

Cas laughed. It had been a long time since anyone had called him sir. Abernathy was like Evie and Yamashita. Either too young or too new to this area of space to know who he was. Cas turned to face him. "Yes, scratch. Or dent, or otherwise injure. I just got her repaired and ready to go. I don't need some inexperienced pilot tearing microfractures in my ship's hull."

Recognition dawned on Abernathy's face. He knew who Cas was, he'd just never seen a picture of him before. "No. I didn't *scratch her.*" He made a noise in his throat that sounded a lot like a curse and turned to leave, passing Box at the end of the ramp and exiting out through the nearest door.

"You do have a way with words," Box replied.

"Get up here and help me do that systems check. I want to make sure they didn't do anything to her."

"Like what?" Box asked, approaching him.

"Like disable the engines so I can't—so we can't leave."

Cas's comm beeped before he could take another step. He tapped it while keeping it on his belt. "Yes?"

"Mr. Robeaux, please report to the bridge. We are preparing to depart," said an unfamiliar voice.

Cas sighed, closing the comm. "Fine. *You* do the full systems check. Look for anything out of the ordinary," he said. "I want to make sure when it's time, we're ready."

“Got it, boss,” Box replied, heading into the ship.

“And no vids until you’re done!” Cas called after him receiving no response in return. He estimated there was a fifty-fifty chance the check would be done when he returned.

He shook his head and made his way back down the ramp. The same guard that had been near the door stood at the very bottom. “You’re my escort?” Cas asked. The man nodded. “Then lead the way.”

***

The doors to the main bridge opened and Cas had to steel himself. The last time he’d been on a Coalition bridge it had ended with him being led off in a pair of cuffs. He never thought he’d see one again.

Despite the relative variety of ship configurations most Coalition bridges were laid out in a familiar manner. Though *Tempest* was completely different and it took him a moment to figure out where everything was.

The spacious room was circular in design, with eight different stations situated around the center, all at different height levels. Sunken into the floor were stations one and two, which were the navigation and piloting stations. They were tilted up at a slight angle to get a better view of the primary navigation display in the middle of the room, which was a three-dimensional projection of what was ahead, behind, above and below the ship. On either side of the two primary stations were the tactical station and the ship control station. They were on floor level with control panels in front of them and chairs, but they also had secondary control systems behind them as backups. On either side of those were the Captain and XO chairs, each with their own consoles as well. While some ships had these two stations directly next to each other it seemed the *Tempest* had set them some distance apart; perhaps to get a better view of the projection in the middle? Cas wasn't sure. Finally, rounding out the circle were two final stations directly across from each other, also at floor level, but about five meters back from the central projection. One of these had to be the engineering relay station and the other—the station closest to the hypervator door—was probably a station configurable to whatever was necessary for the particular mission. It was blank as if it hadn't been turned on.

Along the curved walls of the bridge were various other fold-out stations. Some were redundancies in case of damage and others controlled other aspects of the ship that weren't necessary to be manned at all times. The other parts of the walls sported giant screens that could produce more traditional two-dimensional views of what was happening outside the ship. But the redundancy ensured if one was damaged there were three more the crew could use if necessary. Cas took notice of the heavy-duty carpet under his feet and the decorative details on each of the stations and along the walls. Someone had gone to a lot of trouble to make this place feel comfortable. At least subconsciously.

Captain Greene stood from his chair as Cas entered, taking the three steps down and walking over to stand in front of him. "Mr. Robeaux."

"Captain."

"Crewman Welles, please remain by the hypervator," Greene said. The man behind Cas nodded and returned to the back wall. Greene stood to the side. "Would you like an introduction or…?"

Cas forced a smile. "No, thank you." He glanced to the people staffing each station. Most shot him dirty looks. Though he realized the Ship Control officer wasn't human. It was evident by the dark blue robe he wore covering everything except his face and hands. He looked human, but anyone who'd ever met an Untuburu knew it was nothing more than a hard-light projection. Their natural form underneath was decidedly very un-human. He was the only member of the crew who greeted Cas with a smile.

Cas glanced to Evie, who sat at the executive officer's station. She didn't return the favor, instead focusing on the projection in the middle of the room.

"Take a seat at the empty station," Greene said. "We are about to depart."

Cas walked over, doing as he was told. It was eerie, taking orders from a captain again. Though he much preferred Greene over Rutledge. If he looked past the display in the middle he was staring directly at the engineering control station; the one he *really* wanted to see. The woman in charge of the station didn't glance up, instead stayed focused on task. Though the station was nothing more than a glorified backup for the main engineering station somewhere else on the ship. On most ships it wasn't even manned. On this vessel, with a Claxian in charge down in engineering, he saw they might need a liason. Especially since Claxians only communicated with their minds.

"Commander, are we ready?" Greene said, standing in front of his chair, eyeing the display in the center. The projected image was of inside the shipyards.

"Aye, Captain," Evie said. "All hands, prepared for departure. Clear all moorings and disengage all docking clamps."

Everyone went to work on their respective stations, Cas couldn't do anything other than watch. Why had Greene brought him up here? Surely it wasn't for Cas's own benefit.

The screens showed the ship moving away from the central hub of the station, clear on all sides. Behind them open space beckoned beyond the threshold of the station itself. The pilot didn't bother turning the ship around, instead backed it out using the primary thrusters; something Cas could appreciate. It took a certain amount of skill to send a ship "backward" since most of its propulsion systems were designed to send it forward. The pilot was to his left and he glanced over at the young man with a bronze complexion in the sunken seat, watching his hands move with grace. He was a junior grade lieutenant but he flew like a pro.

As they cleared the station Cas uttered, "Impressive." The pilot turned his head so his hazel eyes landed on Cas. He looked as though he was about to say something then thought better of it and returned to his duties.

"Ensign Blackburn, set course for the BLV undercurrent, best possible speed," Greene ordered to the young woman with long, dark hair sitting on Cas's right. He turned his attention to the rest of the bridge crew. "For those of you who don't know this is a search and rescue mission for the USCS *Achlys*, lost near Sil space ten days ago. Mr. Robeaux is joining us temporarily until we locate the ship and he can confirm it is in good, working condition."

"Sir?" said the man at the tactical station. He had wheat-colored skin and sported a trimmed beard and moustache hiding a gaunt face. To Cas he looked about forty but his hard-edged voice and sharp features made him seem older. "*He's* confirming—"

"Yes, Lieutenant Page," Greene said. "On orders of the admiral himself. Unless that's a problem for you."

"No, sir." Page flashed Cas a quick glance before returning his attention to his own station.

Greene took a seat and turned his attention to Cas. "Mr. Robeaux, we will begin our search in the area where the ship was last seen. I understand it carried a portable spacedock."

Oh hell, the spacedock. Cas had forgotten. Or he'd chosen not to think about it. Either way, it made sense the ship still used it, given its mission. "Yeah, the Coalition built a spacedock that the ship could tow to a remote location. To save it from needing to return to Starbase every time it needed a tune-up," he said. That hadn't been the real reason, of course.

"A portable spacedock," the woman with the light blonde hair at the engineering station said. "That seems terribly inefficient." Cas couldn't quite place her accent, but if he had to guess it was Draconian. Draconian families were some of the oldest in the Coalition; it was rare to see any of them serving on starships.

"Believe it or not," Cas said. "Last I checked it had its own crew, twenty to thirty workers and about a hundred drones and automated pieces of equipment."

"Why would they need their own spacedock?" Evie asked. "It isn't *that* far between starbases or friendly planets. It doesn't make sense." She continued to avoid looking at Cas.

"Regardless," Greene said. "It's out there. We find the spacedock we find the ship. Hopefully."

"Undercurrent in ten minutes," Ensign Blackburn said from the navigation seat.

"Very good. Ronde, once we're in there make sure it's a smooth ride."

"Yes sir," the man who almost opened his mouth to insult Cas replied.

"Ship reports ready," the Untuburu said. Like all of his species his voice was like "death's whisper" as in it had a heavy quality to it. There was just something about when an Untuburu spoke the atmosphere around them seemed to dim in some intangible way. They often sent shivers down his back. Cas always assumed it was the translator the Untuburu built into their hard-light projections. Though they all looked different they pretty much sounded the same. They were also the only species in the Coalition to be given special permission not to wear Coalition uniforms as—according to their religion—their robes were all they were allowed to wear off-world.

Greene nodded. "Then it seems we are ready. Initiate all procedures and may our efforts be fruitful."

Cas watched one of the side screens as they moved through the inky blackness of space toward the invisible undercurrent. This was it. There was no more going back.

17

Box stuck his head into Cas's quarters. "Whatcha doing?"

Cas glanced up from the desk he'd cleaned off. For the first time in years he'd found time to clean parts of his ship that had never seen the underside of a sonic mop. With most of the crew hating his guts and nothing else to do he and Box had retreated to the *Reasonable Excuse.* They stayed there for everything except meals and periodic status requests from the bridge. All of which gave Cas plenty of time to get things in order.

They'd hooked up the *Excuse's* power conduits to the *Tempest*, keeping the batteries charged but also allowing Cas to print anything he needed. The first thing he'd "purchased" was a brand-new set of 1800 thread count sheets. He'd also managed to get rid of so many junk food wrappers he'd started to question if Box had been sneaking food into his system when Cas wasn't looking. And after everything had been cleaned there hadn't been much to do other than brood. So Cas had pulled out all his old star maps; the ones he thought he'd never use again after Veena had wrapped her chain around his neck.

"Just plotting our course." Cas returned his attention to the maps. They were old, printed on paper he kept rolled up and stored in special tubes in the back of his closet. He hadn't even thought about them in years. But they were reliable. Drawn by some of the first explorers of these sectors. They had been the one thing he'd managed to retrieve after deserting the Coalition.

Box entered the room. "I finished *World on Fire*," Box said, melancholy in his voice.

"All forty-seven seasons already?"

"It got better as it went on. I started watching on high-speed. Shouldn't have done that."

Cas scoffed, looking over the maps. "You know you're as bad as I am with impulse control. Speaking of which." He grabbed the bottle from the edge of his desk and took a long drink, exhaling at the end. "That's better."

"She's still not talking to you?" Box asked.

"Who?" Cas asked, struggling to put the bottle down without spilling it all over the maps.

"Commander Diazal," Box replied.

"Why should I care who she talks to?" Cas announced. "She's free to talk to whomever she wants to." He gestured behind him, feeling Box got his point.

"Except it's bothering you. You and women." Box tsked. "First Veena now the commander. Is it because neither of them gave you any sex? Is that it?"

"What? No!" Cas replied, feeling his ears go red. He rolled his map up and tossed it on his bed. It was still messy but at least it wasn't covered in vomit.

"Because the women you do sex don't seem to affect you." Box's eyes blinked.

"Listen to yourself. *The women you do sex*. Who says that?" He took a breath. "It isn't about sex. And it isn't about Evie. It's being back on a Coalition ship. I never imagined myself here. I wasn't prepared."

"For the hate." Cas nodded. "At least you're not sequestered on this ship when there's a whole Coalition vessel to explore. At least you get to leave once in a while." He leaned against the doorframe, crossing his arms.

"What are you doing?" Cas asked, watching him.

"Being casual. You know. Like you do."

Cas shook his head. "Whatever. Maybe I am upset about Evie. At least she was talking to me. Until we got here anyway." He picked up the bottle and took another swig. "Hooray for the Coalition. May she long live in infamy!"

"Boss, maybe you want to—"

"Do you know she hasn't looked at me once? I've seen her a dozen times since we came aboard and she hasn't even acknowledged my presence. What the hell happened? She didn't seem to have a problem at Devil's Gate. Or even on the way to Starbase Eight. But then—"

"What?" Box asked.

Cas smacked his forehead. "Someone told her." He ground the heel of his palm into his forehead. "How could I have been so dumb?" Now he thought about it, it made perfect sense. As soon as someone who knew his past saw him, they told her what he'd done. It could have even been that ensign who'd first escorted him here the day they left.

"Why don't *you* tell her?" Box asked. "If it's bothering you that much."

Cas glared at him through an alcohol-induced fog. "Yeah right. Stellar idea."

"You told me."

"You're not a Coalition officer! Not only does it put us in potential danger, think about what kind of situation it would put her in. Especially since she's been taking orders from Rutledge. What if she reports back to him I told her the truth? Then what?"

Box seemed to consider it. "Space-faring accident?"

Cas nodded. "Exactly. I just finished looking over my shoulder for the first time in a long time, I'm not about to start up again."

Box was silent for a moment. "Get me on the bridge."

Cas looked up. "What? No! These people already hate me enough."

"Are you saying you're ashamed of me?" Box taunted.

"Greene was very clear. You're to stay out of sensitive areas on the ship." Cas took another swig.

"More like *all* areas of the ship," Box replied, leaning into the doorframe harder. "They're just afraid I'll crack the ship's code, lock them out of the system."

"You would, wouldn't you?" Cas asked.

Box shrugged. "If I got bored. But just before they lost all hope I'd turn it back on."

Cas shook his head again. "You're insane."

"And you're pathetic. Locking yourself in your own ship instead of finding everything out about what's going on out there. Did you figure out how the ship moves so fast? No. Did you look into the Coalition files to see if the *Achlys* is still performing the same experiments? No."

"It wouldn't be in there anyway," Cas said. "Greene and the rest of them have no idea what the *Achlys* is doing. Rutledge wants to keep it that way. Why do you think I'm here?"

"There has to be something," Box said, straightening himself. "But you need to go look for it."

"I don't need you to tell me what to do and what not to do!" Cas yelled, the alcohol exacerbating his anxiety. "I'm just trying to get us through this in one piece and outside of any kind of room with bars on it. Isn't that enough?"

"I guess it's going to have to be," Box replied.

***

Evie made her way down the corridor toward Bay One. As the large doors slid open she noticed Welles, still on his post beside the door. “How’re they doing?” she asked as he caught sight of her.

“Same as before. They’re staying put for the most part,” he replied. The crewman’s eyes were heavy. He’d been on the same posting for four days in a row now.

“No trouble?” She looked up at the ship she’d spent five days on. It seemed smaller in the large shuttle bay.

“Not yet. Though I’m not taking my eyes off him,” Welles said. “You know what he did, right?”

Evie nodded. “I know.” She’d been trying to reconcile it ever since the captain had told her and she’d done a poor job at it. The best she could do was avoid Robeaux and his robot for the duration of the trip. But something didn’t feel right about all this and she wasn’t about to let blind hatred get in the way of her judgment. She’d gotten hold of his psych reports after some persuading of Doctor Xax, telling her it was a matter of ship security. Xax didn’t put up much of a fight. Her people were naturally curious and scientific and she hadn’t found a reason not to give Evie the information.

“Crewman, take a break. I’ll stand watch for a while,” she said, not taking her eyes off the ship.

“Sir?” he said.

She turned to him. “Did you not hear me, crewman?”

Welles sputtered. “No, sir, I mean. Yes, yes, sir I did.” He tapped his chest and walked out of the bay, leaving Evie alone with the ship and its occupants. She checked the chronometer on her comm device. It was late, and yet lights in the ship were still on. She approached the ramp and walked up, heading to the ship’s main airlock.

It opened without prompt.

No big deal, she thought. *If they ask why I'm here I'll make something up about a spatial anomaly.*

Why was she there? Didn't she have enough on her plate with the initial crew evaluations due in the morning? Not to mention the primary coolant systems were only operating at sixty-five percent efficiency. And yet she was wasting time here, with these two renegades.

Raised voices filled the hallway and she made her way toward the personal quarters to hear better. The room she'd stayed in was only a couple meters away.

"…ust not willing to give it up," Cas yelled. "I told you I'd get us out of this and that's exactly what I intend to do."

"And if he double-crosses you?" Box asked. He must be in Cas's room with him.

There was a rustling of papers before Cas replied. "We'll be ready before then. The ship is charged and ready and we've got enough supplies for a few seasons until we can get to the nearest non-aligned port. I'm not about to let Rutledge stop me again. Not when we're so close. I promise you, we will never have to deal with the Coalition again."

Evie's heart panged. He thought he'd be able to get away. They still hadn't yet realized Greene had ordered his ship disabled. But then again Blohm was as skilled an engineer as Evie had ever known. If anyone could disable the ship without them knowing, it was her. If they tried to run it would only further incriminate Cas.

The only problem was *he was holding up his end of the bargain*. And Rutledge wanted him arrested anyway. Was it revenge? Or was there something else? Evie had no way of knowing without finding more information. And she couldn't do that unless someone magically granted her a higher security clearance.

"Boss, get some rest, you look like hell," Box said.

"I like looking like hell!" he yelled. He was clearly drunk.

"It's your life." Box appeared in the hallway, staring at Evie who had neglected to even try and hide herself. She froze, at a loss for words. Box turned his head back so he could see inside Cas's room. Evie fumbled to say—to explain, somehow…

Box returned his gaze to her and put one finger against his non-existent lips. Then he strode past her, back toward the ship's cockpit. She watched him go, letting out a breath and thankful for his silence. The last thing she wanted was Cas knowing she'd snuck on his ship. She should have been more careful.

There was a further rustling of papers and then a *thump* against what sounded like a bed. The door to Cas's room remained open and she felt the urge to glance inside but restrained herself. Instead, she turned back toward the airlock and let herself out.

18

Cas stumbled into the cockpit, his shirt off one arm and his pants still undone from tossing and turning the night before. “What time is it?” he asked.

Box glanced up from his vid. “Almost nine. There was a ship-wide announcement a few hours ago. We’re close.”

“What?” Cas ran his hands through his hair. “Why didn’t you wake me?”

“You looked too peaceful. I didn’t want to bother you.” He returned his attention to the vid.

“I thought you finished that show,” Cas said, righting his shirt.

“Spin-off series,” Box replied.

“Of course, spin-off. Why not?” Cas said to himself, adjusting his pants. When he’d woken up he’d been dismayed to see he’d finished the entire bottle last night. And it had been a significant part of his stash. He only had three left. And since he wasn’t welcome at the ship’s bar he might need to ration himself until this was over.

“Feel better?” Box asked, not taking his attention away from the screen.

“No, now I feel sick and hungry.”

“They’re still serving breakfast in the mess,” Box said. “Commander Diazal is there every morning.”

He snapped his attention to Box. "How do you know that?"

"She keeps a regular schedule. Breakfast right before her daily shift." He paused. "Must be nice. All those waffles and pancakes. Syrup and eggs. Toast and rice."

"Stop." Cas closed his eyes and braced himself against the wall. Maybe he wasn't as hungry as he'd thought.

Box turned to him. "Do you need to see the doctor?"

"No, I'm…I'll be fine," Cas replied.

"Then how about the ship's therapist?"

"What?" Cas sat in the co-pilot's chair. "Does this ship even have a therapist on board?"

Box shrugged. "Don't they all? Regardless, you need to talk to someone. This is tearing you up inside. Since we've been here you've been a nervous wreck. You finished off *two* bottles last night."

"I finished off two?" Cas groaned. No wonder his head hurt so bad. He hadn't had that much to drink since right after he'd escaped the Coalition. "I'm *not* seeing a therapist."

"Then talk to the commander," Box said. "You might be surprised."

"Evie? The person who hasn't said one word to me over the past four days? I don't think so." She'd go right to Rutledge. "Plus I told you, it puts her in a precarious position."

"Look at you, concerned with others. I'd almost think you'd morphed back to your human form," Box said.

The words struck him. Evie had said something similar back at Devil's Gate. "Fine," Cas said, standing too fast. The cockpit began to spin. He had to steady himself against the wall again. The alcohol was still swimming around his system. "I'll tell her. I'm not afraid to see what happens. I guess we'll find out if we can trust her or not, won't we?" He burped, not bothering to cover it. "But if it turns out I'm right make sure you've got this thing fired up and ready to go. At the first sign of trouble we're out of here."

Box blinked rapidly, indicating happiness. "Good for you, boss. Getting it off your chest will be good for your misshapen, ugly soul."

"You know I can always replace you with a less talkative 'bot. They aren't hard to come by." Cas tried to flatten the wrinkles in his shirt as he pushed his other arm through the sleeve and made his way out of the cockpit.

"You love me," Box called to him.

"I'll love it when we get out of here," Cas said, reaching his room, then his sink and tossing enough water on his face and through his hair to make himself presentable. He even added a dab of cologne. It was more to mask the smell than anything else.

Box was right. He needed to get this off his chest. Cas thought he'd be able to handle the pressure, but the constant looks, the incessant needling was wearing him down. Someone *needed* to know. If just one other person knew the truth then maybe he could get through the rest of this assignment without having a mental breakdown. There was a good reason he'd left all this behind. Out of sight…out of mind.

***

Cas meant to thank his escort to the mess hall but forgot when the doors opened to reveal a bunch of crewmen walking around and eating breakfast.

The commander sat at one of the far tables of the mess hall, her attention on an honest-to-Kor paper book. Cas hadn't seen one in years. He wondered if she would appreciate seeing his maps before he remembered why he was there and made a bee-line toward her. Along the way he kept his gaze straight but couldn't help but catch dirty looks from the crew members. Though his vision swam, he didn't question his motives, except to briefly consider he might not be there at all had he only had one bottle last night. Cas avoided the food line and pulled up a chair in front of Evie, sitting down uninvited.

Her eyes glanced up for the briefest of seconds before returning to the book. "Make yourself at home," she said sarcastically.

"Got a minute?" he asked.

"We're almost at the quasar," Evie said. "And I'm trying to finish my breakfast."

"This will just take a *minute*."

She sighed, closed the book, and took a bite of scrambled eggs. "I'm not pausing my breakfast for you. So whatever you're going to say get on with it."

He noticed she'd taken a cursory look around the room. Those who weren't staring were in the midst of trying to figure out what the first officer of the ship was doing with a known criminal. But to her credit she didn't seem to let it bother her. Instead, she waited in silence.

"I'm assuming someone told you," he began.

"I've heard the gist of it," she replied, chewing the eggs then swallowing.

"Are you working for Admiral Rutledge?" he asked.

She sat back, the question catching her off guard. "No. It was just that one assignment. Why?"

"Because if I tell you what I'm about to tell you and it gets back to him, it won't end well for me."

Her eyes narrowed. "Tell me what?"

Cas glanced around their immediate area. Anyone who'd been close when he'd arrived had given them plenty of room. It was as if he had his own personal force field around him at all times.

"The reports were faked," Cas said. "The *Achlys* wasn't off course. We were where we were supposed to be."

"In Sil space?" she asked. "That's impossible. There's a treaty. Coalition ships don't violate Sil space."

"This one did. The *Achlys* is classified as an exploration vessel, but in reality it's a cover. It's really a battleship."

"Bullshit," she replied, tossing her fork down. "The Coalition doesn't commission battleships. They haven't for a hundred years."

"They don't commission stealth ships either and look what we're sitting on," Cas replied.

She considered it. "Okay. Keep going."

"Our mission was to *infiltrate* Sil space. On purpose."

"What?" Evie gasped. "That's illegal!"

"Keep your voice down," Cas shushed her. "I know it's illegal. And it's in violation of the Coalition charter and the treaty with the Sil. As well as going against the core values the Coalition purports to represent."

"Why?" Evie asked, skeptical. Though she had lowered her voice.

He wasn't about to give her all the details. If she knew the real reason they'd been out there it would put her in serious trouble, especially if she *wasn't* working for Rutledge. Not even some of the people who'd cleared the project knew what they'd been doing. "I can't tell you. Just know it was Rutledge's baby. I didn't have all the information, but from what I gleaned he and a few choice admirals in the higher ups made the decision. The crew on the ship and spacedock was minimal for a reason."

She leaned forward. "To keep the secret?"

"Can you imagine if that got out? What it would do to the Coalition?" he asked.

“There would be internal anarchy,” Evie said, her eyes glazing over. “The whole thing could break apart from the inside out. What if the Claxians found out?”

“Exactly,” Cas said.

“But why risk going into their space? We don’t need the resources and the Sil aren’t a threat to us. Not since the end of the war almost a hundred years ago.”

“I just know my mission.”

She studied him. “So is that what happened? You *did* disable your ship’s weapons.”

“Only after Captain Rutledge ordered me to fire on a Sil civilian vessel we accidentally encountered,” Cas said. “We’d infiltrated Sil space for two weeks when they spotted us. Rutledge said there couldn’t be any witnesses. He told us to disable the civilian vessel before they sent for help.”

“But you didn’t do it,” she said.

He shook his head. “It was the wrong call. We should have just run. I disabled our ship’s weapons systems so when I refused the order no one else could carry it out. I knew he wouldn’t stop, so I sent out a coded frequency to the Sil alerting them to our presence. I thought he’d leave then, but he was too stubborn, and wouldn’t go.”

“Is that why your crew died?” Evie asked. “Because he wouldn’t leave?”

“If he’d returned to neutral space and just left the damn ship alone we could have made it back before we ran into trouble. But he wouldn’t let it go. He had one of the other officers restrain me while he and the bridge engineer tried to fix the weapons.”

“I take it you didn’t have a Claxian in your engineering section,” Evie said.

Cas shook his head. “No such luck.” He took a breath then let it out. “Anyway. Two Sil warships showed up and we barely made it back to the undercurrent before they destroyed the *Achlys*. On the way Rutledge apologized to me. Told me he knew he was wrong and he'd take responsibility once we returned to Eight. You can guess how well that went."

"He got promoted to admiral," she said.

"For bravery in the face of mortal danger," Cas replied.

"What about the rest of the crew?" Evie asked. "They knew what really happened."

"It seems," Cas said, smacking his lips. He was parched. "They all agreed with him. Or at least that's what I assume since no one came to my defense." He grabbed her glass of water and drank the rest of it in one long draw. "So now you know the truth. I don't know what he's capable of if he finds out I've told you."

Evie was speechless. She only sat in the chair, staring at him, probably trying to decide if he was lying or not. But he had to admit, he felt better talking about it. Even if she didn't believe him, he'd managed to tell his story to *someone*.

"*All hands, prepare for undercurrent exit. Officers report to the bridge.*"

Cas glanced up to the hidden speakers in the walls. They were here. He hoped the ship *had* been destroyed. At least then it couldn't do any more damage.

Evie stood, gathering up her book. "Come with me," she said, depositing what was left of her breakfast in the matter recycler and marching out of the room. Cas swayed slightly, getting his feet under him before he followed. Did she believe him? Was she going to talk to the captain about it?

Or had he just made a fatal mistake?

19

Evie didn't say a word the entire way to the bridge. She'd dismissed Cas's escort, the same crewman who'd escorted him to the mess hall in the first place. When they got in the hypervator she didn't look at or speak to him. Cas could only assume she was about to make a report to the captain. If that's how things were going to go he needed an exit plan. He'd taken some time studying the ship schematics and because the bridge was in the center of the ship it was easy to get to from almost anywhere. So there wasn't just one access point; it also had backup evacuation options in case of disasters. He'd noticed it when he first entered the bridge five days ago. Directly to his right and left had been doors; one leading to the captain's command room and the other leading to a conference room as well as a second hypervator. He could use those hypervator lines to get directly to Bay One. Cas would have to create a distraction to get past everyone and use that hyper to get down there quickly. So long as Box had done his job and didn't start daydreaming he'd get there.

The doors to the bridge opened just as the ship lurched out of undercurrent space. The rest of the crew was already there, save Blohm whose station was occupied by another engineer. And it seemed there was a different pilot as well, Ronde, the kid who'd piloted the ship out of the spacedock with such grace was nowhere to be seen.

Greene didn't look up when Cas entered with Evie; his attention was on the main display in the middle of the room. It showed open space but in the distance was a tiny object Cas couldn't make out. He glanced over to one of the two-dimensional screens but they only showed the same image: a tiny white object moving against a field of stars.

"Can we enhance that image at all?" Greene asked.

Evie took her seat in the XO's chair, leaving Cas standing by himself. No one was paying him any attention. If he wanted he could turn right around and get back in the hypervator. But he was too intrigued by the object on the screen. Instead, he took a seat in the specialist's chair, which was still unoccupied.

"We're already at full magnification," the Untuburu said. "We'll have a better look in a few minutes."

"What do the sensors say?" Greene asked.

"It's composed of galvanium, bortaxium and giving off a high fusion reactor signal," Page said from the tactical station. "It looks to be Coalition."

"It's the spacedock," Cas said without thinking. He'd already recognized its shape as it moved closer in the screens. It had been custom-built for the *Achlys* and was designed to fit around the ship in a way, almost like armor that didn't touch the outer hull. Most of that was for ease of access to certain areas of the ship while in deep space. When Cas has been stationed on the *Achlys* they'd only used the spacedock twice, mostly for minor repairs. Its true purpose would come later.

"Are you sure?" Greene asked. Cas nodded. "Any sign of the *Achlys*?"

"No sir," the Untuburu replied. "Nothing else within two light years."

Greene stood. "Blackburn, as soon as we reach the spacedock, plot a search pattern out from its current position out to five light years. I want to see if she drifted away."

"Aye," Blackburn said, already plotting the search grid. Cas could barely see her console from where he sat.

"Commander," Greene said. "When we reach the station you and Page get over there. I want to know what's going on. I assume they're not responding to communications?"

Page shook his head. "Nothing but a faint power signature from them."

Greene nodded.

"Sir," Evie said. "May I have a word?"

Cas's heart nearly stopped. He glanced at Evie then back to Greene. Neither of them payed him any attention.

"Of course. In my command room, please." Greene turned and left the bridge through the door to the left and Evie followed, still not looking at Cas. As soon as the doors closed Cas felt more like an imposter than he'd ever been. Everyone else continued working at the their stations and the spacedock only grew larger in the viewers, but he didn't belong here. He'd been tethered to this place by a connection he'd probably just cut in half and no longer had any reason to be here. Evie would make her report to the captain, the captain would either arrest Cas on the spot for violating the admiral's orders or he would arrange an accident for Cas as soon as he was off the bridge. And if Greene *was* in Rutledge's pocket, Evie's life could be in danger too.

Why had he been so stupid as to tell her? Because he was still drunk from the night before? Or was it something else? Had he really needed to get it off his chest that badly? Cas realized he should have just kept his mouth shut. He'd managed to do it this long, why had he finally broken his silence?

Just as he was eyeing the hypervator door he felt a presence beside him and glanced over. the Untuburu stood there, a smile simulated on his holographic face. "Hello," he said, the word coming out as an ominous whisper. "We haven't had a chance to meet. Zaal." He reached out with his robed hand and Cas took it, not thinking. What he ended up gripping was not a hand at all but something that felt mechanical and hard in his grip. He let go almost immediately.

"Sorry," Zaal said, his voice deep and heavy, yet somehow cheerful. "I forget to warn humans sometimes. The projection only does so much."

"No, it's fine. It's just been a while since I've met an Untuburu. And I've never known one willing to exchange physical contact," Cas said.

"I'm expanding my horizons," Zaal replied. "I wanted to welcome you…since no one else seems to want to."

Cas appraised him. As an Untuburu, he could make the holo projection display whatever emotion he wanted at any time. Some people said it made them untrustworthy, since you never knew what was going on behind the "mask". But Cas figured you could say that about any human. Humans were excellent liars.

"Thanks," he said. "Though I won't be here for long."

"I was hoping to speak with you longer," Zaal said, drawing out the last word, as Untuburu tended to do. "It isn't every day someone leaves the Coalition. I find you a fascinating person."

"Um…sure," Cas replied.

Zaal's projection smiled and he bowed slightly. The blue robe just barely concealing his face. "Excellent. I will seek you out in due time. Until then…I have my duties." He turned and made his way back over to his station. Cas glanced around and caught Page giving him a dark stare before returning his attention to his own station.

Greene's command door opened revealing him and Evie together. They both returned to their respective positions. Cas cursed Zaal. He'd distracted him from his only chance of escape!

"Robeaux," Greene said. "You'll be accompanying Diazal and Page over to the spacedock."

Cas sat there for a moment, stunned. She hadn't told him after all. "Yes, sir," he finally said. Page's eyes flashed at him.

"Let's do this quickly and correctly," Greene said to everyone on the bridge. "I don't want to draw this out." He turned to Evie. "When you're done on the spacedock, rendezvous back with the *Tempest*. Hopefully you'll find something that tells us where our ship is."

Evie placed her fist to her chest.

"Dismissed."

***

They stood in Bay Two, close to one of the larger support craft *Tempest* carried. Cas hadn't had time to do a full count, but from what he could tell, the ship was equipped with fifteen light support craft ranging from shuttles to tugs to other short-range autonomous vehicles and at least ten or more medium-level support craft. These larger ships weren't as big as the *Reasonable Excuse* but could carry up to fifty personnel and were outfitted for different types of missions. Some could be long-range exploratory missions and others could be diplomatic envoys. In addition, it held a compliment of twelve Spacewing class fighter craft, outfitted with nothing but offensive weapons. Typically, they were used for the defense of a stationary object, like Eight. He'd never seen them on a starship before.

"We're headed for *Kerkini*." Evie indicated the medium-level craft off to the right. Two other crewmen would be accompanying them over to the spacedock, which was now visible through the open Bay hangar, floating out there in space on its side.

Evie climbed aboard first with the rest of them following behind. Onboard it was like a smaller version of his ship without as many amenities. But it was very similar to the shuttle he'd disabled at Devil's Gate in décor and aesthetics. The front section of the ship was partitioned off by a door, which Evie and Page passed through, leaving Cas with the two crewmen in the back. Stacked bunks lined the left side of the craft, each complete with its own sliding door for privacy and on the right was storage. In the center was a conference table and chairs that folded underneath. Cas walked over to check the lockers, finding all manner of scanning equipment as well as ten sets of enviro suits. He moved to the back to find a washroom and toilet. Conceivably a crew of ten could live on this craft for weeks or even a season if necessary.

"Prepare for departure," Evie's voice said over the comm and the primary airlock slid closed, the ramp folding up under the ship.

Cas glanced at the two crewmen who didn't seem to acknowledge him and took a seat at the planning table in the middle of the small room. They followed suit, taking the two seats furthest from him. He tapped his comm.

"Box, we're off. Take care of the ship for me until we get back," he said.

"Be careful, boss. Don't get in over your head over there."

"I won't," Cas replied. The ship shook and he could just barely feel the inertia pull him back as it accelerated through the Bay's force field. He glanced out the window to see the ship's hull flying by and just barely caught a glimpse of Bay One, a corner of the *Reasonable Excuse* peeking out from the edge before it had disappeared and the ship grew smaller.

After a few minutes of uncomfortable silence Page entered, heading for the lockers. "We won't need the enviro suits," he said. "We'll be using the repel fields. Equip yourself with one and prepare to disembark in three minutes." He pulled five field generators out of the equipment locker, tossing one to each of the crewmen then casually sending one in Cas's general direction. He had to stand and back up to catch it before it smashed into the far wall. Page didn't say anything else, only returned to the front section with the remaining two generators.

Cas affixed his to his belt. They were standard equipment for non-hostile environments. All they did was generate a protective shell around the wearer when the generator detected something dangerous, but they weren't impervious. Typically they were used in low-risk situations.

"Fun guy." Cas shook his head. He knew the two crewmen were staring at him but he didn't care. A few more days and this would all be over. And Lieutenant Page could just go shove it up his ass.

20

They didn't land on the spacedock, instead Evie piloted the ship so it matched the spacedock's rotation and speed. They just used the manual docking with the main airlock. Page was the only one armed with a weapon and he went first, everyone else following with their own scanning equipment. All except for Cas, who had nothing.

"I'd be a lot more helpful if I had a diagnostic device," he told Evie as they waited for Page to open the airlock on the station's side.

"You have everything I've been cleared to give you," she replied. He saw the two crewmembers exchange looks.

The second airlock opened and Cas's ears popped as there was a rush of stale air into the ship. The corridor beyond was dark save for a few emergency lights. Page glanced around, assessing the situation. "Everyone stay there until I get the power on," he said, disappearing into the darkness.

"Got any theories?" Evie asked.

Cas turned to her. "About the power? Probably the station going into power-saving mode when it doesn't detect anyone using any of the primary systems. Standard stuff."

"Which begs the question," Evie said. "Why doesn't it detect anyone?"

The lights in the station blinked to life, illuminating the corridor beyond. Page returned from around the corner. "Let's go," he said.

Fifteen minutes later Cas and Evie made their way down one of the side corridors while the others made their way to the main command center of the station. Page had seemed happy to have Cas out of his hair.

"You didn't tell Greene," Cas said as they walked.

"It didn't seem necessary at the time," she replied. "What can he do about it now anyway?"

"He could toss me in the brig," Cas replied. "Or out an airlock."

Evie scoffed. "He wouldn't do that. The airlock I mean. He's one of the most respected captains in the Coalition."

"If there's one thing I've learned, it's you never know who has skeletons in the closet. Usually it's the people you least expect." He peered down the empty corridor. It was so odd to see it so desolate.

"That may be true but Greene is different. He keeps his personal life close to the chest, but I don't think I've known anyone with more integrity."

"Haven't you only been working with him a few days?" Cas asked.

Her brows pinched together.

"Ah," Cas said. "He's got a stellar reputation, then. Those are *never* unreliable. Let me ask you something. If you're so sure of his character, then why not just tell him?"

She turned and grabbed his arm, stopping him. "Because he's my captain. And all I've got is the word of a convicted criminal. Until I have something more concrete, I'm protecting his interests. It's what a good first officer does. *You* should know that." She let go.

"Thanks, I guess," Cas said. "Regardless of your motives. At least you don't think I'm crazy."

"I don't know what to think," she said. "Based on your behavior and what I know about you I'm inclined not to believe any of it. But…"

"What?"

"Something isn't adding up. I'm not so sure you are wrong. But until I can prove it, there's no sense involving the captain."

Cas nodded. He hadn't expected her to actually take him at his word. Or had he? Thankfully he'd had a chance to sober up since the mess hall and now he could see what a monumental risk it was to tell her. It didn't seem that she was working for Rutledge after all. Although…an abandoned station in the middle of space was a good place to get rid of a body.

"What?" Evie said. "You've got a strange look on your face."

"Commander, we've reached the control center. Please rendezvous with us here," Page's voice said over the comm.

"Understood, Lieutenant." She tapped the back of her hand, ending the transmission. She turned back to Cas. "Let's move."

***

"What do you have?" Evie asked, entering the small command unit. It was like a stripped-down version of the *Tempest's* bridge, without the central display system. Instead massive windows on one of the walls showed the other side of the dock beyond.

Page turned to one of the crewmen.

"This room is full of an inorganic residue we can't identify," she said. "But it's been here almost two weeks."

"When was the *Achlys* last heard from?" Evie asked.

"Two weeks ago," Page replied.

She turned back to the crewman. “Is there anything you can tell me about the residue?”

“It’s only in this room. Nowhere else on the station. If it were the remains of the crew, we’d expect it to be all over the dock.”

“Let me see it,” she said.

The crewman moved to the side and pointed to one corner where the other crewman was working, taking a sample from the floor. Evie approached, getting down on her haunches to get a better look. Cas moved closer but Page put out a hand. “That’s far enough.”

“Lieutenant,” Evie said. “He’s here for a reason.”

Page studied him for a moment, dropping his hand. Cas didn’t break his stare until he was well past him. He leaned down beside Evie.

“Any clue?” she asked. “Is this what you were sent to find?”

He’d never seen the substance before, though it bore a striking similarity to what he’d seen on Kathora. He shuddered. “Definitely not.”

“Get a sample and let’s move on,” Evie said, standing. She turned to Cas. “How many crew did this thing have?”

“Twenty-three the last time I was here,” he said. “But that was seven years ago. Though I’m not sure the dock is rated to hold many more. It’s supposed to be mostly autonomous.”

“All the escape pods are still in place,” Page said, looking at one of the monitors.

Evie turned back to Cas. “Is what you’re looking for here?”

He went over and performed a quick scan on the station. It was obvious it wasn’t here. What Rutledge wanted was more than likely on the ship. And there’s no way anyone on the spacedock would have left it unguarded. The dock was nothing more than an accessory; a way to keep everything the

Achlys was working on secret and in good working order. It never would have been on the station in the first place.

Cas shook his head. He really wished the ship had been here. He'd be done and off by now.

Evie nodded. "Download all the logs, we'll take them back with us. Let's get back to the *Kerkini*. Every second we waste here the *Achlys* gets further away."

***

"Hey," Cas said, pulling Evie aside as everyone else disembarked back on the *Tempest*. She turned to him. "I know you're the reason I was over there. I didn't want you to think I overlooked that."

"Is that your attempt at a thank you?" she asked, walking down the short ramp while he kept up beside her.

"No, it's just…I'm glad to know there are people out there that are still capable of fairness."

She studied him a moment. "It's stupid to have you on this ship if we're not going to use you. Taking you along was reasonable. The captain just had to be convinced you could be trusted." Ahead of them Page stood at the main Bay doors, watching as they approached.

"You like staring contests, Page?" Cas asked as they passed. "It seems to be your favorite past time."

Page gritted his teeth. "Permission to escort the criminal back to his…quarters."

"Denied. I want him back on the bridge," Evie said. "We're back to square one here and Mr. Robeaux may have some insight into our next move."

Page didn't say anything else, only fell in step behind them. The two crewmen had already disappeared to what Cas assumed were the science labs to analyze the dust.

Cas's comm beeped. "Boss, you back okay?" Box asked.

Cas tapped the device. “Yep, smooth trip. Box, I’ll—”

“Did you confess your feelings toward the commander?” he asked.

Evie slid her eyes to him without looking over, but didn’t falter. Cas cringed, feeling Page’s gaze boring into the back of his neck. “I will talk to you *later*.” Cas cut the comm. “You’ll have to forgive him,” he said. “He watches a lot of drama. He thinks we’re becoming a bonded pair.”

There was a snort of derision from behind Cas. He ignored it. Evie scoffed. “If he breathed I’d tell him not to hold it,” she said as they reached the hypervator doors. Cas was more embarrassed than anything else, though he tried not to let it show. When he got back to his ship Box was getting all his vid privileges revoked.

A short trip later they were back on the bridge, Page taking his station from a female officer Cas didn’t know. Evie held him back as Greene approached. “Commander,” he said, his eyes flicking between them.

“No luck, Captain. Whatever we’re looking for, it wasn’t on the dock,” Evie replied.

“I wasn’t expecting it to be,” Cas said. “It’s not something that would have ever been removed once…well, once the *Achlys* had it.” He had to be careful. If he revealed too much about what they were looking for Rutledge would have him arrested for certain.

“This is so frustrating,” Greene said, turning his backs on them and staring at the display in the center of the room.

“For what it’s worth,” Cas said. “It wasn’t my desire not to tell you.”

Greene faced them again. “Curious. You’re still following orders. After everything that’s happened to you.”

“Believe me,” Cas said. “It’s purely self-serving.”

Green appraised him a moment. “Suggestions?” he said, turning to Evie. “The search is coming up empty.”

"I believe there's a non-aligned port of call not far from here," she said. "It's small, but they may have heard or seen something. We might want to try our luck there, see if anyone's been talking about Coalition salvage."

Greene pondered a moment. "Very well. Prepare an infiltration team. We'll have to use one of the unmarked shuttles."

"Sir," Cas said without thinking. "We could use my ship. It would attract less attention."

Greene turned his attention to Evie, the intensity of his look saying what didn't need to be said.

After a moment she nodded. "I think it would be better camouflage. Even our unmarked shuttles are recognizable. It's not as hostile as an Sargan outpost, but there are still a lot of non-aligned species who aren't happy with the Coalition."

"It's your show, Commander," Greene said. "Just make sure you cover all your bases."

21

"Where is this port again?" Box asked, standing in the middle of the hallway.

"D'jattan. You know, that place where we picked up that horologist a couple years back. Along the RQ-QS undercurrent."

"Oh, the one on the asteroid."

"That's the one," Cas said, pulling a new shirt on. It was less smelly than the last, though it still needed a good wash. "What have you been doing this whole time? This place is a mess."

"I got bored. Couldn't find one of my data drives," Box replied. "You'll have plenty of opportunity to clean up again on the way back."

Cas grumbled to himself as he yanked on another set of boots. He was going for his classic look, something that wouldn't stand out in D'jattan. Not Sargan, not Coalition. "Have you done *anything* useful?" he asked.

"I emptied the coffee maker. It had all this crusty brown residue in the bottom. Took me almost two hours and I managed not to break it," Box said, poking his head in. "Are you decent yet?"

"Enough, I suppose," Cas said, catching his reflection in the mirror. He'd added an extra-heavy coat and gloves.

D'jattan was cold, even inside. Satisfied with the level of ruggedness he'd self-inflicted, Cas returned to the hallway. "Go ahead and plot the course. I'll wait until—"

The airlock opened revealing Evie. She was wearing the sword again and sported a large leather coat.

"I see you're familiar with D'jattan," Cas said, taking in her outfit.

"I do my research," she replied, walking past him to the cockpit. "An old mining colony on an asteroid hurtling through space where the system's sun only reaches the surface at random times. It's bound to be about as cold as you can get."

Cas had turned his back on the airlock when it opened again, revealing the same ensign who'd originally escorted him when he'd first boarded the ship. She was also dressed in mercenary gear, though she looked less threatening than Evie in her more tailored clothes.

"Ensign…" Cas began, struggling to remember her name.

"Yamashita," she reminded him. "Just call me Laura. I don't need you telling every alien on that station I'm with the Coalition."

Cas furrowed his brow. "You don't think I can handle myself out there? I'm pretty sure I know how to navigate a place like D'jattan. Can you say the same? How long have you been out of the academy, a year?"

Her face turned red but she didn't reply.

"Is there a problem?" Evie asked, approaching them.

"Not with me," Laura said.

"Cas?" Evie prompted.

He let it go, though held Laura's stare for a moment. "We're good." He turned away from them while Laura walked down the corridor, exploring the ship. He looked over at Evie. "Remind me again why she's here?"

“She’s the best exobiologist on the ship. If we encounter something we don’t know how to deal with over there she’ll know how to communicate. I don’t want to leave any stone unturned.”

“I don’t think it’s going to be that hard,” Cas said. “If someone’s heard of or has Coalition parts from a salvage job, they’re going to want to get rid of them. And if anyone’s heard of a derelict Coalition ship, word will have traveled fast. It was a good idea coming over here.”

“Thanks.” Evie had a faraway look in her eyes. Then she seemed to come to herself. “Let’s get going.”

***

Box expertly piloted the ship through the few asteroids left in the field, though they really weren’t close enough to be of any danger to the *Reasonable Excuse*. The *Tempest*—which at this moment was parked behind another planet in the system to obscure it from any non-aligned ships—might have had more trouble but as asteroid fields went this one was pretty typical. Sparse enough for easy transit.

When they arrived at the colony there were already a dozen larger ships in orbit of the small asteroid, all locked into a geosynchronous orbit. Box landed on one of the thirty pads available for passers-by. Cas watched as Box began the shutdown procedures, feeling just the slightest bit of envy at his skill. But he just wasn’t pilot material, never had been.

“He knows how to fly, I’ll give him that,” Evie said as the four of them exited through the airlock into the colony’s tunnels. As soon as they stepped inside a blast of cold hit them. Somehow it felt even colder than the last time Cas had been here.

"He's also not impervious to compliments," Box said from behind them. "He likes to be told he does a good job to his face."

Evie turned, a sheepish grin on her mouth. "Box, I apologize. You are an excellent pilot."

"Thank you, Commander!" Box's optics burned with yellow intensity.

Cas couldn't help but grin himself. "Split up?" he asked, his breath visible as he surveyed the tunnel. It was large enough to drive a small shuttle through, but there weren't a lot of people around. A few passed through but it wasn't nearly as crowded as Devil's Gate. Most of the warm-bloods would be near the heated areas.

Evie nodded. "Laura you go with Cas. I'll take Box. I assume he knows what we're looking for."

"He knows it," Cas replied, shooting Box a look. It was times like this when he wished the robot had a more expressive face.

"You find anything, comm me. And don't lose each other. This is not the place to get lost." Evie was talking to both of them but Cas had the feeling the warning was more for Laura than him. She didn't seem scared, but instead alert. On edge. "Box, let's go."

Cas turned to Laura. "We should start asking around in the main trading areas."

Laura shrugged and turned, leaving him in the tunnel. He picked up the pace to catch up with her.

"You didn't know who I was when we first met, did you?"

"No, and I don't care now," Laura replied.

"Bullshit. You couldn't have a bigger chip on your shoulder if you tried."

"And what?" Laura said, avoiding his gaze. "You don't think you deserve it?"

"All I'm saying is don't feel like you need to hide it. Don't conceal things on my account."

Laura shook her head as she walked. "I don't see why the commander keeps giving you opportunities."

"Let me guess," Cas said. "If you were in her position, you would have run me through with the sword already."

That brought a smile to her face. "Not exactly. But I wouldn't let you come on missions."

"I'm only here because I have to be. On orders from the admiral. Evie didn't have a choice," Cas said.

They turned a corner. This tunnel felt a bit warmer. They were quickly approaching the common areas. "That's disrespectful," Laura said.

"What?"

"It's Commander Diazal, not *Evie*." She glowered at him.

"Maybe to you. But I'm not in the system anymore. To me she's just plain ol' Evie."

"You still shouldn't do it." She clenched her jaw.

"Why does it bother you so much?" Cas asked, narrowing his eyes.

"It doesn't! It's fine," Laura said, picking up the pace.

"Wait, wait just a second," Cas said, a smile spreading across his face. "This is more than just respecting a superior officer, isn't it?"

"I don't know what you mean." They emerged into a large, carved-out space. Shops and eateries had been erected along the walls of the cavern and there were large gathering spaces all around. The area was heated by giant red lamps above that made the space about twenty degrees warmer than the tunnels. "Let's just start talking to people."

"Whatever you say," Cas replied.

***

Evie walked beside Box through the tunnels, moving down into the lower sections of the old colony. They'd already talked to six different people, finding nothing promising so far. The lower sections were more dangerous as it was where unlawful transactions were more likely to take place but they had the best chance of finding information there. Box was surprisingly silent as they walked. The entire time she'd been on the ship from Sargan space to Eight he'd been talking nonstop whenever she'd exited her room.

"Something wrong?" she asked.

"I'm not the biggest fan of enclosed spaces," Box said, his head moving back and forth to survey the walls and ceiling of the tunnel.

"Don't worry," she said. "This place has been here for hundreds of years. If it was going to collapse, it would have done so by now."

He didn't reply, only kept his pace.

"I guess you can't tell me any more about what happened to Cas, can you?" she prodded. He'd given her a lot of information back in the mess hall, but not all of it. There were still missing pieces and she needed to find out what they were before she made any kind of decision whether she should tell the captain. The biggest red flag was Rutledge's insistence Cas be arrested once the mission was over. It hadn't sounded right from the beginning but after what Cas had told her it made a lot more sense. If Rutledge really did order him to fire on a civilian vessel that could be very damaging. Of course without any proof it was a criminal's word against an admiral's.

"Unfortunately, I've been sworn to secrecy," Box replied, then glanced at her. "It's for your own protection."

She sighed. "So everyone keeps telling me. But I'm getting sick of being the last person to know everything."

"I would tell you if I could," Box replied.

"I heard your comm earlier. When we got back from the spacedock." Evie smirked.

"Oh, regarding your future love affair? Yes, I am quite excited about it," Box replied, his posture suddenly better.

"Box, there is no love affair. That's not going to happen."

"But, you're perfect for each other. The daring rogue and the prim officer, star-struck lovers from the moment they met." He turned to her. "I've heard you banter. It's net drama gold."

Evie shook her head, holding back a laugh. "It just doesn't work like that, Box, I'm sorry. Even if it were somehow possible, I'm not attracted to him."

"Then why are you being so…fair to him? Women are only nice to him if they want to sleep with him. Others just brush him off. Either that or try to shoot him," Box said, throwing his hands up.

"Because I believe everyone deserves a fair chance. No matter their background," she replied. "And if it turns out he's right, and Cas got a bad deal the Coalition is going to owe him one hell of an apology." She winced as she said it. Because no matter what happened, he would get a raw deal anyway. As soon as the ship was found he'd be thrown in the brig until they got back to the starbase. And then he's be in there forever. Or until he could be shipped off to a Coalition world for "rehabilitation". Which, in Cas's case, probably wouldn't be pleasant. She had to do something.

She tapped the back of her hand, activating her comm. "Report."

Cas's voice came through a few minutes later. "Nothing yet. No one seems to know anything about it."

Evie sighed, hoping this hadn't been a fool's errand. At the very least there was one thing she could do here. "Rendezvous in twenty minutes in the common area."

***

"Anything?" Evie asked, approaching Cas and Laura. Box walked behind her. He'd seemed more relaxed when they entered the larger caverns.

Cas shook his head. "Though Laura spoke with a Plegarian for the first time."

Laura's eyes were bright with excitement. "It was thrilling. I never thought I'd get the chance."

Evie smiled, then turned to Cas. "Can I talk to you a second. Alone?" She caught the briefest of strange looks from Laura before she managed to right herself. Evie would file that one away for later.

"Sure." He allowed her to lead him into one of the small alleyways between establishments. When she was sure they were out of sight of any surveillance as well as Box's hearing she turned to him.

"I already told you I'm not into kinky stuff." He grinned.

She turned away. "You're being set up."

He suddenly turned serious. "What?"

"The admiral. He ordered Greene to arrest you as soon as the mission was over. Not to let you leave."

"You've got to be fucking kidding me," Cas said, kicking the nearest thing to his boot which happened to a Gresarian block which shattered upon impact. "I knew it. I knew that snake wouldn't keep his word. He didn't the first time, why would he now?" He balled his hands into fists, then turned back to her. "See what I get? See what happens when I try to help? I knew I should have just left you on that station and gone on my merry way."

Evie didn't reply, only leaned back against the wall, watching him. She could be demoted for telling him. She could lose her commission and most definitely her posting. But she couldn't go on any longer with Cas thinking he would be a free man. It wasn't fair to him. She didn't like how the whole situation smelled. It was all contrary to the Coalition's most basic principles. And with everything that happened after he'd told her in the mess hall she hadn't had a lot of time to process it all.

"I thought you should know," she said, feeling the length of the sword press into her back.

"He gave the order as soon as I was onboard, didn't he?" Cas asked.

"Before. Right after you met with him I assume."

"Fine," Cas said, fuming. "That's just fine. If that's how he wants to play then that's how we'll play." He turned, leaving the alley back the way they'd come.

Evie watched him go, hoping she hadn't just made the biggest mistake of her career.

22

Cas stormed from the alleyway toward Box and Laura, who seemed to be engaged in a conversation of their own. "Box, let's go," he said.

Box turned to him. "I was just having a lovely conversation with this fertile female about *World on Fire*. Did you know she's seen it as well?"

"Fertile?" Laura said, resting her hands on her hips.

"I don't care. I need to talk to you. Alone," Cas said. Evie approached from the alley as well.

"Excuse me, Laura, it seems my boss is having a tantrum day," Box said, making a slight bow then following Cas.

"Don't do that," he snapped.

"Do what?"

"Belittle me in front of others," Cas replied. He didn't need Box making this situation any worse. They moved through the crowds, pushing around all the different species packed in close to the heaters. Somewhere off to the left came the sound of shattering dishes followed by a smattering of applause and boos. One of the restaurants.

When they were far from Evie and Laura Cas turned around. "They're going to arrest me."

Box's yellow optics blinked in confusion. "Who?"

"Greene. Under orders from Rutledge. He never intended on keeping his word. Which means I assume he plans on impounding the ship and you too."

"How do you know?" Box asked.

"Evie just told me. They got the orders before we even left."

Box lifted his hand and stroked what passed for his chin. "We shouldn't do anything rash. This might work out in our favor."

Cas shook his head. "No way. I'm not getting back on that ship. We need to leave this place on the *Reasonable Excuse* and never look back. Like we should have done in the first place. Had I actually listened to myself instead of letting my bleeding heart speak for me we wouldn't be in this situation." He was only making himself angrier but he couldn't help it. Everything he'd worked for was on the line. And just when he thought maybe the Coalition wasn't as bad as he'd remembered, it came back and reared its ugly head.

"We can't get away," Box said. "Not with the *Tempest* out there monitoring us. Don't forget, it's a lot faster than any other ship around. They'd have us in a matter of hours."

"Not if we could sneak away," Cas said.

"And what about Evie and Laura? Do we just leave them here?"

"They're adults," Cas said, his mind running through escape scenarios. "They'll figure it out until someone comes to get them." They would need a distraction. Something that would keep the *Tempest* here long enough for them to sneak away. But with it hiding out there behind the third planet in the system it would takes something substantial to keep their attention.

"Commander Diazal just *told* you this information. Don't you think you owe her something more than just to be stranded on a non-aligned station in hostile space? Not everyone in the Coalition is bad. By your own litmus test."

He didn't want to think about Evie at the moment. He needed a plan. *That's* where he needed to put his focus. He hadn't spent all that time working for Veena just to be thrown in prison. Worst case scenario he could always go back to her with a clean slate—if he had no other choice. Right now he was fueled, stocked and ready to go. If the distraction was big enough there would be no way for Rutledge to find him again. Once they were gone they'd be *gone*. Off into the deep reaches of space if necessary.

Box tried again. "Just explain the whole thing. She'll understand. And from what I know about Greene he might too."

"I can't take that chance," Cas said. "I already put too much on the line by telling her what I did. They're not going to give me a second chance. We have to make this happen while we have the element of surprise." The only way this would work is if he could keep away from Evie and Laura. A plan was forming in his mind. He glanced to the side. People moved back and forth, all going about their business. A Spaxksian, about three meters tall lumbered past, his blue eyes the only discernable feature on his furry face. He pulled a white ball from underneath his robe and dropped it in his mouth, crunching as he moved along. It caused Cas to glance up to the cameras. Surveillance cameras ran the gamut of the main common areas, but they wouldn't have them everywhere. They wouldn't have them in the bowels of the colony.

He jogged over to one of the access terminals with Box directly behind him. "I need the manifest transfer schedule for the rest of the day," Cas said.

Box nodded, going to work on the terminal. He was done in a matter of seconds. Cas peered around him to see the full schedule before him.

"What are you looking for?" Box asked.

"A spark."

***

When they returned to Evie and Laura the women had been in the middle of "interviewing" more people in the common areas. They returned to Cas and Box when they saw they were back.

"Have any luck?" Evie asked.

Cas shook his head. "You?"

"Nothing yet. But there has to be something there. There are species here from at least thirty worlds, most of them in relative proximity to this system. A Coalition ship doesn't just disappear."

"No, it doesn't," Cas replied, wishing they'd found both debris *and* nothing at all. Because at least if they'd found debris the search would be over. But if the search was over then so was his freedom. He was done playing nice. "Look, we're heading down to the lower levels. I want to talk to some of the people down there. They might be willing to give up some more information…for a price." He glanced over to Evie. "Transfer me a few thousand?"

"To your personal account? No way," Evie said. "You start bribing people and they'll tell you whatever you want."

"And if you don't they'll never tell you anything," Cas said, his hand outstretched.

Evie huffed and pulled out a small unit from one of her jacket pockets. "Fine, but I'm going with you this time. Laura, you and Box continue finding out what you need up here." She tapped the device and Cas felt his personal comm buzz with the transfer.

"No," Cas replied. "I want Box with me. Things can get rough down there. I need...protection."

Evie gave him such a pitiful look he wished he hadn't tried to cover the lie at all. "Don't worry," she said, patting the sword. "I think you'll be fine."

He could still make this work. Box just had to make sure he was on the *Reasonable Excuse* by the time Cas was done with his meeting. And he'd have to find a way to incapacitate Evie. There was just no other way around it now.

"Box, get back to the ship. I want to make sure no one's poking around."

"The sensors would have alerted us," Box protested.

"Still," Cas pressed. "You never know in a place like this. Someone might have a cloaked refractor or a subsonic emitter. I want to make sure we can take off when we need to." He forced his gaze on Box, doing his best to impress how important this was. After all their close calls, he had full confidence Box could be ready. But his allegiances might be conflicted at the moment. He'd never disobeyed Cas before, but there was a first time for everything.

"Yeah. Sure," Box said, glancing at Laura. Worst case scenario they could fire her out of one of the ships two escape pods and pick up a replacement sometime later. They could even point her back in the direction of the station. That might be ideal, Evie would probably feel better about him if Laura stayed with Box.

"Time's wasting," Evie said, already heading back toward the tunnels.

"See you back on the ship," Cas said to Box as he followed her.

Box only nodded in response.

23

"Are you feeling okay?" Evie asked as they made their way down into the lower levels. The walk was long since there were no hypervators anywhere in the colony. Most of the storage was brought in by cargo transport that docked on the exposed part of the asteroid where shipping containers used to sit, waiting to be filled with alchuriam ore. A couple hundred years ago the ore had been a valuable resource but with the advent of galvanium it had become obsolete and the mine had been abandoned. Strategically Car'pr wasn't an important system and it had no inhabitable planets as they were all gas giants, so it made sense a non-aligned colony would eventually pop up here, out in the middle of nowhere. And from what Cas had seen upstairs it had been thriving.

"Not really," Cas replied.

"I'm sorry I sprung that on you, I just thought you should know. I'm impressed you're sticking it out, though. I half thought you might try to run," she said, trying to keep her voice lighthearted.

"I haven't yet," he replied.

"I know the crew thinks I'm crazy," Evie said. "But I just don't believe one mistake should define a person's life. And if what you told me was true, you didn't even do anything."

"If?" Cas prompted. He was still furious and now she was questioning his story. *She* still didn't even believe him.

"I'm a Coalition officer," she said. "And as much as I'd love to go on someone's word alone, I can't do it. I need concrete proof."

"Concrete proof doesn't exist," Cas said. "So you either believe me or you don't."

She didn't reply, which gave him his answer. That was fine. At least he wouldn't feel as guilty about leaving her behind.

They reached the lower level in silence. It was a wide space full of shipping containers in one direction and a dark corridor in the other. The wide space had different partitions of containers, each indicating a different cargo port. Not all the slots had something to ship, and this place was notorious as a place where illegal goods could be exchanged. Cas wondered just how many valuables were in some of these containers. Probably enough to buy five *Reasonable Excuses*.

Voices drifted over the quiet and two figures appeared from behind one of the crates, approaching Cas and Evie.

Evie put her mouth in a thin line, stiffening which Cas just relaxed back, not wanting to appear threatening.

"What is your business here?" one of the figures asked. Cas couldn't tell if the voice was male or female, the person's face was obscured by a mask of a dragon.

"We're looking to buy a type-four Coalition thrust assembly," Evie said, her face completely straight. "We heard someone might have one for sale down here."

"Hand," the other, shorter figure said. Evie produced hers and a small beam flashed over it. "Hand," he said to Cas. Cas stuck his out and the same light flashed on it. The figure nodded to the other one.

They both moved out of the way as Cas and Evie entered the large area. "I guess it's a good thing we did a DNA scramble," she whispered.

"You did. I have no need to," Cas replied. "Things actually tend to go better for me in places like this when people find out I've defected."

"You didn't defect," Evie said.

"That's not what the record says." Cas chuckled. He should know, he wrote it himself before getting Box to upload it to the Sargan servers.

Evie glanced around. "This place is huge. Where do we start?"

"I'll head down that way," Cas said, indicating straight ahead of him. "You start checking for anyone in that section over there." Another wide corridor branched off from the main one and ran at a perpendicular angle away from the first.

"Shouldn't we stick tog—"

"We don't have the time. We need to find it as soon as possible and we can't wait to play it safe. Don't worry about me, I know how to defend myself."

Evie huffed. "Comm me if something goes wrong. Just beep the comm twice, you don't have to say anything."

"Yeah, you too," Cas replied.

She watched him a second longer than he would have liked, then turned and made her way down the adjacent corridor. He followed his own corridor, knowing full well he was about to betray her. Betray everything she had trusted him with. And for a moment he hesitated. It had been a long time since someone had placed trust in him that wasn't motivated by something other than greed or power or even revenge. But he couldn't go back, and if he didn't take this chance right now, he'd never see the infinity of space again. Rutledge would have him imprisoned forever. His ship was here, fueled and ready to go. Box was set. All he had to do was take a few more steps. Find the Plegarians. It was simple.

So why was he hesitating?

Cas stood there a moment, leaning against one of the shipping containers. It was a large, nondescript box, but somehow it seemed familiar. He'd been too distracted before to notice it, but now he did, he realized he *did* recognize it. It was the same kind Veena used when she was shipping people through one of the larger couriers. She'd pack them inside, as many as the container could handle, then ship them off to some Kor-forsaken planet as laborers or other kind of slaves. Cas had never gotten that dirty. He couldn't in good conscience do it. If he had, he'd never had to worry about parts for his ship again. But he also wouldn't have been able to sleep at night.

The container presented a larger problem. Why was one of Veena's containers way out here, outside Sargan space? The only way it could be here is if one of her couriers delivered it; and Cas wasn't aware of any courier working this far outside her territory. He inspected the container, hoping to find some evidence of when it had been shipped or which transport it had come on, but it had no markings other than her telltale seal that only the couriers knew. It helped keep them from stealing from each other when they were off-world. Veena like competition, but not for her own "goods".

Cas knocked on the side of the container, praying he was wrong. That someone had marked the box incorrectly or perhaps even reused one of her containers. But then there came a light knock in response. It sounded weak.

"Fuck," Cas said. He had two choices: either leave them to their fate, or try and get them aboard the *Reasonable Excuse.* Neither was ideal, considering there could be as many as twenty humans inside. Unfortunately not everyone always survived the journey. He tapped his comm twice to alert Evie.

There was no other choice; he couldn't leave these people here. He'd have to abandon the plan.

As he was looking for a seam to break he caught voices approaching. At first he thought it might be Evie speaking to someone on her own comm but as they grew closer he realized they were familiar for an entirely different reason.

They were the same Plegarians Laura had spoken with earlier. He ducked down behind another set of crates out of sight.

"And you guarantee full happiness," one of them said in their odd lilt. They spoke through a type of translator that didn't always get the words correct as it was trying to interpret the Plegarians' emotions about any given topic. Laura had enjoyed the challenge.

"Of course. If there's a problem just contact my mistress. She will reimburse you," said another voice Cas recognized. Rasp, Veena's first lieutenant. He must have been the one to deliver the cargo out here.

"Insufficient goods will be expunged," one of the three Plegarians said.

"I'm sure you'll be satisfied," he said. "Now. Where is *my* payment?"

"The human is strong any moment," a Plegarian said.

Human?

"And you're sure it's him?" Rasp asked.

"Joyful. We scanned his life earlier. Robeaux confirmed. He set up appointments."

Shit. Backstabbing Plegarians! No wonder they weren't allowed into the Coalition. They were going to turn him in to Veena! But why would she want him now? Evie had compensated her. And how did she find him in the first place? Something was very wrong here; he needed to notify Box.

"We will inspect sorrow," a different Plegarian said. "Afternoon." Cas peeked around the crates to see the four of them standing there. Rasp was nodding.

"Yes, yes, inspect whenever you want. There's enough life support to keep them alive another day or so. But you haven't delivered my *payment.* And if I don't get my payment, you don't get yours."

"Very angriable," the first Plegarian uttered.

Rasp shook his head and walked closer to where Cas hid. He stopped less than a meter from him.

"Yeah. Yeah, it's Rasp. Get her for me." A pause. "I don't care, just get her!" Another pause and Cas risked an exhale. "My queen," Rasp said after another moment. "I've made the delivery, but Robeaux isn't here. I think the Plegarians played us." Another pause. "Yes, of course. They played *me.* I apologize." Cas drew in another breath, holding it. "No, his ship's here. It's docked on the asteroid, I saw it when I came in. They're here looking for it. Him and that Coalition woman."

Cas almost made a noise in his throat. Could Veena know what they were looking for? How? And they knew Evie was from the Coalition. What was going on?

"No, they don't have a clue. I will. *Yes*, mistress. You can count on me." Rasp ended the call. Cas didn't have a choice. He needed to take control of this situation.

It was now or never.

24

As soon as Rasp turned his focus back on the Plegarians and his comm was in his pocket, Cas jumped from his hiding place and tackled him from behind, knocking him to the ground. They both landed with an *oof!* Cas made a move to flip Rasp over and start pummeling him but an ear-piercing screech penetrated the air, causing both of them to cover their ears. Even through his hands the noise was close to unbearable. Cas glanced up at the three Plegarians standing still yet wailing at the top of their lungs.

"Shut them up!" Cas yelled.

Rasp either didn't hear him or didn't care. He struggled under Cas's weight, throwing him off. He got up on his knees, but kept both hands to his ears. The Plegarians remained motionless, screeching. As long as they kept wailing there was no way either of them could make a move for each other. The sound would burst Cas's eardrums if he removed his hands. Cas got on his feet and made a move to charge one of the Plegarians when the tallest one in the back collapsed, his screech silenced. Behind him stood Evie, sword drawn and tiny blinking devices in her ears.

Rasp caught sight of her at the same time and took off running.

Evie took the hilt of her blade and smashed it into the small space between the shoulders of the other two Plegarians, knocking them out cold. The noise stopped and Cas dropped his hands.

Her face was red. "The Plegarians! You were going to make a deal with them?" she yelled, tapping each of the devices in her ears.

Cas shook his head. "We don't have time. Veena knows what we're looking for!" He pointed to the crate behind him. "And there are people in there; they're payment to the Plegarians for info about me. About what we're doing."

She sheathed her sword in one simple move. "I know. I heard. We can come back for them, we have to find Rasp." She took off running in the direction he'd gone and Cas ran after her, pulling his comm from his pocket.

"Box! Veena is close by somewhere. Rasp is here in the lower levels. Make sure you have all defenses on high alert," he yelled into the device.

"You got it, boss, but I doubt she'll try anything this close to the colony. The other ships won't let her fire."

"I knew I couldn't trust you," Evie fumed as they pursued Rasp deeper into the storage areas. "I never should have told you about your arrest. *Of course* you would go to the one species that hates the Coalition more than any other."

"I wouldn't say that," Cas replied. "The Plegarians are just mad because you accepted the Ocarians into the Coalition and made them refugees from their own planet. How would you feel if some hulking organization came to your planet, sided with ninety percent of the population and exiled the rest?"

"That was seventy years ago!" she yelled. "And that was a complex situation. You're over-simplifying it."

"Yeah? How so?" Cas countered.

A bullet struck the wall to his right and he grabbed Evie, pulling them both down. Rasp stood behind the cover of another crate, firing his weapon again. It struck right above their heads as they got behind their own cover. Cas automatically reached for his boomcannon, realizing it was still in the security lock up on the *Tempest*.

"Dammit," he said. "This is why you don't take a man's weapon from him."

"*I* don't need a gun." Evie drew her sword again and gripped the hilt with both hands. She crab-walked out of cover, moving quickly. Rasp fired at her again, only he couldn't get a good bead on her as she was staying low and fast, not repeating a pattern as she moved. He was obviously becoming more panicked the closer she came as he fired fast but wild. Before he knew what was happening she was on him, her sword to his throat and his gun off to the side, having been dropped when she'd nicked his hand with the edge of her sword. "Talk," she said.

Cas double-checked the cover and scrambled over to them.

"Screw you," Rasp said. Cas sucker-punched him, causing his head to bounce on the ground. Rasp spit up blood in response.

"*Don't* do that again," Evie said. It took Cas a moment to realize she was talking to him, not Rasp. "What is your mission here?"

"To…get him." Rasp pointed a bloody finger to Cas.

"Why?" Evie said, pressing the blade against his neck just as she had with Cas. "I paid your boss fairly for him."

Rasp chuckled. "You think she didn't know you were from the Coalition? She wanted to know why you wanted him so badly. And now we know about the *Achlys*…"

Evie winced, pulling the sword back and sheathing it. She grabbed Rasp by the lapels, drawing him up on his feet. Cas stood with them. "What do you know?"

"You're not getting off this rock alive," he told Evie. "And you," he said to Cas. "The mistress has a new job for you."

"The mistress is just going to have to do without," Cas said. "What do we do with him?" he asked Evie.

"I'm placing you both under arrest," Evie said, staring at Rasp. "You for attempting to murder a Coalition officer, and you," she indicated to Cas, "for conspiring against the Coalition."

Rasp only laughed. Evie tapped her hand, activating her comm. "Yamashita. We have a situation down here. Bring me two sets of cuffs and notify the *Tempest* we have prisoners and potential wounded civilians we'll be bringing back."

"Ma'am?" Laura asked on the other end.

"Don't argue, just do it," Evie replied. She led Rasp back to the shipping container but turned to Cas before they got very far. "And if you feel like running now just *imagine* the consequences when I catch up with you. Because you know I will." She turned back and strong-armed Rasp down the corridor.

Cas sighed and followed.

***

Laura met them at the shipping container, handing Evie the electronic cuffs. The three Plegarians lay off to the side, still unconscious. Evie placed one set on Rasp then sat him on the floor. She then indicated Cas put out his hands, which he did reluctantly, and locked the cuffs on him, sitting him down beside Rasp.

"See what happens when you trust the Coalition," Rasp whispered to him. "Veena tried to tell you."

"Don't talk to me. You tried to kill me," Cas replied.

"No, just incapacitate you. If I'd killed you Veena would have been very upset. Just like she'll be upset she hasn't heard from me."

Veena would send others after him when he didn't check in. Cas tried to get Evie's attention, but she and Laura were in the process of studying the shipping container. And Laura's words distracted him.

"...wouldn't let me contact the ship. He said it was too dangerous to send a signal," Laura said.

"So they're both traitors—" Evie replied.

"You can't send a signal from here, half a dozen non-aligned ships will trace it to the source," Cas interrupted. "If Box had let her send a signal she'd have exposed your ship."

Evie whipped her head around. "Just like you were about to do."

"I wasn't going to go that far. I was going to tell the Plegarians there was a Coalition ship close. It would have sent them into a swarming frenzy. They've got to have at least a hundred shuttle-sized ships up there. Enough for an easy getaway."

"And that's all you care about, getting away."

"Yeah, it *was*," Cas said, balancing enough to stand. "Until I found *that*. That's the whole reason I commed you. I couldn't leave those people to be sold into Plegarian labor camps. And if that meant giving up my chance for freedom then I guess I made my choice."

"How noble," Evie quipped. "Too bad I don't believe a word of it."

"Why else would I have told you to come back?" Cas protested, desperate for her to believe him. Why did he care so much about what she thought?

"He commed you to come back?" Laura asked. "Why would he do that if he wanted to meet the Plegarians alone?"

"It doesn't matter," Evie said. "Just help me get this hatch open." She tugged on the side of the container.

"It doesn't work like that." Rasp chuckled. Some of the blood from his nose had dried and crusted on his upper lip. "It needs an access code."

"Then we'll just take the entire container," Evie said, turning to Laura. "Tell Box to move the ship down here, we'll load it just as it was unloaded."

"Commander," Cas said, thinking about how little time they had until Rasp's reinforcements showed up. She didn't reply, only continued to ignore him. "Commander! *Evelyn!*"

She turned on him, fury in her eyes. "What?"

"Do you think he's here alone?" he said, indicating Rasp. "We don't have time to transport the container. We need to get out of here now."

She considered him a moment, then glanced down toward the entrance they'd come through. "Get Box down here, he'll be able to get this open."

Cas put out his hands; he couldn't access his comm unit to call Box with them restrained.

Evie scoffed and turned to Laura. "That's an order, ensign."

Laura seemed to realize she was talking to her at the same time Cas did. She tapped her comm. "Box, we need you in lower level seven. We're about forty meters from the main entrance."

"Be there in a minute," Box replied.

Meanwhile Evie continued to look for some way to access the container, running her hands over the sides.

"Hey, Robeaux," Rasp whispered. "Help me out of here and I'll make sure you're back in good with Veena."

"You can't seriously think I'd go back to her. I'd almost rather be imprisoned in a Coalition cell," he replied.

"She'll make it pretty sweet for you," he said.

He stared straight ahead. "I'm not going back."

Rasp shrugged. "It's your funeral." He wasn't wrong. As soon as Rutledge found out Cas had tried to defect again there was no telling what he'd do.

Box jogged into the space, surveying the area. "Hey, what the hell," he said upon seeing Cas.

Cas put his hands out in a surrender gesture. "It's fine. Just help Evie. Do what she asks you to do."

Box hesitated, but he went over to her.

"Open this," she said, standing back from the container.

Box wrapped his slender fingers around the edge of one side and yanked, tearing the metal away from itself. There was a hiss and a cloud of mist rose from the break in the seal. Box continued to pull, ripping the entire side of the container away.

Cas gasped when he saw what was inside.

Two rows of people, suspended vertically by some kind of harness attached to both the ceiling and floor of the container, tubes running from them into a series of devices built into the floor. Each had on an oxygen mask but they were all conscious. And they looked emaciated. Cas counted five of them, all different ages. The one closest to the wall where he'd knocked was in her early teens.

"Get them unhooked as quickly and safely as you can. We need to get them all back to the ship," Evie said after a moment of silence. Perhaps she was as stunned as the rest of them were.

"You'll never make it," Rasp said, his voice cheery. Cas kicked him in the side for good measure, causing him to double over in pain.

Box went to work disconnecting the people from all their tubes and harnesses while Laura helped them out of the container to sit on the ground beside it.

"How many can you carry?" Evie asked Box.

"Three, maybe four before I won't be able to move under the excessive weight," Box replied.

Evie sighed, approaching Cas. "You and Yamashita get the ones Box can't carry back to the ship. I'll escort the prisoner." She reached down and held her finger to one side of his cuffs. The chain between them lengthened, but remained connected. It was enough so he could move his hands freely enough to help the people in the container.

"You trust me?"

"Not at all," she replied, turning her back on him. She walked over and lifted Rasp up to his feet. His hands remained locked behind his back. But just as he stood a blast of energy hit him square in the chest, leaving a deep black burn mark in its wake. Rasp's eyes rolled up into his skull and he fell back, dead.

The blasts exploded all around them.

25

Bolts of superheated plasma struck the crates all around them as Cas ducked into cover beside Laura. He glanced over to see Evie and Box hiding behind the crate with the five people inside, who had—free from their harnesses—crowded in the back of the container.

Cas risked a glance over what little cover he and Laura had and counted four of Veena's guards, each armed with a plasma rifle. And here they were with no weapons but an ancient sword.

"Box," Cas yelled. "Any ideas?"

"Yeah, but you're not going to like it," he yelled back.

"I don't care! Just do it!"

Box nodded, stepped around Evie to her protestation and reached out in the line of fire, grabbing one of the unconscious Plegarians.

"Wait, Box, you can't—" Before Cas could finish the sentence the Plegarian went sailing through the air, flying like a lawn dart at the nearest guard who didn't have time to register just what was happening to him. They struck skull to skull, knocking the guard back with the unconscious Plegarian landing on top of him. The other three guards were stunned by the scene, long enough for Box to grab the other two and toss them in the same direction.

Box jumped out into the line of fire as the remaining guard seemed to gather himself and point the weapon at Box, only to find his recently-deceased boss, Rasp, heading straight for him. The guard screamed, firing wildly, and while some of the shots struck Rasp they didn't slow his momentum and he collided with the last guard in a sickening crunch.

"Let's go," Evie yelled to the people huddled in the back of the container. They wouldn't have long, but the people were too scared to move. Box lumbered into the container, grabbed three of them and pulled them out, handing one each to Laura, Evie, and Cas. He then went back in for the last two and came out holding one under each arm.

"Now we're ready," he said, his yellow eyes blinking satisfaction.

Evie grabbed her person by the wrist and yanked her down the hall past the moaning guards. Laura followed her with her person followed by Cas and Box. But as Cas passed he took the opportunity to snatch one of the errant plasma rifles from the ground as they ran.

They reached the entrance to the level, guarded by the two men they'd seen coming in. Cas didn't know if they'd heard all the commotion and didn't want to get involved, but he wasn't about to let them stop them from getting back to his ship. One of them reached inside his jacket and Cas fired the rifle at the ground at both of their feet. They both jumped aside, their hands up and their weapons forgotten while Evie and the rest ran through, still pulling or carrying the prisoners.

Cas glanced over to his prisoner, it was the same young girl who he suspected responded to his knocking. Her hair was wild and untamed and her dark eyes traveled over everything, probably looking for potential threats. Cas couldn't help but wonder how long ago she'd been captured.

"This way," Box yelled, indicating the ramp. Thankfully the prisoners seemed to understand Evie was helping them and didn't put up a struggle on the way back to the ship. Cas kept expecting another set of guards to jump at them but they managed to make it back to the ship without another shot fired. Though those guards couldn't be far behind.

Just as he was about to take a step toward the airlock the others had already passed through, a plasma bolt exploded on his shoulder, causing him to scream in pain and fall to the hard, cold tunnel surface. The young girl just stared at him, her face awash in terror.

"Run," Cas yelled, trying to push her to the airlock. Box appeared a moment later and grabbed the girl, yanking her back out of the line of fire.

Behind him one of the guards had managed to keep his pace with them, though he was huffing and bleeding from the head. Cas swung the plasma rifle at him one-handed and pulled the trigger, but the kick of the weapon made the plasma swing wide. The guard grinned and hoisted his own weapon to his shoulder, bracing it and staring Cas down through the sight. Cas fumbled with his weapon, trying to reposition himself so he could get a better shot but he already knew it was over. He couldn't get one off fast enough with the chains in between his hands.

When he looked up a strange frown had come over the guard's face. Cas glanced down to see a very large sword sticking out from the abdomen of the guard, the hilt wagging ever so slightly. He looked to his right to see Evie, standing with her feet prone and her arm outstretched. Her fingers shook, but it was almost imperceptible.

The guard collapsed back just as Rasp had done, his gun scattering across the floor of the smooth tunnel. Evie stood straight and walked over to him, yanking the sword from his body with a *schluck*. The blade dripped red.

Keeping the blade out she strode over to Cas, hoisted him up by his good arm and pulled him through the airlock. "Box, we're good. Go!" she yelled, escorting Cas down the corridor to the kitchen. One of the prisoners sat at Cas's pantry going through the food, tearing things apart with his teeth.

"Hey!" Cas yelled. "That's mine! Get your—"

Evie reached down and pulled the weapon from his hand, tossing it to the counter as Cas felt the main thrusters on the ship fire and the ship begin to rise off the asteroid. She pushed him down into the nearest chair, her eyes burning with an intensity he hadn't seen from her before.

"You have a med-kit I assume," she said, staring at his black shoulder.

"It's over by grabby-hands there. Two cabinets up and one to the left." He surveyed the room. "Hey, where are the rest of them? They're not in my room, are they?" He moved to get up before Evie pushed him back down in the chair.

"What the hell was that back there?" she asked, going over to the metal cabinet and pulling the med-kit from the back. The prisoner ignored her, choosing to continue to gorge himself on Cas's food. Cas eyed his shoulder. Strangely, it didn't hurt. It must be the adrenaline.

"You're asking me?" he said. "I should ask you. I didn't know you could throw swords."

Evie winced. She placed the bloody blade beside the rifle he'd confiscated. "I want to know why I shouldn't turn you in to Captain Greene when we get back to the *Tempest*," she said.

Cas dropped his head. "I panicked, okay? You told me no matter what I did I was going to be imprisoned for it. I couldn't let that happen. You had to expect I wouldn't just sit by. Not when I had a chance."

She sighed, pulling a small knife from the kit. She used it to cut away the charred cloth of his arm. "Maybe I did," she admitted. "But you deserved to know."

"You have to believe me. I wasn't going to put the ship in danger. I wouldn't do that. Not after…everything."

She didn't look at him, instead kept her attention on his shoulder, removing the last pieces of cloth. Beneath the skin was charred and burned. Cas could even smell it. For the first time since he'd been shot he grew concerned. Shouldn't he be feeling something?

"It doesn't hurt," he said.

"That's because it neutralized your pain receptors," Evie said, running a diagnostic scanner over the wound. "Your arm could be missing and you wouldn't feel it."

"Does that mean I'm going to lose the arm?" Cas asked, concerned now.

She pursed her lips at him. "So there's one thing the great Captain Caspian Robeaux doesn't know about after all: medicine."

"Is that a yes or no?"

"You'll be fine, but I can't fix it. You'll have to see Doctor Xax back on the ship."

The ship.

"Box, turn around!" Cas yelled down the adjacent corridor.

"What are you doing?" Evie furrowed her brow.

"Don't you see? Veena tracked us to D'jattan. She knows where we're going and what we're looking for. She's got to have a tracker on us somewhere."

Understanding dawned on Evie. "And we can't return to the ship until we find it."

Cas struggled to stand. "She probably installed it when she was unloading all that contraband back at Devil's Gate," Cas said. "No wonder she was so agreeable." The links between the cuffs rattled as he stood, his left arm hanging limp at his side. "Can you please take these Garth-forsaken things off me?"

She hesitated a moment but then pressed her thumb to the inside of the cuff. Both sides released and clattered to the ground.

"Thank you," Cas said. He turned and made his way down the main corridor to the cockpit. Box sat at the pilot's station and Laura occupied the co-pilot's seat. The young girl prisoner stood behind them, watching the stars go by.

"Box," Cas said softly. He turned. "Put it on auto. Take us away from the *Tempest*."

Box nodded and hit the appropriate switches. He rose from the seat and faced them. "What's the problem?"

"Veena bugged us. We have to find it before we go back. Otherwise she'll know our every move."

"That woman is worse than Maxine Anderson!" Box yelled, jolting out of his seat and storming down through the corridor.

"Who is Maxine Anderson?" Evie asked.

"Probably the matriarch of his most recent net drama obsession," Cas said. "I try to stay out of it."

Evie turned to Laura. "Keep us out of range of the *Tempest*. And if anything looks strange, let me know." Laura nodded and turned her attention to the monitors.

"How much does she know?" Box yelled, heading down to the main engineering access.

"A lot," Cas said, following with Evie close behind.

"Then it's on the comm equipment," Box replied. "Everyone shut up until I find it."

"If you'd done a level four diagnostic *like I told you to,* we wouldn't be having this—" Cas began.

"Shhhh!" Box said.

Cas shut up, taking a glance at Evie. She was struggling to keep a smile from her face. Box began opening panels and removing equipment seemingly at random, taking things apart bit by bit.

"He can get all that back in one piece, right?" Evie asked.

"If he can't I can," Cas replied. There wasn't a piece of this ship he didn't know by heart. Probably only about twenty percent of the original ship remained since he'd first purchased it.

"Are you going to stand there and gawk or are you going to help?" Box said, removing the primary communication drive from its housing.

"We'll check the holds," Cas said, leading Evie away. Veena wasn't foolish enough to put the tracker there, but then again she would probably suspect Cas wouldn't use the holds unless he was transporting contraband for her.

"I just want to say," Cas began as they reached the first hold in the floor. "Thanks for what you did out there. You could have left me."

"No, I couldn't," Evie said, bending and helping him move the piece of floor aside. "You knew I wouldn't let you stay out there alone. I'd have been too afraid you would have hooked up with pirates and been on your merry way."

He avoided her gaze, instead inspected the hold. "I don't know what to say."

"Cas, look at me." He raised his eyes to meet hers. "Can I trust you?"

He sat back, his legs folded underneath him and his arm dangling uselessly at his side. "Sometimes I don't even know if I can trust myself."

"That's *not* a ringing endorsement."

"It's the truth."

She sighed, sitting back herself. "Is that what you were really planning to do? Notify the Plegarians the *Tempest* was out there?"

He shook his head. "My first thought was to send a communique to every hostile species on the colony, but that was never a reality. After what happened on the *Achlys* I couldn't put people in danger like that. The Plegarians seemed like the next-best solution. I set a meeting with them, planning to slip them some intel that a ship was spotted in the area and then watch them go crazy trying to find it. It would have been just enough confusion to slip away unnoticed. Until you couldn't trace our undercurrent, that is."

"And what about me and Laura?"

"I was pretty sure you could take care of yourselves. At least until things calmed down. It's not like I would have been stranding you in the middle of the desert." Cas opened a secondary hold under the first one, searching for anything out of place. It was hard to squeeze into with his arm flopping to the side but it was easier than looking at Evie's disappointed gaze.

She was silent while he searched, sitting at the edge of the hold, looking down. When he was sure there was nothing out of the ordinary he managed to hoist himself back out. There was no avoiding this now.

"I guess the question is: what are you going to do now you know I've tried to betray you?" he asked.

She watched him for a moment, as if she was searching his soul, looking for something redeemable in him. He didn't expect her to find it.

"I wish I knew."

26

"Box?" Cas said, approaching him from behind. The robot was deep into the communication equipment, parts and components strewn all around him. He'd recruited one of the former prisoners to hold parts as he removed them from the main comm hub. The man's arms were full.

"I'm working on it!" Box said, his voice muffled from the depth of the contraption

Cas glanced over to the man with his arms full. He had ochre skin with a mop of blonde hair cut close. Various scars ran down the sides of his face, probably a result of being Veena's prisoner. His clothes were a simple jumpsuit suitable for different climates. "What's your name?" he asked.

"Setsemeh," the man replied.

"What happened to you?" Cas noticed Evie lurking around behind him. He wasn't sure if it was because she didn't want him out of her sight or if she was genuinely interested in the man.

"Kidnapped, off Paxi. Me and my brother. But I haven't seen him since. He must have gone with another group."

"How long ago?" Evie asked.

"Three seasons. Since then I've either been in a cell or stasis. I can't thank you enough for saving me. For saving us."

"Do you know what you were being sold for?" Cas asked.

Setsemeh shook his head. "She told us we were going to Cassiopeia Optima, but then a couple of days ago she rounded a few of us up and stuffed us in that crate. But we weren't going to be inside long enough to go into stasis. She had us hooked up to life support. That asteroid was definitely not Cassiopeia."

"She intended to sell you to the Plegarians," Cas said. "Probably to service their ships."

Setsemeh shuddered. "Those ships are so small. I would have not survived long."

Cas thought about it a minute. "If you were conscious, could you hear everything from inside the crate?"

Setsemeh opened his mouth to answer.

"Will you two shut up!" Box called from where he was. "Until I find this thing there's no telling how much is getting out." He was right. Veena could still be listening to their every word.

"Commander?" Laura called from the cockpit.

Evie turned, making her way to the cockpit. Cas followed, and when he arrived he saw what had concerned Laura: four of Veena's fighter ships in pursuit. They must have been the ships Veena's people had used to arrive on D'jattan. The young girl Cas had rescued stood behind Laura's chair, watching the screens intently.

Cas turned to Evie. "Can you outrun them?"

She jumped into the pilot's seat as Laura moved to the co-pilot position. "We'll see. I don't know what this ship can do but for all the parts I paid for it better be able to outrun a couple of class two gunners." She switched off the autopilot and immediately began evasive maneuvers. Thanks to the gravity dampeners the inertia on the ship didn't change, the only difference was it seemed like the starfield outside was twirling in different directions as Evie navigated.

Cas ran back to Box. "You need to find that thing. Now," he said.

"What does it look like I'm doing?" He was much more agitated than usual.

Cas turned to Setsemeh who continued to stand there with his arms full. "What did you do before you were kidnapped? What was your job?"

"I am an architect," he said. "For orbital platforms."

"Close enough," Cas said. "Drop that crap and help him look."

Setsemeh set the equipment on the ground and went to work disassembling parts. Back here with no windows Cas couldn't tell what was going on, everything still felt perfectly still. He pulled his comm from his pocket and tapped it.

Nothing happened.

He glanced over to the disassembled communications array and mentally smacked himself. Instead, he ran *back* to the cockpit, his useless arm still flapping at his side.

"I can't get away from them as long as they know exactly where I am," Evie said, her voice strained as the starfield moved left and right. A plasma burst streaked by. "And they're getting closer."

Cas glanced down to the young girl. "You, come with me. It's all hands on deck." The girl nodded, following him back to Box and Setsemeh. "What's your name?" he asked as they approached the parts all over the floor.

"Yance," she replied, her voice soft.

"Yance, I need you to fit in through where they can't. You might be able to find it faster. Box will tell you what he's looking for."

"A long-range iridium tracker, right?" she asked.

"Yeah," he said, stunned. "How…?"

"My parents used them to track interstellar creatures. It was the best way to keep tabs on a *tunnel guardian* or a *grandgrade*."

"Ah," Cas said, "Okay, get in there and help them." The ship shook for the first time, knocking them off their feet.

Evie yelled from the front: "These guys are all over us!"

Cas had landed on his bad arm but fortunately hadn't felt much. He struggled to stand, finding Setsemeh and Yance doing the same. Box had remained half-inside the comm unit.

"Box," Cas yelled, "Tiny hands, put them to use!"

Setsemeh motioned for Yance to come over just as the floor shook again. Cas ran back to the cockpit where Evie and Laura were doing their best to keep Veena's fighters off them. At least he was getting his cardio in.

"Doesn't this thing have anything more powerful than a quad cannon?" Laura asked, running her hands over the controls.

"Unfortunately not," Cas replied, watching the fighters buzz by out the window.

"It's not worth wasting our reserve fuel if there's nowhere to go." Evie struggled with the controls. "I'm basically just flying in circles until we can lose them."

The ship shook violently and Cas hit the side wall.

"Breach in one of the hab pods!" Laura said.

"Seal it off," Cas replied, pushing himself away from the wall. "They're designed to be self-sustaining. We can eject it if necessary."

"Got it!" Box called from the back. "You're clear!"

"Now you're talking." Evie narrowed her eyes and jerking the ship into a barrel roll that sent the starfield spinning. Even with the gravitational dampeners Cas could still feel the pull of the g-forces. His little ship had never been put to the limit like this. Evie hit the accelerator and the ship shot forward, swinging around the asteroids of the belt. Car'pr, the system's star, reflected light off the cockpit as she dove down, coming close to an asteroid. She slipped behind it, pulling them to a near-stop when two of the fighters shot right past. Evie turned immediately and shot the other direction. "Laura, if they get on our ass shoot the hell out of them."

"I'll do what I can," she replied.

"Drop the damaged hab suite," Cas said. "It has its own power source, you can use it as a mine."

Laura nodded, preparing herself. "There they are," she replied. She hit the eject button and there was a loud *clank* as the hab detached, falling back behind it. "They're ignoring it."

Cas watched as the two fighters adjusted their headings, so they'd go around either side. But when they were on opposite sides of the suite Laura fired a single shot, detonating the suite and destroying both fighters in the process.

"I thought you said you were an exobiologist," Cas said, impressed with her targeting skills.

"I am. Everyone needs a hobby."

"Still have two more," Evie said. She got a funny look on her face. "What is this ship primarily made out of?" She jerked the controls to the right. A fighter appeared beside them, just barely strafing the hull.

"Uh, it's a composite of cyclax, galvanium and—"

"That's all I need to know," she replied, adjusting her heading for the closest fighter.

"Wait, you can't—" Cas began as the ship shot forward, on a collision course with the smaller ship. "This is my *ship*! You can't just ram it into—"

The entire ship shook with a reverberation as the vessel ahead of them exploded from the impact. The fourth and last fighter took off in a hasty retreat back toward the colony. Evie swung the ship around and set an erratic course to throw off any further pursuers.

"I can't believe you just did that," Cas said as Evie stood from the pilot's chair.

She shrugged. "It's my ship now, technically. I knew your hull reinforcements could handle it. Those class-twos are pitiful things, might as well be made out of aluminum. I just needed to make sure the vibrations of hitting something like that wouldn't shake us apart."

"I'm glad you found it satisfactory," Cas replied through his teeth. He caught Laura looking at them but she glanced away as soon as he noticed.

They made their way back to Box who, along with Setsemeh and Yance was repairing the comm system. "Should be good in another day or two," Box said, inspecting components. "It's always easier to take apart than put back together."

"Let me see the tracker," Cas said, holding out his one good hand.

Yance came over and dropped the device into his palm. It wasn't much bigger than his entire hand but had a giant crack down the middle from where Box had disabled it. "You found it?" he asked.

"She crawled in there and within two minutes had it," Setsemeh said.

"It wasn't hard." Yance beamed. "When you know what you're looking for."

"I bet she used one of her Val cronies to get it in there in the first place," Cas said. Val were about the size of a human child. Millenia ago they'd left Earth to settle Valus which had a much higher gravity, resulting in smaller people over a few generations. Though many left the Coalition these days despite Valus being inside the same solar system as Earth.

"Yep. And it was monitoring not only our comms but our conversations as well. Veena knows exactly what we're looking for and everywhere we've searched so far," Box said.

"Which means she's probably already out there looking for it for herself," Cas replied.

"Wait," Evie said. "Does she even know why she wants this ship?"

"She knows its valuable," Cas said. "And that's enough. If she does happen to find it before we do, it will be bad for everyone."

Evie tapped the back of her hand. "Yes Commander?" Laura said from the cockpit.

Cas glanced at her for a moment before remembering Coalition comms had their own built-in network. They didn't rely on a ship to maintain communication like Cas's outdated pocket model did.

"Any sign of pursuit?" Evie asked.

"None."

"Set course back to the *Tempest*. It's time to get the hell out of here."

27

The good news was Evie hadn't put the cuffs back on Cas. The bad news was she hadn't said another word on the short trip back to the *Tempest*.

As soon as they landed, however, she'd gathered her sword and then ordered a very satisfied looking Laura back to the biology labs, making sure to compliment her on her performance. Cas thought the ensign might burst from the endorsement.

He and the former prisoners were all to report to sickbay while Box stayed on the ship to finish the repairs. Evie even gave Box authorization to use the maintenance crew in Bay One if necessary, prompting a confused look from Box to which Cas could only shrug. He had no clue what was going on in Evie's mind.

They reached sickbay and Cas met doctor Xax for the first time, a Yax-Inax. She was bipedal and lean with small feet balancing her slender frame. Like all Yax-Inax she had four arms, two with three fingers and two with four, set parallel to each other in a series and her head was ten percent larger than a human's. And instead of two eyes she had six black globes on the upper part of her face, each one with beautiful aquamarine blue sparkles inside. It gave the Yax-Inax the ability to see things many other humanoids couldn't, such as wavelengths of frequency and light. Below the globes was a small mouth. Cas noticed her rank was that of full Commander. Which made her the only person on the ship ranked higher than Evie, other than the captain of course.

"Please, take a seat, we'll be with you in a moment," she said in perfect English. One of the nice things about the Yax-Inax was they worked for years on perfecting the speech of whatever culture they assimilated themselves into. Their native tongue was much more complex; outside of the vocal range of many species. When the Yax-Inax joined the Coalition they decided on their own to expand their vocal prowess by learning as many languages as possible.

"What is this?" Xax said approaching Cas. Her lower arm with three fingers picked up Cas's lifeless one, while one of the arms with four fingers ran them over the shoulder wound. "Nerve killer. I hate these. Please come with me."

Evie stopped Cas for a moment. "When you're done, report to the captain," she said. "And I don't mean after you've had a shower. I mean immediately." Her eyes said she was dead serious.

Cas nodded, as if by that small token gesture he had accepted his fate. He'd hoped there might be a chance at redemption after what he'd done; but he knew he'd only been fooling himself.

She left still carrying her blood-stained sword out of its sheath as Xax took a scanning device to Cas's arm. As soon as she was gone Cas glanced around at the rest of the former prisoners, Yance, Setsemeh and the others, all sitting on their own beds as the nurses and doctors inspected them as well. At least he'd done something. It wasn't all for naught.

***

Cas stood at the door to Greene's command room, having fielded dirty looks from the rest of the bridge staff with the exception of Zaal. But at least he'd been allowed to come here without an escort. It felt like a test; as if Evie had placed a bet with Page if he'd actually show up or try to run again.

"Come in," Greene's voice said and the doors slid open.

Cas, his arm healed and working like nothing had happened, walked in to find Evie sitting in one of Greene's two chairs on the closest side of his desk. Greene stood, his imposing figure framed by the window behind him. The planetoid the ship had been hiding behind loomed in the distance.

"Please sit, Mr. Robeaux," Greene said, only taking his own seat after Cas had complied. "I was afraid there for a while you might not be coming back." He smiled.

Cas chanced a glimpse at Evie whose own visage remained set in stone. There was no telling what she'd already reported. Screw it. He was tired of living in fear of what she may or may not do.

He reached over and placed the tracking device on Greene's desk. "Veena had this stashed on my ship without my knowledge. She was using it to monitor our conversations anytime I used my comm as well as track our progress. She's been shadowing us this whole time."

"How do you know it's her and not one of her…underlings?" Greene asked.

"Her first lieutenant was down on the colony. In all the years I worked for her I never saw them apart. He doesn't leave her side. Her ship is close somewhere. And we need to find her before she finds the *Achlys*."

"I can't disagree," Greene said. "Any Coalition technology in the hands—"

"This isn't just about Coalition technology," Cas said. "This is about a weapon."

"A weapon?" Greene asked. Evie finally moved, her eyes finding Cas.

"My mission, as outlined by Admiral Rutledge, is to find the *Achlys*. Not because of the missing crew or because the ship is sentimental to him. But because *its* mission was to develop a new type of weapon to combat the Sil."

Greene leaned forward, but didn't interrupt. Cas took a deep breath. It was now or never.

"Seven years ago, the *Achlys* wasn't off-course in Sil space. It was there on purpose. We were looking for a civilian craft, something we could cannibalize and reverse engineer its weapon systems. Because the Sil weaponry is so much more advanced than ours, Rutledge and a few *choice officers* couldn't stand the idea we were technologically inferior to them. But they didn't want to send us up against one of their warships. We never would have made it. But even their civilian craft are shown to have powerful offensive systems. Our job was to capture one of them, eject the occupants into escape pods to be found later, then tow the ship back to Coalition space for study."

"You were part of his mission?" Greene asked.

Cas didn't bother looking at Evie. "I was. As first officer I was tasked with firing on the ship when we came into range. However when the time came I refused, instead disabling the weapons systems and funneling a coded message to the Sil warning them of our intentions."

Greene watched him intently. "No wonder Rutledge hates you."

"Yes, sir. The rest you know. Rutledge was promoted then put in charge of the project. I'm assuming the mission was a success and ever since they have been working on building the weapon directly onboard the *Achlys*."

"Which is why it has its own dry dock floating out there."

"Yes sir."

Greene turned to Evie. "Commander, did you know about this?"

"No one knew, sir. I kept it under strict confidence. Rutledge even confirmed to me he never told Commander Diazal anything about why she was retrieving me," Cas said before she could speak.

Greene turned back to him. "And now this…Veena, knows?"

"I've been discussing the mission at length with Box aboard my ship. He's been aware of my unfortunate past for a long time. Obviously he's not about to say anything. He knows if he does it would put me in an awkward situation, not to mention I'd disassemble him and incorporate the parts into my ship." He took a breath. "I can only assume Veena's overheard everything we've said."

Greene ran his hand down his chin. "That's very unsettling, Mr. Robeaux." He took a deep breath and stood, turning to look out at the stars beyond, Car'pr itself coming into view. The window darkened automatically to shade their eyes from the intense light. "How close is the weapon to being finished?"

"From what I can infer, close. Rutledge seemed on edge about it, determined to find it as soon as possible. That tells me they were either close or already in the testing phase. He wouldn't be so anxious otherwise."

"Damn," Greene whispered. "If the Sargans get their hands on that we'd have a major war on our plate." He dropped his head for a moment, then turned back to them. "I haven't been happy about this from the start. The subterfuge, the hiding in the shadows. I certainly don't like being kept unaware on my own mission." He took his seat again. "Why would Rutledge and others risk a possible war with the Sil for a weapon we don't need? We haven't been hostile with the Sil in almost a hundred years. We have a treaty for a reason."

Cas leaned forward. "Sir, the longer I served under Captain Rutledge the more I began to see he'd do anything to protect the Coalition. Even against threats he only *perceives*. As time went on he became more open to the idea. I don't know if he developed it independently or as part of a group within the Coalition, but he's always been an integral part."

"And now he's risking the safety of a few trillion life forms because he can't contain his paranoia. No wonder they didn't want us to know." Greene turned to Evie. "Commander, you're being awfully quiet."

"Captain, I must confess something," Evie said. "Cas told me about the mission, but he left out the part about the weapon. Had I known I would have come to you immediately. I've known about the rest ever since before we landed on D'jattan."

Cas couldn't read Greene's face. Evie was resolute, however.

"I see," Greene said. "I appreciate your honesty."

"Sir, there's something else. I also informed Mr. Robeaux about his impending arrest. I believe it almost led to a confrontation that could have put this ship in danger."

"How so?" Greene asked, his face unreadable.

"Because as soon as she told me I panicked," Cas said. "I was going to try and run again, and I almost did."

"Ah," Greene said. "The prisoners. You found them on your way out."

"Something like that."

Greene turned back to Evie. "Commander. Given the circumstances, I can't blame you for your actions. Arresting this man for attempting to preserve life is a perversion of our laws and I do not agree with it. You made a judgment call based on the available information. Though I do wish you'd come to me earlier."

"There's no proof," Cas said. "It's Rutledge's word against my own." Evie glanced at him.

"You were the only one who mutinied?" Greene asked. "Out of everyone else on the ship and the space dock?"

"After the…incident and we lost twenty-four of our crew…" Cas paused, trying not to see their faces in his memory. "Rutledge announced he'd be taking responsibility for what happened. He said it was his crew and he was responsible for all of us."

"As any good captain is," Greene said. "But that didn't happen."

Cas shook his head. "As soon as we were back he threw me in front of the ethics committee for mutiny and as being the person responsible for those twenty-four deaths. No one came to my defense. Probably because they didn't want to share my fate. Anyone who spoke out against him would be court-martialed. But he also recruits loyal officers. Some no doubt agreed with his actions."

"This is almost incredulous," Greene said. "Coalition officers, conspiring to undermine our very principles." He took a breath. "Does Rutledge *want* a war?"

"I'm not sure. I can't speak to that point."

Greene shook his head. "What a mess. It seems our goals are now two-fold. Find the *Achlys*—hopefully someone is still alive who can corroborate your story; and stop the Sargans from taking control of the ship."

"Sir, assuming you're not confining me to quarters for my decisions, I'd like to interview the prisoners," Evie said. "They may have information about Veena's location or plans. Anything they may have overheard."

"Commander," Greene said, his eyes softening. "I'm not going to punish you for making a moral decision. That's counterproductive. There have been far too many bad decisions regarding this matter and we're not going to add to the problem. Interview them as soon as you can."

"Box and I may be able to use that," Cas said, indicating the tracker on Greene's desk. "To ping back on her location. It was sending a signal somewhere; if we can track that signal we can find her."

"What are the odds she'll find the ship before we do?" Greene asked.

"She's intelligent, capable, and resourceful. I don't think we can assume she *won't* find it first. Especially since she has a bevy of ships at her command. They can cover a lot more ground than we can."

Greene stood. "Very well. Begin with your assignments. I want status updates on the hour."

Cas and Evie stood in unison. "Yes, sir," they said almost at once.

For once, it felt good to say.

28

"Why didn't you tell me about the weapon?" Evie asked as they made their way across the bridge to the hypervator.

Cas glanced over to the bridge crew. Page seemed surprised to see them walking out together and produced a sneer of disgust in response. The only friendly face was Zaal's holographic one. He also made a small motion with his hand Cas took as a wave. He waved back.

"I was under orders not to reveal it." Cas shrugged.

Evie scoffed. "You're telling me you didn't say anything because you were *ordered* not to?" The doors opened and they entered.

He relented. "Okay. I didn't want you to have to make the hard choice. I knew if I told you you'd have no choice but to go to Greene. And I didn't want to put you in that position."

"Uh huh. Mister altruistic. What you really mean is you didn't want the captain to know you were involved in an illegal operation to procure military goods for the Coalition."

He smiled sheepishly. "That too. Knowing about the mission comes with consequences. As you've seen first-hand."

She shook her head. "I can't believe Coalition officers did this. It's just…wrong."

"I agree."

She turned to him. "And it cost you your career. Your freedom. Did you know when you disabled the weapons and sent the message? Did you know then what would happen?"

"It was in the back of my mind. I knew the most likely outcome. If the Sil didn't find and destroy us first I'd have to face the consequences. Just like I knew when I commed you about those prisoners. When it's just me, or me and Box things don't matter as much. But when other people are involved—"

"But you were willing to sacrifice the crew of the *Achlys*..."

"To stop a war. Yes."

She smiled. "You're turning out to be more interesting than I first gave you credit for," she said, her shoulders relaxing. "When you're not drunk."

He laughed. "Thanks. I think. I've managed to keep myself out of jail this long, and it looks like I've been given a stay of execution. But it won't really matter in the end."

"What do you mean?"

"Once we get back, Rutledge will have me arrested anyway. I hope he doesn't decide you and the captain were conspiring with me. Greene might have hell to pay for not arresting me immediately."

"The captain can hold his own, don't worry about him. He's also not going to let this injustice continue any longer than necessary. When we get back I'm sure he'll push for a full inquiry."

Cas shook his head. "I just don't know. Without any evidence it still comes back down to my word against his."

"Then we need to find some evidence," she replied. The hypervator doors opened back on the sickbay level. Evie glanced at the tracker in his hand. "Get that down to engineering. They'll help you to find the source."

"When you talk to them," Cas said, still looking at it. "Thank them for me. And talk to Setsemeh; he overheard something. Or…he indicated he did."

"I'll be thorough." She stepped out, turning to look at him. "It was nice of you to try and protect me back there. But I don't need your help. I can take responsibility for my own actions."

"Noted."

"Good luck, Cas."

"You too."

The hypervator doors closed.

***

"So will you be having sex now?" Box asked as they made their way to main engineering. Cas had swung back by Bay One and informed Box of their current plans, dragging him away from the ship repairs.

"No! Stop talking about sex so much," Cas said. "I think all I've done is convince her I'm not a flight risk. That's a long way from a relationship."

"But it's closer," Box said, drawing out the last word. He broke into a tune.

"Back before she hated your face,
and now you're a little closer.
Back before she hated your guts,
And now you're a little closer,"

"Stop, please," Cas said. "Why are you in such a good mood?"

"Because! We didn't have to become fugitives. *Again.* I don't like being on the run all the time. Plus when you get arrested I get the ship."

"How many times do I have to tell you, robots can't—"

"Excuse me." Cas looked up to a young crewman who stood a few meters away, staring at them.

"Oh…did you hear all that?" he asked.

"How did I sound?" Box added.

"Um…I'm here to escort you to engineering to see Commander Sesster," the crewman said.

"Right. Thanks, crewman…"

"Pearson," the young man said.

"Lead the way," Cas said, following him down the corridor with Box tagging behind.

"Have you ever met a Claxian before?" Pearson asked.

"A few. Back when I was in the service. Never been to the homeworld, though."

Pearson nodded. He wasn't being as antagonistic as some of the others. Was the crew warming to him or was Pearson just a one-off case? He couldn't be sure. "I'd never met one until I started serving on *Tempest*. He's a sight to behold."

"Interesting choice of words," Cas said. Pearson chuckled along.

The Claxians were an ancient race, already traveling among the stars by the time humans were inventing written language. They were the primary reason technology had advanced as quickly as it had; having developed most of what the Coalition themselves used today. They were the ones to discover the undercurrents and how to transverse them safely, and thus had a hand in developing every Coalition engine that used them. Unique among all the races of the Coalition, the Claxians had no eyes or optical sensors at all; instead navigating their environments through touch and mental speech. They weren't even technically bipedal, being made up more like a starfish with five distinct tentacles that served as either hands or feet, depending on the need. But at the end of those tentacles-each ending in five smaller "fingers"—were highly sensitive receptors which, combined with their mental abilities, gave the Claxians great insight into how the universe and its underlying properties worked. They were genius engineers, a species Cas had always looked up to, despite knowing he would never be on their level.

"In here," Pearson said, leading them through a large door that rolled to the side as if on an ancient pulley.

Before them stood the main engineering department.

Four giant conduits dominated the room, two starting at the top of the room and continuing down to the floor where they disappeared down two dark tunnels, and two more which started at the floor and extended to the ceiling where they likewise disappeared through two more identical tunnels. These were the power conduits for the emitters that kept the tunnels open during travel, each one ten times the size Cas had on the *Reasonable Excuse*. In the center of the room there was a three-sided master systems display with workstations flanking it to the left and the right. And there, in the back of the room, resting in a mold shaped perfectly for a Claxian, was the chief engineer, lying in the cradle as his tentacles worked different systems within the mold. A catwalk circled above the engineer himself with more workstations up there to monitor not only the ship, but the engineer's status.

Cas was struck by the size of it all. Despite the ship being compact and stealth, main engineering had left nothing to the imagination.

"May I present, Lieutenant Commander Sesster," Pearson said.

As he said the name, one of the tentacles rose, as if sensing something. Sesster pushed himself out of the cradle, then using his tentacles, cartwheeled over to Cas and Box.

Hello.

"Hello, Commander," Cas said, staring up at the four-meter tall alien. "Nice ship you have here."

Your jealousy does not become you, Caspian Robeaux.

Cas laughed.

"What's so funny?" Box asked.

"The commander here just caught me in some self-indulgence," Cas explained. "I forgot you were empathetic."

Not everyone is receptive to my thoughts. Only a certain few. I have heard of your exploits. For what it is worth, I don't believe all of them.

"Thank you," Cas said. "I appreciate that. I'll assume you're the genius behind the undercurrent drive on this thing. They told me it's almost twice as fast."

My kindred developed the technology; I only implement it. I understand you've brought a tracking device for us; may I see it?

Cas held out the tracker and one of Sesster's tentacles reached out, the fingers on the end gently picking up the device and rotating it over in his "hand".

We can work with this. Please follow me.

Sesster rolled to one of the workstations, handing the tracker to the junior engineer manning that station. The engineer nodded at him, receiving all the guidance he would need and began hooking the device up to various diagnostic devices.

Lieutenant Page relayed information you were not to be trusted. But I sense your distrust has been excised. May we trust each other?

"We may," Cas said.

Excellent. Ensign Tyler will assist you further. He is capable. If you have problems, return to me.

"Thank you for your help…sir," Cas said. He didn't want to get back into the habit of addressing Coalition officers with such formality, but he felt this was a special case. He hadn't seen a Claxian in probably a decade. And he'd never met one he didn't respect.

"Okay," Tyler said, looking over the device. "Let's get started."

29

Evie stood outside the sickbay doors, contemplating. She couldn't get the image of the bloody sword out of her mind. The sword that had been passed down through her family for at least a hundred generations. The sword she'd heard legends about, how it had stopped an army at Presipico, or how it had saved the Anulli from certain death. In all honesty probably nothing but rumors and hearsay and embellishments…but fun stories nonetheless for her dad to tell at gathering time. At least, that's the way it used to be. Whenever she'd worn the sword she'd felt the power of her family with her.

But she never thought she'd actually have to use it one day.

It was a good prop, something to scare the locals. It was like an unspoken rule: you just don't fuck with a woman with a sword. But that was all over now.

She'd wanted to clean the blood off immediately, as if doing so would wipe the event from history; the sword having forgotten it had seen bloodshed under her care. But she hadn't done it. Partially because she'd been in a hurry to report to the captain. But also because she never wanted to touch it again. She'd taken a life with that sword, and in return she'd given up a small piece of herself she could never get back. She had taken one dark step toward life in the Sargan Commonwealth, or some other equally nefarious organization. The type of organization that recruited killers for even the most basic of jobs. Before she knew it she would be out there slicing people down left and right, all for a small bit of coin. It was inevitable.

Evie shook her head, willing the thoughts to dissipate. She didn't have time for that nonsense. She needed to find out if the former prisoners knew anything about Veena's plans and where to find her. Because now there was more at stake than just one lost Coalition ship and her crew. The *Achlys* could change the balance of power in this region of space for hundreds if not thousands of years.

She took one step forward and the doors slid open for her. Inside only two of the former prisoners remained, still being tended to by the nurses. Evie sought out Xax, finding her in her office as she interfaced with her console; no doubt writing her meticulous reports she'd heard were more boring to read than the serial numbers off a type seven slipshuttle.

"Where did the rest of them go?" Evie asked.

Xax didn't turn around, only continued typing with her two four-fingered hands while her two three-fingered hands examined a scanning device. "I assigned them quarters and released them there," Xax said. "They've had a taxing few days and need the rest. They were in no immediate danger."

"And those two?" Evie asked, glancing beyond the doorway back into the main sickbay area.

"Just finishing up with them. They both had slight infections."

Evie turned back to Xax. "Nothing contagious?"

Xax turned around, her tiny mouth smiling. "Of course not. Just a side-effect of being cooped up in that box for a few days. I'm surprised it hadn't spread to all of them."

"Can I speak with them? They might have information about our mission," Evie said.

"Be my guest. But they've been through a traumatic an ordeal. They need rest as soon as they can get it."

Evie nodded, leaving the doctor to her work. Both former prisoners remained silent as she made her way over to them, not taking their eyes off her. They were the two who had helped find the tracker on Cas's ship. When the nurses saw her approaching they left to give them privacy.

"I never got the chance to thank you for your help," Evie said, stopping a few meters away from their beds. The girl's short legs dangled off the side, swishing back and forth as if she were on a swing.

"Consider it repayment for rescuing us," the man, Setsemeh, said. "We owe you more than we can repay."

She held her hands up. "The Coalition doesn't require repayment. You're free to stay and become citizens if you like, or we can return you to Paxi. Though, since it is in Sargan space it will take time to return you. Special requisitions will need to be made and a stealth team—"

Setsemeh put his hand up, cutting her off. "I wouldn't dream of going back," he said. "I've always been curious about the Coalition, just never had the means to get here."

Evie turned to the girl. "And you?"

"I'll go back. My parents were captured at the same time I was. I need to try and save them."

Evie's heart went out to the girl and she couldn't help but feel a sense of déjà vu. "Don't you have any other family members? Anyone else you could stay with?"

The girl shook her head.

Evie dropped her gaze for a moment. "I'll see what I can do. But first, I need to know if you have any information about Veena's plans or capabilities. Maybe you overheard something while you were in the container. Maybe something Rasp or one of the others said. You may not even think it is important."

Setsemeh furrowed his brow. "Like I told your crewmate, I was scheduled to be shipped to Cassiopeia. We were with a much larger group from Paxi and a few other worlds I think. But then they pulled five of us to the side and stuffed us in that container. I heard Rasp say we were an emergency payment."

"Where were you being held?" Evie asked.

"Before the container? Devil's Gate, in the lower levels," Setsemeh replied.

Damn. They'd been right under her the whole time and she hadn't even known.

"When you were...*packed*...did you notice anything? Hear anything?"

"She was there," Yance said as Setsemeh opened his mouth to respond.

Evie turned to her. "Who?"

"Veena. I recognized her voice. She was on Paxi too, helping to round us up. That's where I first heard her voice. I heard it again when they were separating us from the main group, but I never saw her."

"Could it have been a comm?" Evie asked.

"I don't think so. She said she wanted to deal with this one personally." Yance continued to swing her feet back and forth. Cas had been right, Veena was close.

"Is there anything else?" she asked.

"She has at least two ships," Setsemeh said.

"How could you know that?"

"Back on the ship, when we were trying to find the tracker, I overheard you say we were being pursued by four class two gunners," Setsemeh said. "I'm assuming they were Sargan Steelravens." Evie nodded. "Those are typically only launched from a battleship. Either a Vortex or Darkness class vessel. But those types of ships are small, built for maneuvering in a planet's atmosphere. They can only carry three Steelravens per ship. So if we were being pursued by four, she had a second ship somewhere."

Evie eyed him. "You know a lot about Sargan starships," she said.

Setsemeh gave her a sheepish grin. "I…I lied to your crewmate about being an architect. But I was afraid if I told you what I really did he'd throw me out of an airlock." He paused but Evie indicated for him to go on. "I used to be a ship designer for the Sargans. Before my gambling and…*entertainment*…debts grew too large. I became more valuable as salable goods than as an employee."

Evie turned to Yance. "And you? Anything you want to reveal?"

The girl shook her head.

Evie returned her attention to Setsemeh. "Technically you're a criminal," she said. "So I'll have to confine you to quarters. But your help won't be without merit. It may just take you longer to earn your freedom."

"I'm no stranger to the inside of a cell," he replied, beaming with anticipation. "I'll gladly pay off my debt as required by the great Coalition."

Finally, Evie thought. *Someone who gets it.*

***

Evie returned to the bridge, her body humming with activity. She'd returned to her quarters to change her uniform and gather her thoughts but had seen the sword again and thought better of it.

As she walked on the bridge she caught a nasty look from Lieutenant Page, but dismissed it. It was no secret he didn't like Cas and now his ambivalence had seeped over to Evie, just as she suspected it eventually would if she continued to interact with "the criminal". But that didn't matter anymore.

She knew the truth and so she ignored Page as she made her way to her station. Greene was in his command room.

"Zaal," she said, taking her chair. The alien glanced up from his console. "Scan the system for twin undercurrent trails, Sargan signatures. We're looking for two or more close together. Possibly a small fleet." They were still hidden behind the third planet of Car'pr, but their sensors should be able to pick up residual undercurrent trails if anyone had jumped from the system.

"Yes, Commander," Zaal said, going about his work with efficient speed.

"Lieutenant," she said, indicating Page. "I want full weapons readiness. Make sure everything is operating at top efficiency," she said.

"Is this because of what that traitor told you?" Page asked. "You have to know he's lying to us. He killed twenty-four Coalition crewmembers, we can't trust—"

"Lieutenant," Evie growled. "Follow your orders or I'll have you relieved."

Page sneered but returned to his station, beginning his preparations for weapons drills.

Evie took a deep breath and sunk back into her chair. Stubborn ass. Despite her short time on the ship she hadn't seen Page this agitated before. In fact, before Cas had come on board he'd seemed like one of the most level-headed officers on the ship. Smart, capable and professional. Was this how everyone felt about Cas? Yamashita hadn't been too happy with him down on D'jattan, but she hadn't been as overtly hostile as Page. What if they all knew the truth? Could she even risk revealing what really happened without risking a court-martial herself? What if the same thing happened and the crew banded together against *her*? Greene wouldn't allow it, though. Not if what she knew about the man was accurate. He wasn't someone who could be bullied into silence.

She couldn't focus on that right now. She had a job to do. If what Setsemeh and Yance told her was true then Veena had been close to or on D'jattan after all. And her goal had been to re-capture Cas. And since she hadn't gotten him she might be even more desperate to find the *Achlys* now. This had just turned from a search and rescue into a race to the finish line.

"Commander," Zaal said. "I may have something, but it's faint. We'll have to move out from behind Car'pr III to get a better lock."

"Captain to the bridge," she announced, the autocomm would notify Greene without her needing to make a specific request.

The doors to the hypervator opened to reveal Cas at the same time Greene's command doors opened. "Somebody call me," Cas said with a smile.

30

"You insolent—" Page said, stepping out from behind his station.

"Stand down, Lieutenant," Greene said, making his way into the center of the room. He glanced over at Evie. "Commander?"

Evie glanced from Cas to Greene and back again. "Sir, we may have a lock on the Sargans." She motioned to Zaal.

Cas turned his attention to Zaal who was working his controls while his "body" remained rigid. The hard-light projection didn't do much as far as realism was concerned. It only looked human, it didn't move like a human.

"We need to move the ship to confirm the undercurrent trail," Zaal reported to the captain.

Cas spoke up. "Where is it?" he asked. "Where does it lead?"

"It's hard to tell from here, but I would extrapolate Quadros Sigma," Zaal said.

Cas shook his head. "It's a false trail. She's got no reason to head in that direction, that's off toward Sil space; the wrong direction. By now she has to know we're looking for her. She'll have set up decoys. Anything to delay us." He turned to Evie. "What did you find out?"

She stood. "You were right. Veena is close…or she was. She has more than one ship searching."

Cas nodded. "She probably brought a small fleet. She won't give up easily."

"So now we're getting dragged into a war with the Sargans? How much trouble is this guy worth?" Page asked.

"That's *enough*, Lieutenant," Greene said. "Mr. Robeaux, I assume there's a reason you're on my bridge."

Cas held up the tracker. "With some help from your very capable chief engineer we figured out how to track her. We managed to rig it to ping the original signal back to its source." Cas caught the eye of Blohm at the bridge engineering station. Her face was impassive but her eyes showed interest.

"We can use it without her knowing our position?" Greene asked.

Cas nodded.

"I thought we were supposed to be looking for one of our ships, not tracking some Sargan scum," Page said.

Greene furrowed his brow. "Zaal, integrate the device into our systems, I want to find out which way they went," he said. Zaal nodded then seemed to float over to Cas, taking the tracker from him. Cas caught the touch of one of his hard-light fingers, it was freezing to the touch. "Commander, your thoughts." Greene took the captain's chair as Zaal returned to his station.

"If we find the *Achlys* and try to tow it back to Coalition space we leave ourselves vulnerable to the Sargans. We need to find them first and throw them off the trail, get them to waste their time searching elsewhere. Then we can bring it back without a fight," Evie said.

Cas stood in front of the specialist's station, which was still dark. "Like I said, she won't give up easily," Cas said. "I agree we need to bring the fight to her, if for no other reason than to make sure she doesn't already have the ship. We should be able to tell by her heading; if she's on her way back to Sargan space then we'll know. She'll already have her prize."

Greene nodded. "Lieutenant Ronde, move us out from behind Car'pr three. Blackburn, plot a course along the trail indicated from Zaal's station. Zaal, activate the reverse tracker and take us in."

Zaal nodded, working the controls and bringing up his information on the primary display in the middle of the room. It also appeared on the 2-D master systems display on the far wall. A blinking dot less than a light-year away highlighted the screen.

"There she is," Cas said. As best he could tell her course indicated she was moving away from Car'pr back to Sargan space. "She must have just left Car'pr. She hasn't gotten very far."

"Ensign Blackburn, set pursuit course, nearest undercurrent," Greene ordered.

"Aye," Blackburn responded, building the navigation plan on the display before them as Ronde re-oriented the ship. Cas took a seat in the specialist's chair, preparing to enter the undercurrent.

"ETA is less than thirty minutes," Blackburn announced once the route was complete.

"How is that possible?" Cas exclaimed, standing back up. Assuming Veena left D'jattan as soon as her last crippled fighter made its way back to her main ship meant she should have at least an hour on them. Was the *Tempest* really that fast?

Greene smiled. "You should ask Commander Sesster," he said, keeping his attention on the primary display. "It's his engine."

"Security to the bridge," Page said.

"Lieutenant?" Evie asked, standing as well.

"Just an escort for our…guest," Page said. "He doesn't need to be on the bridge if we're going into battle."

Cas glanced at Greene. "I'm afraid I have to concur with our tactical officer. Civilians aren't allowed on the bridge during war times."

"Neither are criminals," Page added, smirking with satisfaction.

The main hypervator doors opened behind Cas, revealing two security officers.

"I might be able to help, give you some insight about the Sargan systems," Cas said as the officers came over and stood behind his station.

"We'll take it from here, thank you for your help, Mr. Robeaux," Greene said.

Cas shot a look at Evie, but she only gave a light shrug. He supposed he should have been grateful for as much access as he'd been given. He was sure they could handle the Sargans; he might as well return to Bay One and help Box finish the repairs.

Cas nodded and allowed himself to be escorted back to the hypervator. The doors slid open and the security officers followed him in and he watched the bridge disappear. Why was he feeling such an ache to remain up there? Did he just want to be part of the action? Or was it something more? Box would probably call it a sense of duty; but that couldn't be it. Any sense of duty he'd had died long ago.

"Bay One," Cas announced, as he realized no one in the hypervator had specified a destination. However the computer didn't provide its normal chime, instead blaring the *command rejected* chime. This hadn't been a problem before, had they revoked all of his autonomy?

He turned to one of the security officers. "Would you mind? Looks like I've been grounded."

The officer grinned. "You could put it that way," he said. The hypervator stopped and the officers escorted him out.

Something was wrong. This wasn't the way to Bay One. "Fellas, I think there's been a mistake here," he said.

"No mistake," the other one responded. "Lieutenant Page instructed us to detain you, and that's what we're doing."

"You're putting me in the brig?" Cas shouted. "I don't believe this. Check with the captain. Or Commander Diazal. Neither of them approved this order."

"The lieutenant is head of security," one of them said. "He doesn't need their approval. It's his call."

"Oh, you have to be shitting me," Cas said as they led him down the hallway toward the brig.

As the possibilities ran through this mind, throwing him deeper and deeper into panic as they came closer to the brig doors the ship shook, throwing them all off balance. Cas hit the back wall hard, the wind knocked from his lungs. Lights in the hallway flashed and the general alert sounded. Cas took advantage of the momentary confusion to run back down the hallway to the hypervator, leaving the two security officers still managing to regain their footing.

"C'mon, c'mon." Cas hit the panel as he waited for the hypervator. The ship shook again, throwing him against the side wall. He glanced behind him to see one of the officers' faces hit the ground with a smack. The hypervator doors opened and Cas jumped inside, allowing the doors to close again before the guards could scramble back to him.

Once he was inside he pulled the main control panel from the wall and yanked the two cables connecting the voice command system. The hypervator wouldn't move for his voice, but he could still input a manual test code. Something he'd never forgotten from the academy.

As he worked he pulled his comm out of his pocket and sent a message to Box.

"Yeah, boss," the robot said on the other side.

"What's going on? I'm stuck in the middle of the ship, I don't have any eyes down here."

"According to the *Excuse's* sensors," Box said, "We're under attack by Sargan ships. Hey! I bet that's Veena. She really *doesn't* give up."

"You think?" Cas yelled, inputting the last command. The hypervator began moving again. "I'm headed back to the bridge to find out what's going on. Get the *Excuse* as ready as you can. We might have to make a hasty getaway."

"Already on it," Box said and cut the comm.

As the hypervator rose the ship shook again, this time much more violently than the last two. What had happened out there? Why wasn't Greene running? This ship should easily be able to put enough distance between them and the Sargans.

Finally the hypervator slowed and the doors opened. Except they opened on chaos.

The bridge was a different world than the one he'd only left a few minutes before. A piece of the bulkhead was hanging from the ceiling, having smashed the primary display system in the middle of the room. Greene and Evie were barking orders while smoke billowed from one of the side stations. Page and Zaal were frantically trying to maneuver the ship, and Cas could see why. Blackburn had taken a piece of the bulkhead directly to the middle of her chest. She was dead in her seat as Ronde tried to compensate for the loss of their navigation station. The whole room was flashing red. Cas glanced around the chaos to the 2-D display on the far side of the room. Five Sargan ships were on the screen; the largest being Veena's own dreadnought warship, at least four times the size of *Tempest*. And there, trapped in her tractor beam was his old ship: the *Achlys*.

31

Cas dashed over to Blohm's station, jumping over debris and ducking the bulkhead. She was bleeding from a cut on her head and was seemingly having trouble focusing.

"What the hell happened?" Cas yelled. "They were supposed to be thirty minutes away!"

"As soon as we locked on to their signal they appeared, it must have been a decoy," she said, slurring her words.

Evie ran up beside them, taking Blohm's head in her hands. "She's got a concussion. Take the station!" Evie yelled, helping Blohm out of the chair.

Cas glanced down at the engineering station as the ship shook again. He had to grip the side of the console to keep from flying off his feet. There was an *oof* and a *thump* to his right. He glanced over to see Evie and Blohm sprawled against the wall. He ran over to help but Evie waved him away. "Get the goddamn engines back online!" she yelled.

Cas nodded and returned to the station, wiping part of the console covered in Blohm's blood with his sleeve. He examined the systems; it looked like there had been an overload in the primary conduits when they came out of the undercurrent. The ship lurched to the left as Ronde worked his controls, almost sending Cas out of his seat again. He hit the emergency restraints which shot out from the seat and secured him in. A quick glance confirmed the dampeners were only working at forty-six percent capacity. That would make an undercurrent jump uncomfortable to say the least.

One problem at a time. He had to figure out how to get them out of here. Evie said the engines were off. But as far as he could tell they were working fine, but the primaries were out and the backups hadn't kicked in which meant no matter how much power they shunted to the engines, they wouldn't be moving until the connections were in place. Cas hit the comm button down to main engineering.

"Engineering this is the bridge. Are you seeing what we're seeing up here? The primaries are out."

"This is Ensign Tyler, sir," a young voice answered. "We've almost got them back."

"Transfer to the secondary for now, worry about the primaries later," Cas said.

"Sir, but won't that blow the—?"

"Don't argue, just do it, we stay here any longer and we won't have primaries, understand?"

"Yes, sir," Tyler said, cutting the connection.

"Evasive maneuvers! Page, where is my firepower?" Greene yelled.

"Blades away," Page said. Cas glanced up to the screen momentarily to see two curved energy beams make their way toward the closest Sargan ship. They made a good hit but as soon as the damaged ship pulled back another took its place and continued firing on *Tempest*.

Cas worked as fast as he could on the console, reinforcing the secondary systems with temporary force shields, hoping they could hold the amount of power he was about to send through them. It was just like falling back into an old habit. He'd used the same maneuver on the *Achlys* more than once when they'd been in dire straits. It was amazing how quickly it all came back to him. This ship might be the most advanced ship in the fleet, but it was still a Coalition vessel underneath.

Seconds later the secondaries came online. "Thank you, Tyler," Cas said under his breath. Instead of waiting for an order Cas initiated the array and opened up the nearest undercurrent.

"Get us there, now, Lieutenant!" Greene yelled, pointing at the undercurrent on the screen.

Ronde, sweat pouring down his brow, nodded and focused on the task at hand.

"Page, cover the rear!"

Three seconds later they reached the undercurrent.

"Full thrust!" Greene yelled, his hands gripping the sides of his chair.

"Brace!" Cas yelled, keeping his eye on the dampener fields. He only hoped they'd be enough so the entire crew wasn't turned into soup accelerating so quickly.

The ship lurched dramatically and pulled Cas back into his seat so hard he thought it would break from its housing. Within a few seconds the sensation dissipated.

"Clear," Evie announced. Sometime in the confusion she'd made it back to her station.

Greene slumped back into his chair. "Get me a full damage report." He took a look at Blackburn, slumped over in her chair, her eyes still open. "Medical, to the bridge."

Cas secured the engineering station and made sure everything was stable. The secondaries were holding—thank goodness—which meant they should be able to sustain their speed for at least long enough to get out of range of Veena. He made his way over to Evie.

"What happened? It's like as soon as I left everything went to hell."

"It was a trap," Evie said. "She knew our position the moment we entered the undercurrent. We thought we could sneak up on her, but she was ready with her…fleet. They ambushed us. The ship took a direct hit before we could even get the main shields up."

The secondary hypervator doors opened to reveal two medics who hustled into the bridge. One hunched down over Blohm who was sprawled out on the floor behind Evie's station. The other made her way over to Blackburn.

Cas released his restraints and pulled his comm from his belt. "Box, what's your status?"

"Shaken, but only barely stirred," Box replied.

"The ship?"

"I've got communication equipment all over the place and your room is a mess but other than that she's fine. The ship smells like alcohol; I think your bottles broke."

"Get up to the bridge as soon as you can, I need you up here." Cas heard what sounded like a high-pitched squeal on the other end as Box cut the communication.

"Diazal, report," Greene said from his chair. He was out of breath and sweat peppered his brow, but he was focused, determined not to let his crew down. For the first time in a long time, Cas saw a captain he could actually admire.

"We should be out of range by now," Evie said, "Cas got the engines back up and with our advantage if she's coming after us it will take her twice as long to reach our position if we stop now."

"Understood, full stop," Greene said.

Ronde worked the controls and the ship lurched to a halt, the dampeners still only providing minimal protection from the inertia. Cas took a moment to survey the bridge; it was a mess. It would take weeks in space dock to repair. Somehow Veena had known right where to hit them.

"I want to know what the hell happened. How was she there waiting for us?" Greene asked.

"I can take a pretty good guess," Page said, looking at Cas from the tactical station. He had a cut above his right eye and the blood had run down the side of his face.

Greene ignored him. "Zaal?"

"Checking now, sir," Zaal said. His hard-light simulation was unscathed. Though Cas wondered if the creature underneath had suffered any injuries.

The doors to the main hypervator opened to reveal Box, his yellow eyes blinking rapidly in excitement. Cas jumped up from his station and ran to his companion. "Help us over here, we have to get this bulkhead off Blackburn." Cas glanced over at the medic who was trying to reach the ensign but with the massive piece of metal in the way was having little luck. Blackburn deserved more than to stay pinned to her station like a piece of skewered meat.

Box jogged over and pulled the bulkhead away, the sharp piece of metal that had penetrated Blackburn's sternum coming out easily. Box set the bulkhead down as the medic reached the ensign, closing her eyes. Behind her, Ronde seethed. They must have been close.

Box stood back. "This isn't exactly what I had in mind during my first visit to the bridge," he said.

"Sir, I believe I've found the issue," Zaal reported. "The tracker provided by Mr. Robeaux had a failsafe built into it. It didn't activate until we were within a certain proximity of the Sargan ships."

"I knew it," Page said, coming out from around his terminal. "Just can't help yourself can you, Robeaux? Have to kill crewmembers on every mission you're a part of."

"Lieutenant!" Greene shouted, standing again. Page froze but didn't take his eyes off Cas. "Mr. Robeaux, Commander, with me. Right now!" He turned and made his way to his command room. "Page, you have the bridge."

Cas noticed the other medic was already helping Blohm to the hypervator.

"Backup shifts report to the bridge," Page yelled as Cas followed Greene into the command room with Evie right behind him.

As soon as the doors closed behind her Greene laid into him. "I do not take being played for a fool easily, Mr. Robeaux," Greene snapped. "Tell me I haven't misjudged you."

"You haven't," Cas said. "Sir." Adding the last bit because it felt wrong not to do so.

"Did you have any idea about a backup in the tracker?" Greene asked.

"No, sir. But it's my fault. Box wanted to destroy the tracker as soon as we found it. But I thought we could use it. It was my idea to use it to trace her position back. I guess she was counting on that."

"She knows you," Evie said. "She knew if you found it you wouldn't want to let her get away."

Greene walked around behind his desk. "It seems she's had the upper hand this entire time." He pressed a panel on his desk. "Lieutenant Zaal."

"Sir?" Zaal's voice came through the comm.

"Destroy that tracker."

"Yes, sir."

Greene cut the comm. "It appears I have underestimated the Sargans' desire to have that ship."

"It's not even about the ship," Cas said. "Veena probably still doesn't know what it can do. She's more interested in selling the weapon to one of the other Sargan dealers. Someone who will use it to their own ends. She might even try to sell it to the heads of the Sargan Commonwealth themselves."

"And then we'll have a war on our hands," Greene said. "If they have a weapon based on Sil technology nothing will stop them from breaking right through our borders and taking whatever they want."

"I don't understand," Evie said. "She already has the ship and crew in her possession. Why does she still want you?"

Cas shrugged. "My bet would be she doesn't like losing things. There's an old Sargan saying: *once inside doors disappear*. It means you can come and go, but you never really leave. I'm her *possession.* Also if I had to guess the crew of the *Achlys* isn't being very cooperative. Maybe she thinks I can help her use the weapon."

"Do you think she captured the crew of the dry dock as well?" Evie asked.

Greene shook his head. "I don't know." He tapped his panel again. "Lieutenant Page, report to my command room."

A moment later the doors opened to reveal page. Blood still smeared the side of his face. He shot a nasty glance at Cas but kept his composure.

"Lieutenant, give me a tactical analysis of the Sargans out there," Greene said.

"Five ships in total, we disabled two of the smaller vessels. But the largest ship, the dreadnought, we're no match for. We need a Coalition Warship or Destroyer to take on something of that size. We can't survive another confrontation like that. Especially if they know we're coming."

"We've taken care of that issue," Greene said.

"Are you going to tell him about how you tried to have me arrested?" Cas asked.

Page furrowed his brow as Greene stared at him. "Lieutenant?"

"It was for the safety of the ship," Page said. "I didn't want him roaming around when we were going into a combat zone."

"Couldn't just confine me to quarters? Or to my own ship?" Cas asked.

"That's enough," Greene said. "This bickering gets us nowhere. Lieutenant, return to the bridge and oversee repairs. Commander, as you're the only one who doesn't hate Mr. Robeaux I want you to escort him back to his ship where he will remain until we have sorted through this mess."

"Yes, sir," Evie and Page said together.

"And get that robot off my bridge," he added.

"Wait, what are you going to do?" Cas asked.

"I see no choice but to make my report to Admiral Rutledge and await reinforcements from the fleet," Greene replied.

"You can't do that; Rutledge won't just send reinforcements," Cas said. "He's already skittish enough. You tell him the ship was captured by the Sargans he'll probably make a case for all-out war to the Coalition council himself. Remember he's not the only one who knows about this project."

"What project?" Page asked, glancing between the three of them.

"Then what would you suggest, Robeaux? You heard the lieutenant. We're outclassed and outgunned. They have the ship. What am I supposed to do?" Greene asked, flustered.

"Send me over there," Cas said. "Send me and I'll blow it up."

32

Page had to contain himself to keep from bursting out laughing. "You? We're supposed to trust you to go back over to the woman you used to work for and *blow up your own ship*?"

Cas nodded.

"Give me a break." He glanced over to the captain. "You can't seriously be considering this. As soon as he gets over there he'll reveal our position and the Sargans will have two ships to tow back instead of one."

"Seems to me if he'd wanted to betray us he would have already done it by now," Evie said.

"What do you call that out there?" Page shouted. "They were *waiting* for us! He led us straight into a trap with that damn tracker of his!"

"And if he'd wanted us to stay dead in the water he wouldn't have gotten the engines back up and running," Evie argued. "The Sargans had us dead to rights."

Page turned back to Greene. "Sir. Don't do this. He's a convicted criminal. Twenty-four deaths because of his actions. Another five today. He's a walking slaughterhouse."

Five. A pit erupted in the bottom of Cas's stomach. He'd hoped the casualties had been limited to Ensign Blackburn. But he'd been wrong. Maybe he didn't deserve to take down the *Achlys*. Maybe he deserved to spend the rest of his life in prison. Was Page wrong? After all, if not for Cas, all those crewmembers would still be alive.

Greene faced Cas. "How would you do it? Get to your ship?"

Cas shook the thoughts away. He needed to focus. "I would need the *Tempest* to create a distraction. I'd launch the *Excuse* here and follow you through the undercurrent, both of us coming out at the same time at different points. *Tempest* would take a strafing run at the nearest ships while I got the *Excuse* close enough to dock with the *Achlys.* My ship is small enough that a big distraction should keep me off their scanners long enough to match the hull frequency of the *Achlys*. I know it by heart; it won't be hard. Then I get on, enable the self-destruct, and get out. Meet back up with you here."

Page sent him a hard stare. "Or how about this? You never show up at the fight at all and run away, just like you did five years ago," Page said.

"Commander?" Greene said to Evie. "Your thoughts."

"It's a sound strategy, but I agree he can't go alone," Evie said. Cas shot her a look. "If something goes wrong, if there's a malfunction we won't get another chance. There needs to be at least two people on the mission."

"No way," Cas said, stepping forward. "I'm not putting any more lives in danger. If it's just me, no one else can get hurt. I can do this, captain. I just need the chance."

"See?" Page said. "He just wants to do it himself so he can run if it gets tough."

Cas turned and decked the man, sending him sprawling back. Page's eyes turned to fire as he regained his balance, holding himself up against the wall. He bared his teeth and made a lunge for Cas, only to find Greene standing in his way. Cas tried to move forward but Evie had wrenched her hands around his, holding him back. He tried to lunge against her but found he couldn't quite move as much as he thought he should be able to. She was *strong*.

"Dismissed, Lieutenant," Greene shouted at the man seething in front of him. "Take care of the bridge. I'll be back out there in a moment."

Page took a deep breath and straightened his uniform. He then turned and exited the room.

Greene spun on Cas whom Evie still had in a hold. "It's a damn good thing you aren't an officer anymore or I'd have you demoted for that," Greene scolded. Cas relaxed his body and felt Evie ease her hold on him. "Now if you really think you can destroy that ship I'm all for it, but I want a backup. Commander Diazal goes with you."

"Sir—"

"This is not up for debate, Robeaux. You either do it my way or we call the admiral."

Cas shut up. Evie let him go, standing beside him.

"We know where the Sargans are at the moment, so we need to be fast. I don't want them moving on us. We'll move closer, launch your ship and then return to their position at regular undercurrent speed. Once you're away, we'll use our full resources to get out of their weapons range. You'll be on your own."

"Understood," Cas said.

"You try anything funny, or you abscond with my officer, I'll hunt you down and destroy you myself, is that clear?" Greene stared at him with an intensity Cas rarely had seen from another human. He had a deep desire not to disappoint the man.

"I won't let you down," Cas said.

"We don't have long. Get down there quick and let me know as soon as you're ready to launch," Greene said. "Dismissed."

Cas nodded and turned, exiting the command room. Evie remained a moment and the doors closed, leaving the captain with his XO. Cas took a moment to survey the bridge again. The medics had managed to remove Blackburn and her destroyed controls had been transferred to the specialist's station, manned by a new Ensign Cas didn't know. Page sat in the captain's chair barking orders and reviewing reports. He ignored Cas as he made his way around the outside of the bridge.

Box sidled up to him. "Principal's office, huh? Did you get detention?"

"More like a bunch of extra homework," Cas replied. The command room doors opened again and Evie came out with Greene, who took the captain's chair from Page.

Cas led Box over to the main hypervator doors where Evie met them. "Your captain is uncommonly fair," Cas whispered.

"Why do you think I wanted this assignment so bad?" Evie replied.

The doors to the hypervator opened and the three got inside. "Bye bridge!" Box called. "Nice seeing you!"

Once the doors were closed Cas turned to Evie. "I wanted to thank you for standing up for me back there, but you didn't need to do that. I can handle myself," he said, remembering a similar conversation with her earlier.

"No, you couldn't." She smirked. "Your ass would have been grass if I hadn't been in there to back you up."

"Ass would have been grass?" Box asked, his eyes blinking confusion.

"An old colloquialism. It means he would have been in deep shit," Evie said.

"Now wait a second, I can hold my—"

"He's good at doing that," Box spouted, pointing at him. "It's an apt metaphor."

Cas turned to Box. "Would you please, for once, shut up? I'm trying to relay some real emotions here."

Evie scoffed. "Are you even sure you know what those are?"

"See? This is why I wanted to go alone. The two of you are going to drive me to an early grave."

"That's the idea," Box sing-songed. "Cause I get the ship!"

"Robots can't own ships!" Cas yelled.

Evie turned to him, getting into his personal space. "You need to tell me everything you're going to do. And you need to instruct me on how to do it too."

"Holy crap, Cas, she's close enough to kiss," Box said.

Without taking his eyes off Evie, whose face was impassive as stone, Cas pushed Box toward the wall, the clink of metal meeting metal echoing through the hypervator as he bounced off and righted himself. "Sorry about him. Are you saying you don't trust me to get the job done?"

"No," Evie said. "But if something happens to you over there we need a backup. I need to know everything you know."

"It doesn't hurt that it prevents me from springing any surprises on you," Cas added.

Evie shrugged. "We'll just call that a bonus. Now, tell me how to enable the self-destruct."

***

Ten minutes later they were all aboard the *Reasonable Excuse* helping the maintenance crew put the comm system back together.

"I don't know why we didn't have one of these before," Box yelled from the back compartment.

"What? A maintenance crew?" Cas sat up in the cockpit with Evie, going over their plan of attack.

"Yeah! They're so much faster than you in every way conceivable," the robot yelled back.

"Maybe if *someone* had gotten off his metal ass and done something other than watch *net dramas* all day we might have had some extra money for one!"

"I need those dramas! They help my stress level!"

Cas rolled his eyes.

"Has he always been like that?" Evie asked.

"Like what? A royal pain?" Cas smiled.

"No. He's so....un-robot-like."

Cas tapped the nav panel in front of him showing them the course. "We didn't meet under ideal circumstances, but I always knew there was something...off about him. The first words out of his mouth to me were a lie, only it took me some time to figure that out. But at the time I needed a pilot and wasn't asking questions. Later on I became curious, and started investigating his internal systems. Someone programmed him very differently than any other machine I've met before. So I figured why not take him to the next level? I opened up his learning centers, increased his memory and emotional capacities. The problem is I never knew when to stop. Before I knew it, he'd kinda..."

"Come alive?" Evie suggested.

"If you want to think of it that way. I tend to think of it more as just a very complex interaction between millions of programs in his cortex. It led to some...interesting results."

"I'll say," Evie said. Box's humming reached them even all the way down here.

"They're not that different from non-artificial life forms," Cas said. "I guess I was curious to see how much his systems could handle." He tapped the screen again, confirming the course. "He hasn't hit the limit yet."

"It's amazing if you think about it. He's like your offspring," Evie smiled.

"Don't say that. You're making it weird." Evie chuckled. Cas stood, checking the rest of the systems in the cockpit. "How are we doing down there?" he called down the hall.

"They're just finishing now," Box called back. "Ready to go in five minutes."

Cas turned to Evie. "Okay. I think we're good. Call the captain."

"Yes, sir," she replied, tapping the back of her hand.

"Go ahead," Greene said through the system.

"Five minutes," Evie replied. "And we're good for launch."

"Understood," Greene said. "Good luck out there, Commander." He cut the comm.

For the first time in a long time Cas was nervous. It had been a while since people had counted on him for something. Something other than money that was. But not only would his plan get rid of the *Achlys*, it would show Veena he wasn't *anyone's* property. No matter what she did. She'd wanted a fight and losing Rasp had probably only enraged her further. But he didn't care. She wasn't getting this weapon and neither was Rutledge. He'd have to start all over again. Sure Cas would probably go to jail for the rest of his life but at least his conscience would be clear.

"Coming up on undercurrent jump," Evie said as Box entered the cockpit, taking the pilot's seat.

"Thanks for keeping it warm grass ass," he said, settling in.

Cas ignored him. "Is the maintenance crew off?"

"Affirmative, boss."

"Retract the landing ramp and prepare to launch," he said, taking the co-pilot's seat. Evie stood behind them, monitoring the *Excuse's* systems.

"You act like I've never done this before. No need to spout orders to impress the lady."

Cas felt heat rushing up his cheeks but he stamped it down as best he could, keeping his focus on Bay One's opening. He made a mental note to thank Sesster for fixing the dampeners so quickly; he'd barely felt the jolt into the undercurrent this time.

"Approaching jettison point," Evie said.

They exited the undercurrent, coming back into normal space. "Launch!" Cas said.

Box pushed the throttle forward and the ship shot out of the Bay, entering the inky darkness of space. He turned the ship immediately to come alongside *Tempest* as it opened another undercurrent. The *Excuse* used its own emitters and followed along, keeping pace with the ship now that it was moving at a normal undercurrent speed. Cas wished he'd had more time down in engineering to examine the systems that made *Tempest* so fast, but there just hadn't been time. He would have liked to use some of those upgrades on his own ship if possible.

"ETA, ten minutes," Evie said. "Here we go."

33

The *Tempest* pulled ahead in the undercurrent, far enough they could no longer see her through the windows though she was still visible on the viewscreen.

"Ready, Box?" Cas asked.

"I want my own quarters," Box replied, his concentration still on the controls.

"What?"

"As payment for this. You owe me quarters," he replied.

"You're asking for this *now*?" Cas glanced at Evie then back at his pilot. "Fine. Whatever. You get one of the hab suites. Are we on course or not?"

"Sure. *Now* we are."

"Box, were you going to jeopardize this mission for quarters?" Cas asked, his words strained.

Box turned his head to him. "No. *Of course* not," he said with sarcasm dripping from his voice. He continued to stare at Cas as he dropped out of the undercurrent.

"Heads up!" Cas yelled. Ahead of them *Tempest* had already exited and performed the strafing maneuvers. Three of the smaller Sargan ships were in pursuit, apparently having broken formation around Veena's dreadnought. They'd come out of the undercurrent closer than Cas had anticipated.

"Whoa!" Box jerked the throttle to the right, sending the ship spinning. The dampeners kept them from feeling the effects as the ship cartwheeled over itself three times before he righted them again.

"Are we good? Can we get in without getting spotted?" Evie yelled.

The *Achlys* sat below Veena's dreadnought, held in place by a green tractor, despite the fact neither ship was moving at the moment. She wasn't about to take her hands off that ship no matter what happened.

"We're close!" Box yelled, punching the normal engines sending them rocketing forward. The *Achlys* only had one docking bay located on the rear of the ship. But like *Tempest* it didn't have a retractable door, instead relied on force fields to keep the vacuum of space out.

"Have we been spotted?" Evie asked.

Cas checked the equipment. As far as he could tell all the Sargan's attention was on *Tempest* who was still performing strafing runs, and getting hit in the process.

"We need to get in there now," she yelled. "Give *Tempest* time to get away."

"Twenty seconds," Box said, pushing the engines to their max. Cas prayed they weren't big enough to register on Veena's scanners. Her dreadnought was huge; at least two thousand meters long. It dwarfed the *Achlys* not to mention Cas's ship.

"Hurry," Evie said. "Tempest is going back into the undercurrent."

"Ten seconds," Box said.

"They're gone," Evie replied.

Cas glanced out the main window to see *Achlys's* bay approaching with disturbing speed. "Box. Slow down." He turned to his pilot. "Box?"

"Three seconds," Box replied.

"Evie, hang on to something!" Cas yelled.

They breached the bay's force field only for Box to throw the thrusters into full reverse as the *Excuse* came dangerously close to slamming into the wall of the bay. They all jerked forward, the dampeners unable to compensate for such a move, but the ship came to a floating halt.

"We're in," Box said, smugness in his voice. He lowered the *Excuse* to settle on the deck of the bay.

Cas turned to Evie. "You okay?"

"Fine. Let's get in there and finish this." She reached down to a small case she'd brought on board, opening it. She grabbed the weapon inside and handed it to Cas. It was his boomcannon. "You might need this. Just don't shoot me in the back with it, okay?" She holstered her own weapon: a standard Coalition pistol.

Cas beamed at her, taking the weapon and holstering it inside his jacket. "You're alright, Diazal. After everything I've done…I'm not sure I'd trust me with this if I were in your shoes."

"I guess that's the difference between us," she said, straightening her uniform shirt. "Let's move."

Cas turned to Box. "Keep it on hot standby, okay? We might need a quick exit."

"Just don't forget you promised," Box replied, initializing the main coolant tanks.

"I won't," Cas replied, following Evie out of the cockpit. As he reached the main door lock he heard Box call "*Be careful!*" from the front.

"Awww," Evie said, hitting the main lock door to open.

"Yeah, yeah," Cas replied, following her. He pulled his comm out, thankful they'd taken the time to fix the system before leaving. "Box, give me a scan of the immediate area. Anything we need to worry about?"

"No life signs, boss," he replied as they walked down the ramp. "No one on this ship anywhere as far as I can see, but all the power systems are still active."

"We need to find that weapon," Evie said. "Disabling it should be our first priority."

"Blowing up the ship *will* disable the weapon," Cas replied. "And to do that we need to make it to the bridge."

She pursed her lips. "Indulge me," she said. "Backups, remember? If we for some reason can't blow up the ship I want to make sure they can't use the weapon."

Cas relented. "Fine. It will probably be in main engineering. But we'll have to take the long way. If we use the hypervators it might register as power spikes in the system. And if anyone on Veena's ship is monitoring, it will look suspicious."

"You mean we have to use the access corridors."

Cas forced a smile. "Yep."

She sighed. "Lead the way."

***

Twelve minutes later they were crawling on their bellies through the access corridors that connected deck eleven with main engineering. They'd already been through seven of the things and Cas's arms and legs ached in a way he hadn't felt in some time. The access corridors weren't more than a meter in any direction, mostly made for maintenance bots and the occasional worker to reach sensitive systems. They certainly hadn't been designed for comfort or ease of access for the crew to get to certain parts of the ship.

"What do you think happened to the crew?" Evie asked as they crawled.

"Probably in holding cells on Veena's ship. She wouldn't kill anyone she couldn't sell or use later," he replied.

"That's comforting. How much further?"

"Another three meters in this corridor. Then another ladder, then another short corridor and we'll be there," Cas replied. Stepping back on the ship had been like being home again, only it was a home he'd been kicked out of. He'd heard the saying you could never go home again but he wasn't so sure. It all felt familiar to him. He'd even remembered being in this particular corridor before; back when Mason had needed a power realignment and had been too wide to fit. The man spent most of his off-time at the ship's gymnasium and his shoulders were as wide as Cas was tall. Cas smiled at the memory. Mason couldn't have crawled through these things if he'd wanted to.

"Almost," Cas said, exiting the main corridor into the junction with the last ladder they needed to climb. Engineering would be only a few steps away. Evie grunted along behind him and he was glad she decided not to bring her sword. It would have been a tough fit getting that thing down the tubes. As he reached the top of the ladder it occurred to him they would have to come back this way as well. He groaned.

"What's wrong?" she asked.

"Nothing, just thinking about the return trip." The last corridor was wider than the others, enough so that he could crouch-walk to the engineering access door. But when he approached the doors they wouldn't open for him.

"I'm locked out," he said.

"Let me try," she replied. "Only one of us isn't a known criminal. Your organic ID is in the system. Prevents you from accessing any sensitive areas of the ship." She stood in front of the door and it opened for her.

"Did you revoke that restriction on Tempest?" he asked. "I didn't have any trouble accessing the bridge there."

She winked. “I might have had something to do with it. Plus, it pisses Page off and that makes me just the slightest bit happy.”

“That guy needs to learn how to control his temper,” Cas said.

“He wasn’t the one who struck first.”

She had a point. They entered main engineering. It was similar in layout to Tempest’s engineering department, except without the giant cradle for the Claxian engineer. Cas wondered if all Coalition ships would eventually be outfitted with Claxians from now on, since it seemed to help with the ship’s speed and efficiency. Would a bunch of Claxians even want to serve on ships? From what Cas knew about them, most preferred to stay on their homeworld. Though Commander Sesster had obviously been an exception.

“Oh,” Evie said. Cas had been too lost in the nostalgia of being back on his old ship to notice the massive modifications that had been made to engineering.

In the middle of the room where the master systems display should have been was a gyroscope, or at least what looked like a gyroscope at first glance. As Cas drew closer he could see while it had the appearance of one, it had to work completely differently. None of the circles was complete, each was missing segments in their rotations and in the center of the device was a golden ball which glowed gold. He could almost feel the energy pulsing off it.

“Is this the weapon?” Evie asked.

“Has to be. This is not Coalition tech,” he replied. He had the overwhelming urge to turn it on, just to see what it did, but doing so would register a power spike and they couldn’t risk being caught. “It’s attached to the main weapons array. This must be the primary power source for the weapon’s destructive capability.”

"Cas." Evie bent in front of the device. He leaned over to see what she'd found. In front of the base of the device was a pile of black dust, as if something from the device had incinerated and collected on the ground. Now that Cas looked, it was everywhere.

"This is the same stuff that was on the dry dock," he said. But there was so much *more* of it here. "Did they ever identify it on *Tempest*?"

"I never saw a report," Evie said. "But you're right. It looks exactly the same."

Cas went over to one of the main engineering stations and initiated a scan of the room. There was forty-four cubic meters of the dust scattered throughout engineering. But nowhere else on the ship. "This doesn't make any sense. Why would it just be in this room and on the command floor of the dry dock? Why isn't it anywhere else?"

"We can figure it out later, right now we have a job to do. I need you to permanently disable it."

"Right," Cas said. The wheels in his mind were turning. He couldn't stop thinking about that dust. Where would it all have come from? It didn't make any sense.

He walked over to the gyroscope and opened the access panels below it, which required pushing small mounds of the dust away. Inside it was a mess. Nothing like he'd ever seen before. The parts had obviously been manufactured by the Coalition, but they'd been assembled in a way that didn't make sense at all. Is this how Sil technology worked? You just threw a bunch of things together and all of a sudden you had superweapons? He wished he could take some time to study the device, understand how it worked.

"You'll need to purge all references of the device in the computer," Cas said as he examined just how he was going to disable this weapon he knew nothing about.

"Won't that show up as a power surge?" Evie asked.

He shrugged. "You were the one who wanted the assurances. And until this ship is in a billion pieces floating through space, the information is vulnerable."

"Damn," she muttered under her breath. She made her way over to one of the consoles while he continued to examine the device. Probably the best way to disable it would be to take apart as much of the inner-workings as he could. He thought about just shooting the thing but without knowing more about it he didn't want to risk an overload of some kind.

"Okay then," he said. "We'll do it the hard way." He got up and jogged to the other side of engineering to grab a maintenance kit from the wall. Inside were all the tools an engineer could ever need: spanners, ratchets, bolt-sealers, fusion guards; etc. He returned to the device and began work on removing its guts, piece by piece.

After the third panel came off, he stopped cold. "Evie?"

"Hmm?" she said from the console station.

"Your people were right about the dust. It's the crew."

34

"What?" she asked, turning from the active station. He moved to the side to reveal the inside of the gyroscope's base. "Is that…"

"A negative-mass interdimensional particle," Cas finished for her. "I don't know if it's what powers the weapon or if it's a byproduct of it." When Cas had removed the last panel it had revealed a transparent casing of some kind, and within the casing was a very bright object, almost like a miniature sun. Something that shouldn't even be able to exist in this dimension.

"Is it really a one-dimensional object?" she asked, leaning in closer.

"That's the theory," Cas replied. "But somehow this one is stable and large enough to exist in a three-dimensional space."

She was getting too close, Cas took her shoulder and pulled her back.

"What?" she asked.

"ID particles are theorized to emit a type of thorian radiation," Cas replied. "It robs molecules of carbon and other proteins. Leaving nothing but inorganic materials behind. If the weapon uses this type of radiation as its power source it would explain all the dust."

"They tested the weapon," Evie said.

"And it ended up killing them," Cas added.

She stepped away from the device. "But if they knew it emitted this kind of radiation, why use it in the first place?"

Cas shook his head. "I don't know. Did you find anything in the records?"

"Not yet. I finally got the system up and running. I had to use my own credentials to get in."

Cas took a glance at the computer interface. "It probably won't even open for a rank less than Lieutenant Commander. I guess it's a good thing you came along after all."

"Can you still disable it?" Evie asked.

"I don't want to be anywhere near that thing," Cas said. "I don't know enough about it to shut it down without it killing both of us. Our best bet is my original plan: blow up the ship and let it take care of itself."

Evie's eyes fixed on the dust collected all around the gyroscope. "You're right. But give me a minute to download all the technical specifications. I'm not letting Rutledge get away with this," she said. "They court-martialed you for twenty-four deaths. As far as I'm concerned, he's the one responsible for the death of every member of this crew. And the space dock."

"There were a hundred and seventy-one people on this ship," Cas said. He couldn't believe this was all that remained of his former crewmates. If he hadn't been kicked off the ship he would have ended up just like them.

"Can you set up the self-destruct from here?" Evie asked, returning to the computer.

"Probably," he replied. "Assuming my codes still work. The captain may have changed them or they could still be in the system, I won't know until I try."

"Get on it, I want to get this done and out of here as fast as we can."

"Boss?" Box's voice came through his communicator.

Cas pulled it from his pocket. "Yeah?"

"You've got company. Fifteen non-friendlies headed your way."

Cas bared his teeth and surveyed the room again. They were out in the open here. "Where did they come from?"

"I don't know, I picked up their life signs three decks above you. They're on their way down in the hypervator now," he replied.

"Scan for a shuttle. Or anything," Cas yelled.

"There's a small shuttle docked at the top of the ship," he replied. "It probably dropped down from the dreadnought. You better get back here."

Cas glanced at Evie who was working the controls at the station. "I've only got about half of it," she said.

"Leave it, fifteen to two aren't good odds." He grabbed her arm.

She wrenched it away, staring daggers at him. "What about the self-destruct?"

"There's no time. It would take me at least five minutes to set it up, and we'll be lucky if we have thirty seconds. Accessing the computer must have tipped them off after all."

"I'll draw them off." She pulled her weapon from its holster. "You finish downloading the logs and set up the self-destruct."

"Draw them off where? You don't know anything about this ship," he replied. "You're just as bound to get lost and lead them right back here as you are to get away."

Her face was a mix of fury and indignation. "It's a standard Constellation class ship, *Mr.* Robeaux. I think I know how to get around. And I don't need you reminding me what I can and can't do."

He put his hands up in defense. “I’m sorry. I didn’t mean that. But you drawing them off is just going to get you or me cornered somewhere. We need to go. Figure out another plan.”

She winced, her eyes darting between him and the console. “Fine,” she said, pulling her uplink from the computer and replacing it in her belt.

Cas drew his weapon. “Box, which way are they coming in?”

“Access E-2 and E-6,” Box replied.

Both sides of engineering. They meant to box them in. “We’ll have to go back the way we came.” Cas indicated the access door to the side.

“That will take too long,” she replied. “Talk about making for easy targets.”

“Then what do you suggest?” he asked.

The main engineering door rolled away, revealing eight of the soldiers behind him. Evie raised her weapon. “A frontal assault.” She fired as Cas ducked, spinning around and using his own weapon on the men scattering away from the opening.

Blasts of plasma flew past them as they got into cover behind one of the consoles. “If they hit that gyroscope…” Cas said.

“I guess we won’t have to worry about blowing up the ship then, will we?” Evie smirked. She jumped out of cover again and fired three more times. Behind them the E-6 doors opened on the upper level and six more soldiers emerged, taking stock of the scene before them.

“Oh shit, time to move,” Cas said, pulling Evie back as a blast of plasma hit the ground where she’d been standing only a moment ago. “I bet you wish you had your sword right now, could be really handy.” He took a few shots at the men on the upper balcony, but they all managed to duck the blasts. They couldn’t keep this up for much longer otherwise they’d be completely pinned in.

The main door was still open, all they needed to do was get through it and they could sprint the hallways to the closest hypervator, which was hypervator three if Cas remembered correctly. That would take them directly back to the ship. But there was so much fire coming from that direction it would be nearly impossible to get over there.

"It's too much," he yelled over the blasts, still holding Evie's uniform as she laid down some fire of her own. They were obscured from the view of the upper level but the soldiers only had to move a few more meters to the right and they'd be in their crosshairs again.

"I can do this!" Evie yelled back. "Just give me some cover!"

Cas let go of her uniform and put both hands on the boomcannon, pointing it at the upper level where the men would come around. The first one popped his head out and Cas squeezed the trigger, sending the blast sailing up and smashing into the bulkhead where the man's head had been only a second before. The man jumped out again and Cas fired three more times, one of the blasts catching him in the chest and sending him back to the wall. Evie continued to fire at the group in the front but Veena's soldiers wouldn't stay put. They'd find a way to make their way around the stations to ambush them.

"Ah, damn!" Evie drew back. One of the blasts had caught her in the arm which was now missing a significant chunk from the upper part. She fell back to his side, her hand over the wound. "Lucky bastard, that was a one-in-a-thousand shot," she said through gritted teeth.

That was it. She was injured and they were still pinned down. And they'd only taken out maybe two or three of the soldiers. Cas glanced over to the access corridor exit. They didn't have another choice but could Evie even crawl now with an injured and bloody arm? He should have just made her go.

"Aaaaaaggggghhhhh!"

Cas exchanged looks with Evie and they both peeked over the wall to see Box running in through the main door, an old chair in his hands swinging it wildly back and forth. The soldiers in cover turned to fire on him but he was quicker than they could anticipate and one-by-one he smacked them with the metal chair, sending their weapons, equipment, and sometimes teeth in all directions. He was like a robot possessed. Cas had never seen him so enraged.

"C'mon!" Box yelled after he'd hit the last one. A blast hit him in the side but he paid it no attention. Cas glanced up to the upper level where the soldiers were still in position and were now taking shots at Box.

Cas pushed Evie forward as Box hurled his blood-soaked chair at the closest soldier on the upper level who tried to scream and run but only succeeded in making a brief noise before the chair smashed into him, sending him sprawling. Box stood by the door ushering them forward as more shots peppered the ground around them. Cas pushed Evie forward, praying to Kor he could get her out before any other hits landed.

They reached the door and Box hit the panel beside it, rolling the massive door closed again. "Hurry, there's another ship approaching," Box said, grabbing Evie and hoisting her under his arm as he took off in a sprint for the hypervator. Cas took off after them, checking behind them every few seconds to see if the other soldiers were still in pursuit.

"I can run on my own, I'm not an invalid!" Evie yelled.

"What are you doing up here?" Cas called as they made their way down the hall.

"Making sure I get my room!" Box yelled back.

"Yeah? I thought you wanted the whole ship. All you had to do was leave us and it could have been yours," he replied, checking behind him again. Still no pursuit.

Box turned to him just as they reached the hypervator. "It's more of a long-term plan. I can start small."

"I've never seen you so…enthusiastic," Cas said.

"I was re-enacting Lady Regina Thornhouse's reaction to finding out Lord Thornhouse cheated on her with the chambermaid."

"She beat people with a chair?"

"A wooden one."

Cas nodded in approval. "Good call then."

The doors opened and Cas followed them in just as a blast ricocheted off the side of the door. Cas fired back as the doors closed. "Shuttle Bay," Box announced and the hypervator began dropping. He set Evie down on the ground, inspecting her wound. "You've lost four percent of your upper arm mass."

She pulled her hand away to reveal a deep gash. Box was right, part of her arm had been torn away by the Sargan's' weapon. Evie sucked in a breath as she saw all the blood.

"It's probably not as bad as it looks," Cas said. "Can you still feel your fingers?"

She wiggled them. "Yeah, but it hurts. I would have much rather been shot by whatever hit you," she replied.

Cas couldn't disagree. Dealing with temporary numbness had to beat getting half your arm ripped away anyday.

"We have to stem the flow of blood!" Box announced and grabbed Cas's shirt underneath his jacket, ripping a perfect strip all the way down the center of Cas's chest.

"Box! You did not—"

"Would you rather her bleed out?" he asked, applying the makeshift bandage on the wound, tying it tight.

"Aaaa!" Evie grimaced as Box cinched the wound.

The doors opened to the Bay access and Box picked Evie up again against her protestations while Cas ran ahead to make sure the area was clear. No sign of anyone. "Let's move, we got lucky," he yelled as Box bolted past him, up the ramp of the *Excuse* and through the locks. Cas took one last look around and followed.

Inside Box deposited Evie in the kitchen then went to the cockpit to confirm the startup sequence. "Fast as you can, Box!" Cas yelled. He went over to check on Evie. "Are you okay? Can you make it another few minutes to the rendezvous?"

She squinted, still holding the wound and nodded. "Go. Get us out of here."

He hated to leave her, but she'd be okay for a few minutes. Cas made his way to the cockpit just as Box had fired the engines. "Punch it," he said and the ship lurched forward, bursting out of the hangar bay into open space. "Somehow I didn't think we would make it," Cas added, scanning the surrounding space. The only other ship in the area was the dreadnought which quickly fell behind them.

One of the indicators beside Box began blinking. "Uhh, boss?"

Cas glanced over. "Is that the *Tempest*?"

Box shook his head.

"Caspian!" Veena's voice boomed through the internal speakers. "How nice of you to visit."

35

"Veena," Cas said as her image appeared on the screen in front of him. "I hoped I'd never have to see you again."

"Now that's not a very nice thing to say, you hurt my feelings," Veena replied in that sickeningly insincere voice of hers.

"Two of her ships have changed course and are on our tail," Box said, pushing the engines even harder.

"What do you want?" Cas asked, readying the undercurrent drive. Even if they couldn't outrun Veena's ships they could at least keep pace in the undercurrent. But he'd have to lead them away from *Tempest*.

"Why, you, of course. You're my key to a unique and special lock," Veena said. "The prize is no good without someone who knows how it works. And based on what I've learned you are the perfect person to help me operate it."

"I just got a pretty good look at your superweapon down there—sorry about your men by the way—I can tell you one thing: it's pretty much useless."

Veena waved her hand in front of the screen dismissively. "Somehow I doubt that. The Coalition wouldn't have gone to so much trouble to build such a weapon if it didn't work. Even if it doesn't; the information itself it worth more than its weight in kassope. Just imagine what the Claxians will do once they find out humans from their precious Coalition have conspired to build a superweapon based on Sil technology."

Cas cursed. She really did know everything.

"Aww, now don't be upset, Caspian. You didn't really think I'd let you go without a little insurance now did you? That mercenary act by your new girlfriend was pretty pathetic."

"She's not his girlfriend, they're not initiating sexual encounters!" Box yelled.

Veena grinned in the screen. "I'm glad to see *my* robot is still in good working order. I feared you might have tried to disassemble him after you left."

"What do you mean *your* robot?" Cas asked.

"I mean he's been the one transmitting all this wonderful information to me," Veena said, grinning even wider. "Didn't you know?"

Box turned to Cas. "What's she talking about, boss?"

Cas shook his head. "No, that's not possible," he said. "We found your tracker; it was in the communication equipment."

"Oh, you found the decoy. Yes. Very good. Bravo, Caspian. You're too clever for your own good." She mocked clapping.

"Evie, get up here!" Cas yelled. He turned to Box. "Are you compromised? Have you been spying on us this entire time?"

Box's eyes blinked wildly. "No! Of course not, I don't…I haven't…"

"Oh, he doesn't know about it, poor thing," Veena said. "The best type of informant is one who doesn't even realize he's informing. My maintenance crew managed to get the drop on him while we were unloading my wares before you left. Made a few modifications, you could say."

"Box, get away from the controls," Cas said.

"Boss, I'm fine. She's lying. I'm not—"

Evie made her way into the cockpit, still holding the bandage on her arm. "What's going on?"

"There's our mercenary now!" Veena said, making small claps with her hands. "Now that we're all together—"

The ship shook with the force of a plasma blast and Evie was knocked to the ground. Cas grabbed on to the nearest thing he could to keep from being thrown from his chair.

"We're caught in a tractor," Box said. "Wait, this can't be right. We're back under the *Achlys*. We haven't gone anywhere!"

"Thank you, Box, for delivering my cargo undamaged," Veena said. "You've been more helpful than you can imagine."

Box slammed his hands down on the controls. "I'm not your slave!" he yelled.

Cas jumped over the seat to help Evie back up. The bleeding around her arm had gotten worse. He bent down to her ear. "Can you still fly? I need you to get us out of here," he whispered.

She nodded. "Yeah. I think so."

Cas stood back up, turning his attention to the screen again. "All of this, it's been nothing but a ploy to get the ship?" He motioned for Evie to move behind Box.

Veena pursed her ruby lips and tilted her head, like she was explaining basic math to an infant. "I didn't know what I was in for when little miss merc there showed up willing to pay your debts, did I? But I figured it must have been something important if the Coalition was willing to infiltrate Sargan space just for *you*. I knew you were an outcast, but it gave me unending pleasure to find out exactly why. All this business with the *Achlys*, so serious," she said, *tsking*. "But once I learned, from you no less, that the Coalition was in possession of Sil technology well…how could I refuse? The opportunities were just too wonderous."

"She's pulling us in," Box said from his seat. Cas kept his eyes on Veena but motioned with one hand behind his back to Evie.

"The only problem is you've done nothing but find a dud," Cas said. "The weapon doesn't work, all it does is kill every living thing in the immediate area once it's activated. The crew of the *Achlys* didn't know its power source makes it unusable."

"Does it now?" Veena said, tenting her fingers under her chin. "Well, that explains why the ship was empty when my men found it." She paused, thinking.

"Still pulling," Box said, watching the monitors. Cas risked a glance at Evie. She nodded to him.

"Regardless. It could make a wonderful present for some of my enemies. And when they try to activate it…yes, that will do quite nicely. Caspian, you are just a bundle of good information. You should have known I'd never let you go. I love you too much."

Evie hit the hab ejection button and Cas reached down, targeting and firing the quad cannon at the hab, destroying it. The ship rocked with the explosion, sending all of them tumbling. Veena's image disappeared from the screen, replaced by static waves.

"Get in the pilot's seat!" Cas yelled as Box was thrown against the far wall.

Evie had landed on her side again and scrambled up. It didn't escape Cas's notice that she was leaving a trail of blood in her wake. But she managed to get to the seat and engage the engines. "Jumping to the nearest undercurrent now," she said, hitting the emitter.

The tunnel opened before them and the small ship pulled away.

"We've only got three stabilizers working," Evie said, jerking the controls. "This is going to be rough."

"Signs of pursuit?" Cas crawled over to where Box lay against the bulkhead.

"I can't tell, all the sensors are down. I'm flying blind here," she replied.

The ship continued to shake back and forth. Without the fourth stabilizer, they wouldn't be able to stay in the undercurrent long. The friction would tear the ship to pieces. "Box?"

"I'm sorry, boss, I didn't know."

"I'll trust you on that," Cas said. "But you can't remain active. If she's seeing everything you're seeing…"

"I know," he said, his eyes blinking. "Just promise me you'll turn me back on. I don't want this to be it."

"I promise." Cas winced. He wasn't sure it was a promise he could keep. If they couldn't find the bug inside Box and remove it without destroying his cortex, he might not be able to reactivate him.

Box nodded and his yellow eyes went dark, his lifeless body slumping to the side.

"Don't worry, buddy, we'll get through this," Cas placed his hand on the machine for a moment. He jumped back up and returned to the co-pilot's seat. "Status?"

"We've maybe got another two minutes in this undercurrent then we'll have to go back to normal space. See if you can't get the sensors working," Evie said, piloting with one hand. Her other was back on her wound, blood seeping through her fingers.

"Is the comm down too? Can we call the *Tempest*?" Cas asked. The forward and aft sensor arrays were out; not only was she flying blind he had no idea if they were being pursued.

"Comm is still up." Evie tapped a series of buttons. "*Tempest*, come in. Mayday, gamma stabilizer is out, can't maintain heading long."

"*Excuse* this is *Tempest*," Greene's voice said over the comm. "We're coming to you, standby."

"Any luck?" Evie asked, indicating the sensors. Cas shook his head. "Then I guess we'll find out if anything is behind us pretty quickly." She pulled back on the throttle and disengaged the undercurrent emitter. Normal space appeared around them. She swung the ship around to give them a visual of what might be coming behind them. Evie took deep breaths through her teeth to control the pain.

"Let me take the controls," Cas said. "You're in no shape to fly anymore."

"No, if they come out of that tunnel after us you won't be able to maneuver us to safety," she replied. "You told me yourself you're a terrible pilot."

Cas was about to argue the point when a tunnel opened to their right, revealing the *Tempest*. "Stay where you are," Greene said. "We'll bring you in." The ship came around in front of them and lined up Bay One with their position. Evie sat back in relief as *Tempest* enveloped them into the hangar. She pushed the controls to set the ship down.

"C'mon." Cas helped her to her feet. "We need to get you to Xax." He draped her arm around him and helped her to the lock, where they were met by a group of security officers and medical staff. "She's been seriously injured," Cas said. "She needs medical attention right now."

"What about you?" One of the medical officers asked as Cas helped handoff Evie to the others.

"I'm fine, but I need to go get my robot. I don't want to leave him aboard."

The officer nodded and tended to Evie as they walked her down the ramp into the main part of the bay.

Cas jogged back over to where Box lay slumped against the ground. "I'm not leaving leave you here." He hooked his arms under Box's frame, dragging him back along the hallway. Box's metal legs scraped along the floor.

"Never…realized…how much you…weigh," Cas grunted as he pulled Box further down the hallway. When he reached his personal hab suite he yanked Box over the threshold and left him in the middle of the floor. "Sesster can help you," he said. "And Evie knows what's wrong. You're going to be fine."

He took one last look at his friend and ran from the room, sealing the door behind him. Cas bolted down the corridor back to the cockpit and began the initiation sequence for the engines. He may not be the best pilot, but he could at least get the ship out of the Bay.

The engines rumbled back to life and he retracted the landing gear as well as the main ramp, making sure all ports were sealed. Finally Cas toggled the switch that would release his own hab suite with Box inside, hearing the rumble as the suite dropped to the Bay floor.

"Okay, Veena," he said. "You want me? You got me."

Cas hit the engines and blasted out of the Bay back into open space.

36

It took a minute to get used to the steering as the ship wobbled back and forth but as long as he was moving away from *Tempest* that was a good thing. The comm button beside his chair chirped three times. Cas decided to ignore it. This was what was best for everyone. The *Reasonable Excuse* was already hanging on by a thread; he'd lost three hab suites and a stabilizer. There was no future for him in either the Coalition or the Sargan Commonwealth. Veena would either keep him a slave forever or Rutledge would have him locked up for the rest of his life. And he wasn't going to go out like that. He was going out on his own terms. If the last seven years had taught him anything, it was life never turned out how you wanted. But at least he'd have control over how it ended.

The comm chirped again. Cas ignored it, plotting his course back to Veena's ship, or at least its last-known position. It wasn't as if he'd never *flown* before; it had just been a long time. His vector drifted as he tried to re-enter the coordinates back along the route he'd just come through. The ship could survive one last small jump. She'd been better to him than he deserved, holding together long after any other ship would have long fallen apart. She was like a friend who'd always been there for the ride. And she was going to help him end this once and for all.

Finally he got the coordinates inputted and made the necessary arrangements for the jump. "Emitter power is…active," he said, feeling the rush of adrenaline as the emitter opened up the undercurrent tunnel and the ship shot forward.

Two minutes. In two minutes, he'd be right back at her ship then all of this would be over. His only hope was the previous explosion had permanently taken out that tractor beam. Because if not he might be in a world of trouble.

The comm chirped again. And again. And again. Cursing, Cas finally hit the accept button.

"What the hell do you think you're doing?" Greene's voice said on the other end.

"I'm taking care of this, once and for all. Maintain your position," Cas said. "I don't know how large this explosion will be but you need to keep your distance. The weapon on board can affect things beyond the confines of one ship. That's how the dry dock crew died too."

"What the hell are you talking about, Mr. Robeaux?" Greene asked.

"Talk to Evie once she's better. She'll explain everything," he replied.

"Was she in on this? Was this *her* idea?" Greene demanded.

Cas shook his head even though Greene couldn't see him. "No sir, this was all me. She didn't even know about it. This weapon must be destroyed and we don't have time to wait for Coalition reinforcements. I'll regret I won't get to see the look on Rutledge's face when you tell him his ship was lost. When you tell him *I* did it, but we're out of time."

"Caspian," Greene said. "I know you think there is no other way out of this, but this isn't the answer." His voice sounded softer, more understanding than Cas had heard before.

"Sorry, sir, I think it is. This will be best for everyone. Including the Coalition," Cas replied, cutting the comm link. It chirped again but he ignored it. Less than thirty seconds to go. The ship shook like it would fly apart at any second and warnings flashed in front of Cas letting him know the structural integrity wouldn't hold much longer. All he needed to do was get close enough. The *Achlys* wouldn't be able to sustain a direct hit from his ship, despite being much larger. Plus, Cas knew right where to hit its most vulnerable spot: the underbelly. Based on his speed he should be able to penetrate at least one of the main emitters which would be enough to destabilize the matter conversion system resulting in a complete self-destruct.

The screen in front of him flashed an urgent *WARNING*. He wouldn't be able to hold it; he had to come out of undercurrent space. But he hadn't reached his destination yet. That was fine, it would just give him more time to speed up. Maybe he could reroute some of his extra power to the emergency thrusters. Anything to get him to critical velocity.

Cas pulled back on the throttle and re-entered normal space. In the distance sat Veena's ship. He'd come close, but not close enough. It would take another few minutes to get there using the normal engines and he'd probably burn most, if not all of his reserve fuel.

"Computer scan for additional…" he began before remembering the scanners were offline. The best he could do was stare out the main window and count how many ships he had to avoid for the next five minutes. Veena's dreadnought was the largest, obviously, though it didn't appear to be moving. The hab suite might have done more damage than he'd thought. Around Veena's ship patrolled two of the smaller Sargan ships. Setsemeh had been right, they were Darkness class vessels. He hadn't gotten a good look before when the *Tempest* was making its strafing runs but there they were, clear as day. All three Sargan ships were well-armed. But he just needed one shot. One well-timed shot.

The comm chirped again and Cas hit the button, swearing this was the last time. "Listen, Captain, you're not going to convince me—"

"Oh, so it *is* you again," Veena said. "I thought that little girlfriend of yours might have gotten all heroic. But look at you, back again to finish what you started." There was a certain amount of sarcasm and pity in her voice which only enraged Cas more.

"You were the one who wanted me back so badly," he quipped, double-checking his approach. He was dead-on target for the *Achlys*. This flying thing wasn't so hard after all.

"So I did. I must have done *something* right in a previous life because here you are. Ready and waiting. What are you thinking? A suicide mission? Oh, Cas, how quaint." A bolt of high-energy plasma strafed across the bow of his ship, having originated from Veena's. He hadn't even seen the imminent weapon indicator. With all his focus on the heading and keeping the ship straight he couldn't afford to split his attention.

"While you are quite capable," she teased, "There's always been something you never mastered, hasn't there?" Another bolt flew to the side of the ship and Cas jerked the controls, sending the ship sailing starboard. He struggled to right the *Excuse* again. "I thought maybe all those years with that robot might have taught you something but…alas. Still just an engineer."

Only a few hundred thousand kilometers. I can make it that far, Cas thought, readjusting his angle back toward the *Achlys.* It was a clumsy attempt and he knew it, but he only had to survive long enough to actually hit the damn thing. That was all that mattered.

Plasma strafed the left side of the ship lighting up ten different warning indicators. She'd burned out one of his engines; he'd have to reroute additional power to the others to compensate. And his heading was off again. She was just toying with him. There was no way he'd ever make it to his target. The destroyers would see to that much.

"Once you're back home safe we might give you a new job," Veena said. "Unfortunately you can't have Rasp's old position since you're the reason he's gone, but I do have space in my entourage for a new servant. Which would fit you nicely."

Cas shuddered. Servant only meant one thing: sex slave. He'd rather go to jail.

"Come now. Doesn't that sound nice? Catering to my every whim? My every desire? You couldn't ask for a better assignment."

He had half a mind to blow up the *Excuse* right there. But he had a job to do, and he'd see it through. There had to be some way of getting around all these obstacles.

Yeah, if you were a better pilot you could fly circles around them. There was only one thing left to do. He pulled back on the throttle and threw the ship into a barrel roll as he'd seen Box do so many times before. Indicators went off all over his panels and he completely lost his vector, but at least plasma blasts weren't scorching his ship anymore. "This would be a lot easier if the sensor arrays were working," he grumbled, orienting the ship back into a stable flight plan. Only when he looked up he found himself staring at the nose of a Darkness class Sargan Destroyer. They had positioned themselves directly between him and Veena's ship.

"Fuck." He stared at the green ship in front of him.

"Take comfort in knowing you never had a chance," Veena said over the comm. "It was always going to turn out this way, no matter what you did."

He had to think. There had to be another way. What if he just rammed the Destroyer? Would that create a large enough shock wave?

Just as he was about to try a bright pulse of light caught his eye, coming from the left side of his ship. Cas could barely believe it as the *Tempest* exited an undercurrent and fired on the Destroyer, causing it to dip down to minimize the damage.

A new voice came over his comm. "Robeaux, get in there and do what needs to be done!" Greene said.

"Yes, sir!" Cas replied. With the Destroyer out of the way he had a straight shot for the *Achlys.* He gunned the engines, causing the dampeners to fail momentarily and pull him back into his seat.

"All ships, fire on that small one, don't let him get close!" Veena's voice screeched. But it was too late, he was too close. She had let her overconfidence get the better of her and now it would cost her everything.

"Really enjoyed the job, Veena," Cas said, "But if you don't mind…I quit." He cut the comm and focused all his attention on plowing the *Reasonable Excuse* right into the side of the *Achlys*. Soon this would all be over.

***

"You're not going out there," Xax said, running down the hall behind Evie.

"The hell I'm not, who else do you know who could get out there and save his wretched ass?"

"Someone not missing part of their upper arm!" she yelled back.

She spun on the doctor. "Am I in danger of losing the arm? Right now? Will I lose it?"

Xax took a step back. "Well no, I've stabilized it but that doesn't mean—"

She held up her hand and resumed running down the hall to Bay Two. Cas was out there making a suicide run and she wasn't about to have another dead man on her conscience.

Evie reached the main doors which opened for her, revealing the large Bay. Glancing to the side she saw the firefight outside the ship. Greene had brought *Tempest* through a short undercurrent to catch back up with Cas once he'd blasted out of the Bay. She should have known he would try something stupid. Had she not been injured she never would have left him alone in his ship. At least he'd had the decency to leave Box behind, which told Evie everything she needed to know. He was going out and he wasn't coming back.

"Clear the way, I need a Spacewing ready," she yelled. Two crewman looked up from their jobs and hurried over to the small fleet of vehicles stashed on the side of Bay Two. They were designed to operate short-range only, but they were highly maneuverable and carried a large complement of offensive weapons. They could also fly in a planet's atmosphere, and thus they were more aerodynamic than most Coalition ships.

They had been her favorite ship back at the academy.

"It will take a moment to warm, ma'am," one of the crewmen said, beginning the startup procedure and popping the access hatch.

"I don't have a moment, emergency startup," she ordered, climbing the ladder and hauling herself in with some difficulty, given her arm wasn't functioning right. As long as it could hold a stick and push a button, she'd be good. The other hand was the one she needed for navigation.

"Just what the hell are you doing with one of my ships?" A harsh voice said from below. Evie looked down to see Chief Master Rafnkell with her hands on her hips.

"I need this. For just a minute," she replied, flipping on all the startup procedures.

"Commander, you're not authorized—"

"Chief, don't. We've got a man out there and I'm not leaving him."

"Then let my squad do it. We can have him—"

"No time," Evie interrupted. "Executive order. Now move."

Rafnkell watched her for a beat then took a step back, working her jaw. The Spacewing hummed to life under her as Evie yanked the hatch back down and hit the "seal" button on her console. She tapped the top of her hand.

"Put me through to Cas on the *Reasonable Excuse*," Evie said into the onboard comm.

"It's locked down," Page replied. "And if you haven't noticed, we're a little busy up here."

"Page, shut up and put me through to his personal comm. That one won't be active."

She heard her colleague grumble but he did as she asked and the small beep around her told her she was connected.

"Hello?" he asked. He sounded surprised.

Evie dropped the moorings and hit the main thrusters, pulling the ship into a direct line of launch from the Bay. "Cas, you don't have to do this." She hit the accelerator and the ship blasted out of the hangar bay.

"A little late to back out now," he replied.

Just as she suspected, his course was locked on the *Achlys.* "No, it isn't. Take the last hab suite. Get out of there." *Idiot thinks he's going to be a martyr.*

"It's better this way, Evie, trust me. I don't belong in the Coalition any more than I belong with the Sargans. This solves everyone's problem."

She shook her head, yanking the ship around into a pursuit course. She wasn't sure if she could catch him in time. The

Excuse had more powerful engines than the small Spacewing. "Including Rutledge?" she challenged. "You dying would be his greatest gift. Don't let him win, Cas. Don't give him the satisfaction. The only way this won't happen again is if you speak out against him. You're the only one left who can."

He didn't respond. She pushed the accelerator harder, willing it to move faster even though she knew she was at full speed. She checked her instrument panel which told her *Tempest* was engaging both the destroyers. The dreadnought still hadn't moved. And Cas was headed directly for it. She needed to be more persuasive.

"Cas, please. The Coalition may have failed you, but that doesn't mean you give up on the rest of us. Some of us still believe in this institution and it needs people like you who are willing to fight the corruption for it to survive." If he was right and there was a thread of corruption running through the Coalition, his death would bury it forever. Without him any hope of bringing Rutledge to task would be destroyed. Plus, she had to admit to herself she didn't want to see him die. He was a good person who deserved better.

She waited, trying to think of something else to say while the *Excuse* only flew closer to the Sargan ship. If he'd already made up his mind she needed to turn back now.

"I'm on my way," Cas finally said.

Thank Kor. Evie leaned forward, urging the ship to move faster, all the while checking her surroundings to make sure there weren't going to be any surprises. Her arm throbbed in pain, but she pushed past it. Why wasn't the Dreadnought firing at Cas's ship? It was like it was just sitting there, dead in space. Had something happened?

Evie watched as the last hab suite detached from the rest of the ship. But due to the inertia it didn't slow down, only kept pace with the *Excuse,* flying right beside it. She adjusted her heading to match the new object, hoping she hadn't done all this for nothing.

"Evie, you better be able to grab me," he said. "This is gonna be close."

She watched his ship inch closer and closer to the *Achlys,* flying at full speed. The impact would not be pretty, not at these speeds. The hab suite was just out of reach. Evie reached down with her damaged arm and readied the grappler. As soon as the reticle turned red she fired, the grappler digging into the side of the hab and jerking it back. She immediately reversed thrust and whipped the ship around, throwing all her power into heading away from the *Achlys*. On the panel to her right she pulled up a visual of the ship as the *Excuse* grew ever closer to its target. She only had seconds to get out of range. A bright blast filled her screen. That was it. The shockwave would hit them any second now. She could only hope they were far enough away.

Evie braced herself.

37

From the bridge of the *Tempest* Greene watched the tiny ship plow into the *Achlys*, obliterating both ships. The resulting explosion began a chain reaction in the dreadnought. "Report!" he yelled.

"It's a massive shockwave explosion, sir, whatever was on the *Achlys* had more destructive power than I've seen from—from anything," Zaal said.

The weapon, Greene thought. "How far away is Commander Diazal?"

"Forty-thousand kilometers, sir," Page replied.

"Will she make it out?"

"Not before the shockwave hits."

Greene turned to Zaal, knowing the answer to his question before even asking. "Can a Spacewing survive that kind of destructive power?"

Zaal shook his head. "No, sir. Neither can the hab suite she's towing."

His crew may have been fresh compared to some of his other shipmates in the past, but that didn't mean they were worth sacrificing. There was no choice, he had to try and save them, even if one was a convicted criminal. Cas had tried to sacrifice himself for the Coalition, *despite* everything they'd done to him. And Greene wasn't about to let them get away with it.

"How long until it hits them?" he asked, watching the screen with intensity. The waveform was massive, closing in on his executive officer's ship. He'd never seen anything like it either. Whatever this weapon on the *Achlys* had been, he was glad it was destroyed. Watching the destruction he couldn't help but wonder how long it would spread before it could dissipate. Even supernovas didn't generate this kind of power.

"Thirty-two seconds, sir."

Greene turned to his helmsman, his mind made up. "Ronde, you did an excellent job last time enveloping Mr. Robeaux's ship. Think you can do it again?"

"We're too far away, sir. If we were closer—" Ronde said in an uncertain tone, frowning.

"Ensign River, plot an undercurrent course to the commander's ship," Greene said. "And make it quick."

"Aye," River responded with an unsure voice of her own. He watched her hands move over the controls faster than any normal human could. Despite her lack of confidence, she was talented. Greene had to admit, if he'd had a non-augmented officer at the navigation station this maneuver probably would not be possible. But that was the beauty of the Coalition. Anyone could become an officer.

"Course plotted," River replied.

"Lieutenant Ronde, if you please," Greene said, staring at the screen on the far wall. He braced himself. This was definitely off-book as far as standard rescue procedures were concerned.

The image turned into a blur for a split second before re-pixelating to show the commander's small craft directly in front of them, the shockwave closing fast. Her ship then moved past the image of the monitor out of view. Greene barely had time to appreciate the beauty of the wave itself. It was as if someone had spun paint and oil in water and lit it all on fire.

"Got them!" Ronde whooped.

"Blohm, full power to engines and punch it," Greene ordered. The ship made one fluid motion around and within an instant they were in an undercurrent.

"We're clear," Zaal said.

"Well done everyone," Greene said, tapping a pad on his chair. "Xax, prepare to receive wounded."

"Oh, I'm already waiting," Xax replied causing Greene to smile.

"Ensign River, set course for Starbase Eight. Full speed ahead."

38

"Oh look, he's coming out of it."

"He might be better off sleeping a while longer."

"He only likes extra sleep when he's hungover."

Cas opened his eyes. Box stood in front of him, his yellow eyes blinking approval. Cas groaned and turned over, his body responding to the movement by sending a surge of aches and pains through his system. "You better not be recording this," Cas said.

A small circular device landed on the bed beside him. Cas picked it up, examining it between his forefinger and his thumb. "Sargan tech."

Box shrugged. "It wasn't buried deep. Sesster was able to get it out without much trouble."

Cas squinted. "And I'm assuming because I'm sitting here talking to you I made it out okay." He tossed the device on the small table beside him.

"That depends on your definition of okay," Xax said, siding up to him as if from nowhere. She stared at Cas with her six black eyes, as if she were staring into his soul. "You sustained a concussion and three broken ribs which I have since repaired. But you may experience some vertigo over the next twenty to forty hours."

Cas sat up and in response the room did a quick three-sixty before settling again. He rubbed his temples. "Thanks," he said, swinging his legs off the side of the bed. "What about…?"

"Over there." Box pointed to where Evie lay on one of the beds, a med droid beside her, stitching new muscles and skin together inside a self-enclosed chamber.

"We had to reconstruct her arm from scratch," Xax said. "She re-injured it rescuing you. She'll be out another twelve hours until her immune system has healed enough to prevent any infection."

Cas got on his feet, the floor wobbled under him but he managed not to fall over. That was a beginning at least. "Box…what happened?"

"I was in shut down. But from what they told me you decided to make a suicide run."

"I know that part, what happened after that?"

"Oh," Box said. "Well, Evie went after you, because she secretly has a crush on you, and then Captain Greene went after her because he secretly has a crush on her."

"Box—"

"And then I woke up under the care of the engineers because they secretly have a crush on me!"

Cas coughed. "People don't rescue other people just because they have crushes on them, you know."

"But it makes it that much more plausible, doesn't it?" Box said. "The girl going off to risk everything to save the man she loves? It makes my servos flutter."

Cas rolled his eyes. "Yeah, okay. What happened after that?"

"You managed to plow *my* ship into the heart of the *Achlys*, which caused a cascade reaction completely destroying both ships. I watched the footage. Veena's dreadnought was obliterated in the subsequent explosion. As in, atomized. Turned to dust. Kaput. So, you don't have to worry about her anymore."

Cas caught Xax giving him a look, but it was hard to interpret. He wasn't fully versed in Yax-Inax body language. If he had to guess he'd say the doctor wasn't too happy about the loss of life on Veena's ship. But the universe was a better place without her.

"Which means you now owe me one ship," Box finished.

"I never said I'd give you the ship. I said I'd give you quarters. And I kept my word."

"What good is a hab suite if it isn't connected to a usable ship?" Box complained.

"Guess you should have been more specific in your request." Cas made his way to the door as Box grunted behind him.

"The captain wants to see you," Xax said. "As soon as you're able."

Cas nodded and exited sickbay, taking one last look at Evie, lying unconscious on the table. He wouldn't forget what she'd done for him, she had saved his life. And he wasn't going to let it go to waste.

***

The doors of the hypervator opened on the bridge. Much to Cas's relief he saw much of the damage had been cleared away. The viewscreen on the back wall still served as the focal point since the central display was still in dozens of pieces. It would need a full replacement. All of the stations—save the two sunken into the floor—had turned to face the display. But because navigation and helm control already naturally faced that direction, those stations didn't need to turn. Cas noticed Ensign River now occupied Ensign Blackburn's post permanently.

Greene wasn't on the bridge. Cas cleared his throat and Page glanced back at him and Box, dismissing them with his eyes. "He's in the command room," Page said, turning back to his work.

Cas ignored his urge to go and punch the man again and instead led Box to the command room door, entering only when given the all-clear from the captain on the other side.

"Feeling better?" Greene stood as they entered.

"Alive is better than dead, so yes. Much better," Cas replied.

Greene stuck out his hand for Cas, which caused Cas to gape at him for a moment. "You were willing to do what was necessary. That's a trait I respect," Greene said.

Cas took the man's hand and gave it a firm shake. "Thank you, Captain."

"I'm curious. Why did you change your mind?" Greene asked, his eyes penetrating.

He'd almost gone through with it. But then Evie had reminded him there were more important things than sacrificing yourself for a cause. Sometimes it was more important to keep fighting. "Ev—your first officer reminded me I wasn't done yet. And I didn't want to give the admiral the satisfaction."

Greene nodded. "Which brings me to why I've asked you here. Please take a seat."

Box sat in the seat directly across from the captain. Cas couldn't hide his smile as he took the other. Greene was momentarily flustered but turned his attention to Cas. "You have a problem, Mr. Robeaux."

"I think the Coalition has a problem," Cas replied.

"I agree. And you are the only one who can help us remove that problem. You are the last eye witness to a terrible atrocity that never should have taken place. And I want to make sure the man responsible for it is taken into custody and punished for his crimes."

"I would love to do that, sir, but without any evidence it's like I told Evie—"

Greene held up a small data recorder. It was exactly like the one he'd taken off Maddox back at Devil's Gate. Standard-issue. "Commander Diazal had the forethought to download the *Achlys* logs while you were over there. I've taken some time to examine them and some of the crew's personal logs back up your story. It seems a few of your fellow officers weren't happy about what Rutledge did to you, but were too afraid to speak up."

"Their personal logs, sir? Aren't those protected?"

"Not when the subjects are deceased. They become Coalition property and I have every right to review them in order to seek out and end an injustice. With an eye witness and corroborating evidence, I don't see any reason Admiral Rutledge will remain at his post much longer."

Greene set the recorder down on his desk.

"Wow. She really does care," Box whispered, staring at the recorder.

Cas was stunned. "She did that, for me?" he asked. "Why?"

"I haven't known the commander long," Greene said. "But from what I know about her and her service record, she has a real problem with bullies and people who don't believe in the sanctity of the Coalition. What Rutledge has done goes against everything we stand for. Perhaps she took it personally, having been assigned by him to go get you. Whatever it is, she wasn't going to let it go."

Cas furrowed his brow. "I can't say I'm not appreciative—"

"Of course she also violated protocol by going after you and saving your life," Greene said. "Fortunately, records of the incident have been conveniently misplaced." He grinned.

Cas grinned back. Maybe the Coalition wasn't so bad after all.

***

"I never thought I'd see the day," Cas said as they watched Rutledge being led from his office by three security personnel. He and Evie reclined on the couch in his quarters on Starbase Eight—provisionally given to him by Admiral Sanghvi, the new ranking officer for the station—watching the feed repeat over and over. The official Coalition news station hadn't been showing anything else for the past six hours.

"You think you'll be ready for the trial?" Evie asked. Her arm was still in a hyperbaric wrap, but only for another twelve hours.

"I doubt he'll let it get that far," Cas replied. "He's got too much pride. He'll take whatever deal they offer him. I can't believe Greene made this happen." He turned to her. "That you made it happen."

She placed her hand on his forearm for a moment. "We all made it happen. And hopefully after this the Coalition will think twice about commissioning experiments based on alien technology. I think it was for the best you destroyed that ship."

"I think you're right," Cas replied.

"So what are you going to do now? No ship. And stuck in the middle of Coalition space."

Cas glanced around. His quarters were on the upper levels in the starbase; from here he could see *Tempest* under repairs down below. It had been a rough few days, but he hadn't had a lot of time to think about the future. Between all the meetings with admirals and providing his testimony to the

Coalition security forces he'd wanted nothing more than sleep. Box had been adamant about staying in "his" hab suite, but the maintenance crews had already disassembled it, leaving him to bunk with Cas again.

"I'm not sure. Without a prison sentence hanging on my neck I was thinking about working my way back to the inner systems. Figure out a way to get another ship. Nothing fancy, just something that will get me from here to there."

"You could always join up again," Evie suggested.

Cas recoiled. "And go through everything all over again? The academy was tough enough the first time. I'm not sure I want to put myself through all that again."

"They might be willing to grant you something provisionally—since, you know…"

Cas shook his head. "It's been seven years. I doubt I'd even be able to qualify for lieutenant anymore. No, I think I want to take my robot and start exploring. Without any kind of weight dragging me down."

"You don't think the Sargans will come after you? After what happened to Veena?"

He shrugged. "Maybe. But I'm not too worried about it. I can start on the far side of Coalition space. About as far from the Sargan Commonwealth as I can get."

"That's where I used to be stationed. Out near Epsilon Lyre."

Cas leaned back, putting his arms behind his head. "I'm talking about even further out. Archellia, or Beta Stromgren. You know, the real untamed frontier."

Evie scoffed, sitting back and taking a sip of her tea. "Just can't stay in civilized society, can you? It will take seasons, if not years to even get out that far."

"Yeah, but what's life without a little adventure?" Cas replied. He would never be able to express how thankful he was to her for saving his life. And in all honesty, he would love to stay here in the middle of the Coalition, find a way to stay on *Tempest*, but it wasn't realistic. He'd never be anything other than the criminal-turned-revolutionary to the crew. And even if people no longer looked at him with disgust, it would still be in the back of their minds. He was still the reason twenty-four people from the *Achlys* were dead, nothing could ever change that. But at least now he'd taken steps to make it right.

"Well," Cas said, standing. "I guess I should go start booking passage. What about you? Headed back to *Tempest*?"

She stood as well, nodding. "We'll be in repairs for another week then we'll get our next assignment. But I think it will be hard to beat this last one."

He smiled. "Yeah. It was one hell of a ride." He paused, trying to draw out the moment. "Thanks."

She watched him a moment before heading toward the door. At the last moment she turned. "Thanks yourself," she said, then disappeared through the other side. It was only when she was gone Cas realized it was probably the last time he'd ever see her. And for all his protestations to the contrary, he couldn't help but feel a pang in his heart as the doors slid closed.

Epilogue

"Ready?" Cas asked, approaching the airlock.

Box trudged along behind him, dragging three crates which scraped along the floor. "Are you sure we *have* to go?"

"I suppose you could stay here, *if* you wanted to be assigned to exhaust cleaning," Cas said.

"I should have rights!" Box announced, banging on his chest, sending an echo of metal on metal through the space. "I should be able to go to the academy if I wanted!"

Cas scoffed. "Keep dreaming, bud." He turned to the airlock. Beyond was the USCS Winston; a survey ship headed for Pryocyon. He'd managed to book passage for them as far as Pryocyon IV, but once they arrived he'd have to make new arrangements. He'd been given free passage through the Coalition but that didn't mean things would be easy. The Coalition had been very enthusiastic about keeping the events surrounding the *Achlys* quiet. Which meant few people beyond the crew would know the actual story. The cover was Rutledge had been arrested for a separate charge having nothing to do with the crew of *Tempest* or Cas. The two events were to be kept as separate as possible, though any arrest warrants for Cas had been quietly rescinded.

Cas understood. They wouldn't want word getting out to the Claxian homeworld or any of the Coalition's enemies that there had almost been a coup within the Coalition itself. Rutledge had brought them to the brink of war and it had only been the actions of Cas and the crew of the *Tempest* who had prevented it all. And no one would ever know about it.

Cas had been given a clear record—all war crimes expunged—but in his experience, people had a long memory. People like Page would never stop suspecting him, so what reason did he have to give them the chance? He was sure once they got to the far side of Coalition space back out into non-aligned territory he'd be able to find another ship. And not a courier this time. Something much nicer.

Cas's comm beeped. He creased his brow and glanced at Box. "I bet it's Evie," Box said. "She's going to come running down the corridor at any minute and throw herself into your arms, begging to come with us."

Cas pursed his lips. "Somehow I highly doubt that." He tapped the comm. "Robeaux here."

"Mr. Robeaux, you haven't left yet?" Why would Greene be calling him?

"No, we were just about to board the *Winston*."

"I need you to report back to the main officer's ward. Admiral Sanghvi's office. Immediately," Greene said.

"Is there a problem?"

"Immediately, Mr. Robeaux." He cut the comm.

That was odd. What could they still need with him? Rutledge had opted not to go to trial; everything regarding the *Achlys* had been wrapped up. Cas turned to Box. "You stay here, don't let that ship leave without us. I'm sure this won't take but a minute," he said.

"Fine," Box said, pulling a screen from the crate and turning it to the closest wall. A net drama immediately popped up. "I'll just sit here and wait. Like always." He slumped down so he was sitting on the ground.

Cas jogged to the closest hypervator. This had to be some sort of last-minute farewell or something. He'd heard people did that sometimes...surprised their friends with a going-away party or other equally sappy gesture. Not that he wouldn't be happy to receive it; it just seemed odd that they would wait until he was leaving to tell him. Add in the fact he didn't have any friends meant it would be a small party. Which was fine, he wouldn't be able to stay long anyway; the *Winston* would be departing within the hour. And they still needed to check in and get settled in their temporary quarters. Pryocyon was two hundred light years away; a good forty days away on a ship that wasn't equipped with *Tempest's* advanced drive.

Watching the interior of the station fly by as he transversed from the docking ports to the habitable sections, he figured most Coalition ships would probably be equipped with the drive within the next five years. It had been their only saving grace in the fight with Veena. Had the *Tempest* not had the speed it did Veena's ships could have easily pursued and destroyed it. But that also meant a Claxian on every ship; something Cas was keen to see happen as he'd felt it had been a long time coming, even back when he'd still been an officer.

The hypervator doors opened on the admiral offices level and he made his way down the large corridor, reading the names on each one. This was the same level Rutledge had been stationed on. If they were throwing him some kind of going-away gathering, he could already tell it was going to leave a bad taste in his mouth. He'd hoped never to see this corridor again.

Cas reached Admiral Sanghvi's office and touched the panel to the side.

"Come in," a man's deep voice said.

The doors opened to reveal the admiral himself, a tall, dark-skinned man with jet-black hair standing with his arms locked behind his back as he stared at Cas. In front of him sat Evie and Greene. There was a third chair, empty.

"Mr. Robeaux, thank you for coming on such short notice," the admiral said, indicating he take the third seat. "We've been discussing your exploits in the Car'pr system. Please have a seat."

Cas shot Evie and Greene a look but they seemed reassured he was there, not worried. "I'm not sure I'm supposed to be here," Cas said.

"I'm sure it seems that way. However, upon speaking with Captain Greene and Commander Diazal I've concluded we can't ignore your unique position in the Coalition."

"Okay," Cas said, taking the seat. *Unique position?*

"The blunt truth of why you are here is simple: Admiral Rutledge was both wrong and right."

"I'm sorry?"

"As I'm sure you know, he was not alone in his wish to build a weapon based on Sil technology." Sanghvi took his seat.

"I thought that was the entire reason he was arrested," Cas said, not liking where this was going.

"What you don't know is there was a very good reason for what he did. A few seasons ago, our long-range telescopes out past Starbase Five at the edge of Coalition space detected something we're calling *Andromeda*. We know they are an alien species and we know they are incredibly destructive and that's about it. And they are headed for our region of space and will arrive in about a year. And so, based on my conversations with your colleagues here, and your unique position in this situation we've decided to bring you back into the fold. The question is: are you willing to help the Coalition? Are you willing to help defend us against this threat?"

Cas couldn't believe it. An alien presence? And they were heading for Coalition space?

"I know you said you wanted the quiet life." Evie grinned. "But this seemed like more your style."

Cas returned her gaze, then glanced at Greene, whose face was still, yet his mouth was upturned at the corners. It looked like he wouldn't be headed to Pryocyon after all.

Cas returned his attention to the admiral. "Tell me everything."

Thank you for reading **CASPIAN'S FORTUNE!** If you enjoyed the book, please consider leaving a review on AMAZON. And look for future installments in the series! The easiest way to keep up is to sign up on my website, and you get access to all the INFINITY'S END short stories, absolutely free!

The adventure continues in **TEMPEST RISING**. Turn the page for a sneak preview!

TEMPEST RISING: INFINITY'S END BOOK 2

PREVIEW

Caspian Robeaux wasn't used to this.

Typically when he sat at a bar and drank himself into a stupor the place was a seedy hole-in-the-wall; the type of place where illegal transactions were the norm and everyone who came in looked like they either wanted to fuck you or kill you. The type of place that often maintained a lingering odor of something moist but no longer ripe. Those were his places, where he went to feel comfortable. A place where he could disappear into the back wall and no one would give him another glance.

But this was not that place.

The bar was too clean, too sanitary for his likes. An automated bartender stood behind the polished wood surface separating them, waiting to take Cas's next order. Not that he was sure there would be one. When he'd come down to the concourse to get away from it all he'd hoped he'd be able to find a place to hide out for a couple hours until he could get his head straight. But staring into the yellow eyes of the bartender as it glared back, he couldn't help but wonder if the bartender himself was some sort of deterrent. As if he'd been placed there specifically to make the patrons uncomfortable and thus keep them from overstaying their welcome. Perhaps that was how the Coalition kept their officers from getting drunk all the time. Back when he'd still been one, he'd never ventured in a place like this. It wasn't until after his arrest, parole and escape-slash-exile before he started frequenting imbibing establishments. And sure, maybe the Sargan Commonwealth wasn't the safest place in the galaxy and you had to carry a blaster on your person at all times, but they knew how to set up a bar. And mix a drink.

"This tastes a little weak," he remarked, hoping to give the machine something to do.

"I apologize, sir. Would you like me to fix you another? I can adjust—"

"Just, pour another shot in this one, will you?" Cas asked, pushing the small glass away from him.

"Yes, sir."

Cas glanced around the rest of the bar. It was relatively empty, which didn't surprise him. These were duty hours after all; he wouldn't expect a bunch of Coalition officers to be skipping work to day-drink. It wasn't their style. And that was fine with him. It was a good thing Admiral Sanghvi had called him into his office early in the day, because after his news, Cas needed something strong and he didn't want to have to push through a throng of people to get it.

"There you go, sir," the machine said, pushing the drink back towards him. Cas had been too distracted to actually watch and see if he had added anything substantial to the glass or not. He picked it up and gave it a swirl before knocking the contents back into his throat, nearly coughing on the burn. "Better?" the bartender asked.

Cas cleared his throat as the warmth traveled down his esophagus where it disappeared into the acid of his stomach. "Yeah. One more just like that."

"I'm sorry, sir. You have reached your daily allotment. You may return for another in seventeen hours, fifteen minutes." The bartender picked up the empty glass and it disappeared below the other side of the bar.

He should have expected this. "Fine. Then I'll take a bottle for the road." Cas glanced up to the hundreds of bottles of liquid perched on shelves behind the bartender, each varying in color and label. Alcohol from all over the Coalition.

"I'm sorry, sir," the machine repeated. "But bottles are only available for ranking officers."

"What if I said I used to be a Lieutenant Commander, would that make any difference?" Cas asked, slightly slurring the words.

"Only current ranking officers may access alcohol stores." The machine's eyes blinked on and off once; an indication Cas's question had now been reported somewhere. Ever since he'd found and modified his robotic travelling companion, Box, he'd become accustomed to their mannerisms. Where most humans just saw a machine's eyes go out momentarily, Cas knew it was the signal that something inappropriate had happened or was about to happen, and someone needed to be notified.

He grumbled, wishing Box where here at the moment. He could shove right past the bartender and grab as many bottles as he wanted; or at least push him out of the way long enough for Cas to grab a Firebrand or Scorb.

"Is there anything else I can do for you today, sir?" the bartender asked.

Cas stood, his legs wobbling under him as he pushed himself off the stool. "I guess not," he replied, automatically preparing to reach over to pay. He withdrew his hand at the last moment, remembering where he was. The Coalition worked without money. *Service is its own reward.* The mantra had been drilled into his head from the academy. But experiencing life outside the Coalition had shown him a different reality. One where people *were* motivated by money, and greed, and the accumulation of goods. And sure, sometimes maybe someone got a little overzealous and put out a hit on someone for not paying their bill, or stole someone else's transport to sell for spare parts, but were things really worse in the Sargan Commonwealth than in the Coalition? If you really stripped everything down wasn't a little bit of murder and theft worth being able to drink as much as you wanted at eleven hours past on a Selday?

Cas's communicator beeped. "Boss?"

"Speak of the devil," Cas said, tapping the small device on his arm.

"I've been pinging you for the last hour. The Winston left without us," Box said on the other end.

Cas sighed, stopping at the door to the bar, staring out into the concourse where civilians milled about, moving from shop to restaurant to shop again. While Starbase Eight did have a contingent of permanent civilians, most of these people would be family members of Coalition officers, or off-duty personnel taking in the beauty of the station. He was the only one who was neither. "Yeah. Something happened. I'll tell you about it when I get back." Cas ended the call, closed his eyes and pressed his fingers to his temples. Box deserved to know the truth, and he shouldn't have left him waiting on a loading dock for a ship he knew they wouldn't be taking anymore. But after the meeting with the Admiral, their trip to Procyon on the USCS Winston had been the last thing on his mind. He and Box had just been about to board when the call had come in for him to meet the Admiral in his office. And when he got there—

"There he is," a low, gruff voice same from somewhere off to the right.

Cas's eyes snapped open, his vision swimming for a bit as the room righted itself. Three large men approached him from the concourse, their eyes fixated on him.

Oh shit. Maybe coming down here without an escort hadn't been such a good idea after all. Most people did consider him a criminal. Cas took a step back into the bar, trying to remember if he'd seen a back exit or not. He didn't think he had. His comm chirped again but he ignored it.

The man in the front spoke up again first. "You think after what you did you can just come in here and waltz around like you're a regular person?" He had at least six inches on Cas and looked like he might bench press small shuttles for fun. He was in civilian clothes but somehow Cas instinctively knew, even through the fog of inebriation, they were officers.

"Listen," Cas said, backing up further into the bar with his hands up. "I'm not looking for trouble."

"Maybe you should have thought about that before you deserted," the one on the right said. He was smaller, but still a hefty guy. Had the three strongest guys on the station gotten together and decided on an old-fashioned beat down?

"How is he even allowed to be down here?" the third one asked. His voice was pitched higher, and he wore a shirt so tight Cas could see his pectoral muscles tighten and loosen as they grew ever closer. They were mesmerizing in their own way.

"I guess you haven't heard," Cas said, taking a few steps back but keeping his eyes on the man's pecs. Through his inebriation it seemed like the safest place to look. "My warrant was rescinded."

"Yeah, by who?" the first one said, only a few steps away from Cas now.

"Admiral Sanghvi," he replied, stopping as his back reached the bar.

"How can I help you today, gentlemen?" the bartender asked from behind him.

"What the hell are you staring at?" the third one asked, having finally noticed Cas's gaze.

"Your..." Cas put his hands out in front of him, making a circular motion with them. "Are very nice." The man narrowed his eyes. "I mean why else wear a tight shirt if you don't want to show them off?"

"George, I think he's making fun of you," the one in the front said, not taking his eyes off Cas.

"No, that's not what I meant at all!" Cas said, scrambling. He really wished he hadn't had that second Firebrand. "All I was saying was you should be proud of yourself. It takes commitment to go to the gym every day. Or in your case, five or six times a day."

"I don't care if you were pardoned or not," the middle one said, sticking a finger in Cas's chest. "We don't tolerate deserters in the Coalition."

Now *this* was more like it. Cas had been in his fair share of fights with the Sargans, and because there were virtually no police, other than the Guard (who could be paid off easily), fights tended to be final. It gave the fighters a healthy respect for each other. Not like these guys. These guys were nothing but bullies with extra time on their hands. And since he was backed up to the bar, there was only one way out.

"Then I guess it's a good thing I came back," Cas said, pulling back and plowing his head directly into the face of the man in the middle, his forehead connecting with the man's nose in a sickening crunch.

"My fucking nose!" the man yelled as blood splattered everywhere. Cas reeled to the right, holding his own head as he stumbled and eventually fell on the ground, his forehead pounding with pain. Wasn't headbutting supposed to hurt only the attacked, not the attacker?

"George, Ivory!" The man yelled, his words wet with fury. Cas pushed himself into a half-standing position and reached for his boomcannon, only realizing too late it wasn't there. Weapons weren't allowed in Coalition facilities. And as this realization washed over him striking a match to his adrenaline, something large and solid plowed into him, knocking them both back into a series of tables that toppled as they fell. Something metal dug into his side and he cried out in pain while simultaneously pounding on what he suspected was the man's head, but he couldn't be sure. George or Ivory, depending on which one hit him, was all muscle and everything felt like hitting a steel beam covered by a thin layer of cloth.

Pain exploded in his head again, this time from blunt-force trauma and white dots peppered his vision. It was a good thing he was drunk otherwise he'd probably be in a lot more pain than he actually was. Another explosion of pain knocked some of the inebriation away as his adrenaline kicked into overdrive, willing his body to get out of the very bad situation he'd found himself in. He kicked with his legs but nothing connected while a robotic voice in the background was saying something urgent. But it seemed his ears weren't quite working like they were supposed to as he couldn't make out the words. All he could discern were the white dots and the increasing levels of pain in his face as something plowed into it over and over again.

This was fine; this would be the fight that would take him out. And it was all because of the Coalition and their stupid rules about no weapons. Had this been a Sargan bar, it would have been over in seconds.

As he felt himself drift further and further into unconsciousness, the pounding finally stopped. Just in time for him to take a nap.

To be continued in TEMPEST RISING, available soon!

Glossary

Planets

Vetar VI – Sargan world home to her Royal Highness of Cloistria

Pryocyon IV – Standard Coalition Planet. Used to refine metals for production

Quadros Sigma – An unknown system inside Sil territory

Cassiopeia Optima – Sargan homeworld (settled by humans millennia ago)

Claxia Prime – Claxian Homeworld

D'jattan – Old mining asteroid turned into a trading depot

Devil's Gate – Sargan Outpost near the edge of Coalition space

Starbase Eight – Coalition stronghold and first line of defense against Sargan incursions

Paxi – Small world just outside Sargan space in non-aligned territory

Meridian – non-aligned colony world subject to raids by the Sargans

Species

Human – one of the founding members of the Coalition and central to its operation. Humans can be found on any of a hundred different worlds in the Coalition and often hold high positions of power within the organization. Worked with the Claxians to be the founding members.

Claxian – Founding members of the Coalition and pacifists with advanced technology. Lived as isolationists until first contact by the humans two thousand years ago. Helped form the Coalition to spread peace through the galaxy.

Untuburu – Early members of the Coalition. Highly religious to their god Kor. Untuburu are the only Coalition members not required to wear uniforms as their religion requires the sacred blue robes be the only garments worn off world.

Yax-Inax – Early member of the Coalition. Studious, have perfect memory and can retain huge amounts of information. Often integrate themselves into other cultures to learn as much as possible.

Sargans – Generally human but can also pertain to other species who have joined the Sargan Commonwealth. Sargans are humans who want to be lawless, or at least out from under the thumb of the Coalition.

Plegarians - Speak through a translator that translates emotions, doesn't always get it right. Have a high-pitched scream. About human height, though faces are smooth and angular, like a fish. Seventy years ago the Plegarians were driven from their homeworld by the Ocarians.

Ocarians - Physically identical to the Plegarians, but with a different moral base. Once shared a homeworld with the Plegarians. Recent members of the Coalition.

Sil – Unkown species of great power. The Coalition has reached a tentative treaty with the Sil not to violate their borders under any circumstances. Their empire is large.

Erustiaans - Seven and a half feet tall, all muscle. Sharp bone or hoof grows out of their hands. They generally associate with the Sargan Commonwealth and are used as enforcers or bouncers.

Miscellaneous

Lett'ra – a type of gambling wheel

Scorb – a heavy-type drink

Firebrand – liquor close to whiskey

Tooth Melter – a sweet, sugary alcoholic drink

Rank – a drink brewed from the hops of Caldonia

Galvanium – a type of metal used in ship construction

Cyclax – a type of metal used in ship reinforcement

Alchuriam ore – an obsolete type of metal

Author's Note

Thanks for reading Caspian's Fortune! If you've made it this far I'm hoping it means you enjoyed the book and are thirsty for more. When I first set out to write this series I don't think I understood just how large the universe would become, and we're only at the end of book one! Needless to say, the scope of this series is already much larger than my last series, which took place on one planet over the course of a few months, whereas here we've been introduced to an entire galaxy with hundreds of millennia of history to consider.

It's a daunting task to say the least. But I'm glad you've come along for the ride.

If you haven't already, consider signing up for my VIP list on my website. Once you do, you'll be the first to know about future books in the series, and you'll get freebies such as short stories, star maps and other exclusives pertaining to the Sovereign Coalition Universe, none of which will be available anywhere else.

You can also find me on Twitter, Facebook and Instagram. If any of those strikes your fancy.

This world is heavily influenced by some of the great Space Operas of our time: *Star Trek, Star Wars, Battlestar Galactica, etc.* These were influential to me as a kid and are a big part of what makes this universe what it is. Keep an eye out for easter eggs in future installments.

I'd also like to take a minute to thank my friends, family and everyone who has helped support me to make this series a reality. I couldn't have done it without you.

See you in the future!

About the Author

I've always been an author, but I haven't always known I've been an author. It took a few tragic events in my life and a lot of time for me to figure it out.

But I've never had a problem creating stories. Or creating in general. I wasn't *the* creative person in any of my classes in school, I was always the kid who never spoke but always listened. I was the one who would take an assignment and pour my heart into it, as long as it meant I could do something original.

I didn't start writing professionally until 2014 when I tackled the idea of finishing a novel-length book. Before then I had always written in some capacity, even as far back as elementary school where I wrote pages of stories about creatures under the earth.

It took a few tries and a few novels under my belt before I figured out what I was doing, and I've now finished my first series and am hard at work on my second (which you hold in your hands now!). I am thrilled to be doing this and couldn't imagine doing anything else with my life.

I hope you enjoy the fruits of my labor. May they bring you as much joy as they bring me.

Having lived in both Virginia and California in the past, I currently reside in Charlotte, NC with my very supportive wife and two small pugs.

Visit me at my website

45950381R10175

Made in the USA
Lexington, KY
21 July 2019